SKIN

Caroline Venetia Annis

Caroline Venetia Annis

Two Soups
Publishing

First published in eBook edition in 2021 by
Two Soups Publishing
This print edition published in 2021 by
Two Soups Publishing

Copyright © Caroline Venetia Annis 2021

ISBN: 978-1-3999-0478-0

Cover image - photon64 at Getty Images

For Jeff

1

SATURDAY

The sun presses hot on my skin. I hope my cheeks aren't burning – Luca might think I'm blushing. I want to move but Sophie and I have agreed it's better for Luca to see me side-on, with my legs stretched out in my new jeans.

'Chloe!'

Mum calls from inside the caravan. I ignore her. She and Dad are still unpacking, as well as getting ready for the traditional first night barbeque. Dad is setting up his 'outside man cave', as Mum calls it. The barbeque has been cleaned and the metal camping shelves carefully stacked with his 'special equipment', which basically means tongs, oil, and some kind of hot sauce that will burn your mouth off. Dad is fiddling with the gas canister, checking connections, and twisting random knobs.

Mum is coming down the steps of the caravan carrying a stack of plates. They are blue with a white trim just like the sky above her head, wisps of cloud framing a perfect day. Her footsteps creak on the rickety metal stairs.

'Chloe, help your mum,' says Dad automatically, not looking up.

'I've done loads,' I say. 'Ask Ella, she's just making a mess.'

Ella, my sister, is sitting on the grass sorting through our beach fun bag. She has laid everything in a rainbow on the ground: red ball, yellow bat, pink frisbee, green skittles, orange football. She looks up and whines in that know-it-all voice which she uses when she knows nothing. 'I'm *tidying. And* I got all the knives and forks out *and* wiped the plates.'

Ella is nine and so annoying. Mum says it is Ella's job to be irritating because she's the little sister. My friends think Ella is cute but she's really not.

The sound of a car horn lifts the seagulls off the caravan roofs. 'They're here,' screams Ella, scattering her rainbow as she jumps up and hurtles towards the approaching car. It moves slowly and quietly, the wheels muffled by the overlong grass. I have to concentrate hard to keep my pose and not run to the car like we always do. Ella is circling the car, waving and flapping her arms like a seagull looking for somewhere to land. I manage to stay sitting on the sun lounger and look down at my phone without seeing it. I'm going to glance up and wave when the car stops.

Every August, in the last week of the school holidays, we meet the Rossi family at the caravan site in Dorset. Dad says that Uncle Toni is from Italy-upon-Thames which means he was born in Italy but grew up in London. Mum says Dad shouldn't say that, but Dad says it's just a joke from when they were kids. Toni and Dad went to school together. Toni's accent is the same as Dad's except he waves his arms around a lot as if he is talking to a deaf person who is sitting a really long way away. Mum says Dad shouldn't say that either. Uncle Toni and Auntie Helen are not a real uncle and aunt, we just call them that because, well... we always have.

Auntie Helen has dark hair like the others but she's not Italian, she's from Basingstoke where they all live. Luca is in the same year as me at school. His brother, Marco, is a year older so he's 14 now. He's not with them this holiday as he's away with his school on a football trip. We've known them all forever.

I'm finding it hard to stay put, however, I am not the only one holding back. Mum is arranging the plates on the picnic table. She waves to the honking car. I can just see the corners of her mouth turned up and the beginnings of her slow smile. Most of her face is hidden by her huge straw hat, the wide brim pulled low. She wears it all the time now, a permanent shadow over her face. The doctor said that she has to keep her scar out of the sun, so she plasters herself with even more sun cream than normal, and never leaves the house without a sun hat. Since she came back from the hospital she is obsessed about Ella and I going out in the sun. The doctor told her most skin damage occurs in childhood. *Great*. Just as I'm about to leave the house for school in the morning, she appears with a selection of sun hats I wouldn't be seen dead in. I'm 13 not three. *Who wears a sun hat at secondary school?* Of course, I take one to shut her up, and bury it at the bottom of my bag. I get it, we're ginger, redheads, *whatever*, we have to be careful, but I'm not going to burst into flames on the way to school. It's only a ten-minute walk.

Luca. I can see him. Well, I see his head and one arm waving from the rear door window. He is trying to extract himself from the back seat dragging duvets and pillows with

3

him. Everything tumbles after him from the overpacked car like clowns in a circus. Luca straightens up grinning, pushing up his hair with one sweep of his hand. A spiky quiff, different for him. I like it.

*

Luca is my 'true love'. Yeah, I know, it sounds like something a Disney princess would say, but he's 'the one' apparently. *Kute* magazine said he was the one, not me or Sophie (she's my best friend). I told Sophie it was stupid but the more we talked about it, well… I don't know why I never noticed before. Sophie says I always talk about Luca. Maybe I've always liked him.

It all started when Sophie and I found her mum's old magazines in the loft room at her house. Sophie says her mum's a hoarder and she can't throw anything away. Their house looks okay to me. Nothing like those houses you see on the TV where people have hoarded so much stuff they can't sleep in their bed and they have to climb through a window because their hallway is full of junk. Sophie's house is a bit cluttered, I suppose, but there's a lot of people in it as Sophie has three brothers, two older and one younger, as well as her, and her mum and dad. There are books, DVDs, board games and video games overflowing from every shelf and surface, and piles of washing, papers and random stuff in every corner of every room. My mum wouldn't like it, she's a neat freak, but I think it's cosy. The kitchen table is always covered in Sophie's little brother's Lego and they never clear it away. If you're not careful you might eat a piece of orange brick instead of a carrot when you stay for tea.

On the top floor of their house, they have a loft room which is sort of an office and spare room, with a double bed squeezed between the desk and piles of uneasily stacked cardboard boxes. Sophie wants the loft room to be her bedroom and she hangs out up there hoping her mum and dad take the hint. Sophie and I had a sleepover in the loft room in the Christmas holidays. We started watching a film on her laptop, but we got bored. Then we watched a load of videos on YouTube and Insta and stuff until we got bored of that. We even made a video ourselves of us trying to rap a Christmas carol. It was really funny, but we didn't post it. That would be too embarrassing, and I'm not allowed anyway. Then Sophie started opening some of the boxes in the loft and nosing inside. We found some old baby clothes and I took a photo of Sophie wearing a tiny, pink knitted baby hat. She said she would kill me if I showed it to anyone. I only showed it to a few people at school. Most of the other boxes were full of boring stuff like office files and tangles of cables. Then we found a slightly squashed box that looked like it hadn't been opened in a million years. The tape holding it shut was brown and brittle and barely held the lid together. Scrawled on the side in faded black marker pen, it said 'Judy's stuff from home'. Judy is Sophie's mum's name.

The box was full of copies of an old magazine called *Kute – the maga-zeen for the modern teen.* Cringe. On the front of all the magazines was a label with an address: 16 Queen's Avenue. Sophie said that's her Grandad and Grandma's address and they still live there. Her mum told her she loved getting her magazines delivered to the house when she was our age. We spread the magazines over the bed like a colourful, crinkly quilt. We couldn't stop laughing. The shiny covers had celebrities posing with goofy smiles or staring moodily at the camera. They had crazy stuck up hair and make-up streaked in blues and pinks. Some of the celebs we recognised, and they looked so young compared to how old they look now on TV.

There were interviews, letters, and problem pages; girls worrying about periods and boyfriends and spots. Not much has changed, I thought, feeling the small lump on my chin which I knew would look red and gross by tomorrow. There were also pages of black and white photos where people acted out stories with the words in speech bubbles like a comic. It all looked so old. The fashion pages were hilarious. Most of the make-up tips were bizarre and the clothes might be vintage but I wouldn't be seen dead in them. Sophie and I were screaming with laughter at one point. Her mum shouted up to ask if we were killing each other.

Every issue of the magazine had a quiz where you had to answer A, B or C and depending on which letter you got the most of, it would give you an answer to the burning question of the week.

Are you the best of the besties? How good a friend are you? Take our quiz and find out.

Party queen or shy sixteen? Answer our quiz and we'll pick the perfect birthday night for you.

There were loads of quizzes about finding the right boyfriend but as it was Christmas, we decided to do the 'King Crush' one.

Kute Magazine. December 1983
Who's your King Crush? Don't look too far
from the mistletoe,
Prince Charming could be right under your
nose.
Take our quiz to find out where true love is
hiding for you.

Sometimes I think I'm the only girl in my class who hasn't had a boyfriend. Sophie says she has but I'm not sure. I didn't know her at primary school. When she tells me about her old boyfriends, they just sound like boys in her class at school that she hung out with. The girls at our school are always sharing pictures of themselves posing with their boyfriends or going on about parties they go to every weekend. I'm really boring, I never go anywhere. Mum says it's normal to be at home with your family when you are 13, and that probably some of the girls will be exaggerating. I bet they're not. She doesn't know.

Sophie grabbed a pen and a scrap of paper. Someone had already circled the answers in the magazine and written 'Simon' at the bottom of the page with a big love heart round it. 'Ew!' shouted Sophie when she saw it; her dad's name is *not* Simon. Sophie's mum had got mostly 'A' for her answers, so her King Crush was an 'old love rekindled with Christmas fire'. So cheesy.

I got mostly 'C' for my answers so apparently, for me, 'the one' was 'someone I've known for ages and might not have noticed yet'. At first, I thought of Sophie's brother, Ned, who is two years older than us. However, Sophie's face went a bit funny when I said that, sort of cross and worried, so I quickly laughed and said, 'Only joking!' and she looked relieved. Ned is nice though. He always says hello to me at school without laughing or making any stupid jokes like some of the boys.

So, who was my *King Crush*? It was Sophie that thought of Luca. She was telling me about the holiday to America that her mum and dad had just booked. It sounded amazing. I felt that awful jealous stab in my stomach because I knew I'd be going to the caravan again. I think Sophie was trying to make me feel better by reminding me about how much fun I had last year on holiday at the caravan, how we all get on great, and how the beach is amazing. It's all true, it's just, I'd like to go to America on holiday, or anywhere different really.

I've known Luca since I was little, but I'd never thought about liking him until I did the quiz in *Kute* magazine. Sophie went over the questions again to convince me. We got really excited. This summer was going to be amazing! Maybe this year I would have something to talk about when we got back to school. Luca and I get on great and he's even good-looking now. He's six months older than me which is good because another issue of *Kute* said it was often better for girls to go out with older boys because they are more mature.

The night we found the magazines Sophie fell asleep before me. We started watching the film again, but she didn't see the end. I wasn't tired so I started reading more issues of *Kute* magazine. There were lots of things about getting the right boyfriend, but half of the advice seemed to contradict the other. *Be confident* but *don't be too forward. Don't go after your best friend's boy* but *don't let anything stand in the way of true love.* I read all the problem pages as well. Everything was stupid and old-fashioned but weirdly not so different from what me and my friends talked about at school: parents, homework, teachers, boys, hating what we look like. At least we have less tragic hairstyles and clothes now than they did in those days.

When I finally felt sleepy, I put the magazines back and tried to stick the battered box back together with the broken tape. Next morning it was the first thing Sophie wanted to talk about, Luca and me, and what would happen that summer. I didn't feel so sure when I woke up that morning, but I went along with it. I had closed the lid on the box last night but this subject wasn't going away. Sophie did the quiz too, but her true love was supposed to be a 'close neighbour' which means he has to be the ugly boy from Year 9 who lives next door and has six computers. She didn't want to talk about that at all.

*

Our corner of the caravan site is filled with noise and cheerful shouting. The grown-ups are talking about the journey and what route they took in that weird way they do. Dad is man-hugging Uncle Toni with big playful slaps on the back. Mum is by the car now chatting with Auntie Helen. I watch Mum kiss her on the cheek awkwardly as her huge sun hat gets in the way. Ella is still screeching like the little show-off she is, running from one person to another. I hang back waiting for Luca to notice me. Sophie and I read in *Kute* magazine that you should look natural when you were waiting for a boy and not look cross or anything because he was late, or too excited if you were pleased to see him. But what *is* a natural expression? As soon as you start thinking about it, it doesn't feel natural anymore.

> *Kute magazine. March 1984*
> *Real girls get real boys. Don't be too cool*
> *for school or you might look the fool.*

Uncle Toni is swinging Ella around by the arms, lifting her feet off the ground. Then he spots me. Dropping Ella gently he walks towards me pointing and shouting although I'm only a few feet away. Toni is very loud.

'Who is this beautiful young lady? Where is little Chloe-bear?'

I suddenly feel shy as everyone turns to look at me. Toni scratches his head and pretends to be looking for me, looking out over the caravan site, and even behind me.

'Chloe, where are you hiding? Come give your Uncle Toni a big bear hug.'

I can't help but giggle as he moves towards me arms outstretched, growling. Uncle Toni is nuts. I wince at his big stubbly kiss on my cheek then, smiling, rub where it scratched.

'Stop it, Toni, you're embarrassing her,' says Auntie Helen giving me a sympathetic look.

Uncle Toni turns to Mum and Dad and throws up his arms dramatically as if in despair.

'I told you not to let her grow up. I'll have to lock up my sons!'

I go red at Toni's comment, which is stupid because no one knows about Luca and me. I put my hands up to my face as though I'm covering my mouth laughing but it's really to hide the blushing. I hate it when that happens. Luckily, no one is looking at me. All eyes are on Toni who is shaking his head in his hands like he's got a bee stuck in his ears. Dad says that Uncle Toni is wasted at the post office and he should be an actor. I dare to sneak a glance at Luca. His face is a mixture of amusement and embarrassment. As though he could sense me watching him, he suddenly looks at me and rolls his eyes. I grin back, smiling inside and out. My stomach flips as easily as one of Dad's gorgeous home-made burgers.

The Rossi gang know what happened to Mum, about her 'procedure'. I've heard her talking on the phone with Auntie Helen since it happened. Now, face-to-face everyone is pretending that things are normal. It is a shock, though, when Uncle Toni pulls off Mum's sun hat and throws it to the ground. She hasn't taken it off outside since we arrived, and I wondered if she ever would.

'How can I see you properly under this umbrella!' Toni announces.

As usual he kisses her on the hand like someone from an old movie, however, today he also sweeps her backwards into his arms so that her back is arched, and she only has one foot on the ground. Everyone is laughing. Uncle Toni kisses Mum confidently on each flushed cheek and then looking directly into her eyes he kisses her quickly on the lips. He then sweeps Mum back up to a standing position, her face a cocktail of confusion and shock and laughter. She staggers slightly as though dizzy or drunk. She touches her lip. I wonder whether he has hurt her, but she is smiling.

'Beautiful as always!' cries Toni dramatically. 'Run away with me.' He kisses her on the hand again. Mum gently shoves him away.

'Idiot,' she says, cheeks still pink.

'Go on, Lizzie,' Auntie Helen calls out. 'Do me a favour and take that madman off my hands.'

Now everyone is talking at top speed about everything and nothing. There's so much to catch up on. People talk over each other catching up on news and planning what we will do in the week ahead. I wouldn't normally feel confident enough to join in like this if I was in a big group at school but it's different here. It feels cosy and exciting. Dad has his arm around Mum's shoulder. She doesn't put her hat back on straight away. Suddenly Luca is right in front of me. I blink, unprepared.

'Swim?' he says, eyebrows raised like question marks.

He's taller. He has a faint moustache, and his face is thinner. His cheekbones stand out more than I remember. I suppose I look different too, at least I hope I do.

Swim? Yay! I think. *No, hang on. I have spent ages doing my hair and now it would be ruined for tonight.* This is not what Sophie and I planned. *Should I text her?*

Ella is excited, jumping up and down. A swim would be lovely. The thought of the cool water makes me feel hotter. I desperately want to get out of these jeans.

Kute magazine. April 1983
Life's an adventure. Don't say no, just go
with the flow.

'Good idea,' Mum interrupts my thoughts. 'I can finish getting the caravan sorted and you can pick up some things I need at the shop.'

Ella and Luca disappear in opposite directions to get their swimming things. Mum follows Ella up the caravan steps. Dad is helping Toni and Helen empty their car. Everyone knows what they are doing and where they are going. I try to calm the butterflies inside me. The school counsellor came to our form last term to teach us breathing techniques. She said if you were ever feeling stressed or overwhelmed you should breathe in through your nose and out through your mouth. We had to practise all together and me and my mates could not stop laughing. I thought we might get a detention. I haven't got one yet at school and I don't want to. I wish I could get the breathing right now. I draw in a long breath but the butterflies seem to rise up with it making my chest feel tight and anxious. I must be doing it wrong. I look around at the familiar site of the field and the caravans and the people I know so well and take another deep breath. I feel better.

*

The caravan site is not what most people think of when I tell them where we are going. It's just a big field with a bunch of old caravans dotted about. There's no swimming pool or arcade or anything interesting. There is a big modern

13

caravan site next door which has all that. We can buy day or week tickets to use the pool and clubhouse there. Mr Jones, the farmer that owns the field, gets us a special discount. Ella and I always beg Mum and Dad to let us stay at the modern caravan site, but no, we have to stay in our field in Gran and Grandad's old caravan next to Marco and Luca's grandparents' old caravan.

Mr Jones, the farmer, says that the company who own the big caravan site want to buy his field. Every year, when we pick up the keys at his farmhouse, Mr Jones shakes his grey head sadly and tells us he doesn't know if he can carry on another year. Maybe, at least, one year he could get WiFi, I think. There is WiFi in the bar at the other caravan site but Mum and Dad won't let Ella and I go in there without them. We use the shop all the time to get things for Mum like milk and bread. This was the first place that Ella and I were allowed to go shopping together for sweets which was amazing when we were little. At home I go shopping in town all the time now with my friends, but Ella's not allowed to do that so going to the little shop is still a big deal for her.

Our caravan site is in a field on the edge of Mr Jones's fruit farm. It's enclosed by tangled hedges and tall trees on all sides. You can't see anything through the thick branches, so you feel cut off from the rest of the world. Ella and I used to love pretending that the hedge was the one that surrounded the castle in the 'Sleeping Beauty' story. We'd take turns pretending to be Beauty and the other had to be the Prince cutting through the hedge of thorns, which was really one of us hacking through a hole in the bushes with a big stick. The Prince had to shout: 'One kiss and you will

14

awake!' We tried to make Luca and Marco do it a few times on holiday, but they never got the words right and eventually they would get bored and disappear to play football.

The other modern caravan site is much more fun but our field has its own private, secret path down to the beach. The path has a rocky wall and high hedges on both sides so if you don't look at the sky it feels like you are walking down a tunnel to the sea. The path twists and turns so you can't see the beach until your toes are literally digging into the sand. Mum calls it 'The Big Reveal' like on those TV makeover programmes when they turn someone's horrible house into something a lot nicer but don't show them until the end. Then they cry and get excited about the same rooms painted a different colour. Every year, when we first see the beach, Mum pretends she's on a makeover show, saying, *Oh, I love the colour of the sky. I wouldn't have chosen it, but it really works. Wow, the sand is so soft. I love the seaside theme. Thank you, thank you!* She's so embarrassing. She hasn't done it yet, this holiday, but then she's hardly left the caravan.

There are about 20 caravans that sit around the edges of the field, some newer than others. Most are pretty old and the people who own them are even older. They sit in camp chairs outside their caravans and don't move all week. They remind me of big garden ornaments who wear baggy shorts and drink tea. They call Dad and Uncle Toni 'son' because they remember them from when they were little. We knew everyone when Gran and Grandad used to bring us here. They'd take us 'visiting', walking from caravan to caravan to say hello to their friends. Ella and I loved this as we'd be given sweets and treats dug out from pockets or the bottom of handbags or battered biscuit tins. Some of their friends have sold their caravans and they've been replaced by more modern versions. A few sit empty. Gran and Grandad still own the caravan, but Dad looks after it now.

Not everyone is at the caravan site at the same time so it is always pretty quiet. That makes it feel even more like 'our' place. A couple of years ago, Dad and Toni dug out a fire pit in the middle of the field. They also made wooden benches for us to sit around. Sometimes, we have big fires there and toast marshmallows. People from the other caravans join us, even the old people. Dad and Toni help them carry their chairs over. That's the most lively it gets here but it's very pretty at night. Sometimes the music from the clubhouse bar next door will drift over the hedge as though carried by the breeze, but it all feels a long way away from us. The field shrinks to just a circle around us as we watch the flames jump around the fire pit. If the sky is clear, Dad will point out the constellations in the stars: Orion, the Big Dipper, the Great Bear. Ella and I sit with our heads flipped back until our necks ache, desperate to be the first one to see a shooting star.

> *Star light, star bright,*
> *The first star I see tonight;*
> *I wish I may, I wish I might,*
> *Have the wish I wish tonight.*

If we didn't see any shooting stars Mum would say that they must have landed in the fire when we weren't looking and we should look out for the sparks. Ella still believes that. When we were supposed to be in bed, we would sneak to our bedroom window to watch the dying fire and try to wish upon a star. Mum told us she would find us later, heads on one side, eyes closed, cheeks mushed into the window frame.

*

Ella's head bobs below me in the water. I'm standing on the side of the swimming pool above her, toes curled over the edge. The sun is hot on my shoulders. Zig zags of light are caught in the rippling surface of the water. My ears are filled with that swimming pool sound, waves of high-pitched shrieks and fun.

'Come on!' yells Ella. 'It's not cold.' She crosses her eyes and chatters her teeth making me laugh. The water refracts the shape of her arms and legs. From where I'm standing she looks like a weird, disjointed pink frog. I don't care about the cold. I haven't seen Luca yet and I'm trying to decide whether I should stand by the side of the pool casually or sit on the edge with my legs in the water. I am wearing my new bikini. I've never had one before but I told Mum that all the girls at school wear them now. I smooth down my hair, wondering if I can keep it dry in the pool. Something flits by me and a bomb goes off on the surface of the water.

SPLASH!!

I gasp as a huge wave drenches me in cold water. A whistle is blowing. The shock of the cold makes me wobble.

I am too close to the edge of the pool to stop myself falling. I hit the water in a painful belly flop and bubbles rush up my nose. I come up choking and spluttering. My eyes are blurred but I can just make out the shape of Ella and Luca's faces in front of me.

'What – did you – do that – for?' I cough out the words in angry bursts.

'What?' Luca lifts up his goggles and rubs his eyes. He stares at me bewildered.

'She fell in the water when you splashed, *idiot*,' says Ella. 'You're not supposed to bomb in here. You'll get in trouble.'

Ella likes to tell everyone the rules. She swims closer to me and tries to pat my back looking concerned. I push her away but only gently as she can't reach the floor here. Her legs and arms are moving like crazy as she struggles to keep her chin out of the water. Luca's hair is plastered to his head. The spots on his forehead are red and bumpy.

'Sorry,' he says his usual grin fading, 'I didn't see you.'

He looks more worried as I keep coughing. My stomach smarts where I hit the water. I feel sick and embarrassed.

'She fell on her belly,' says Ella. She slaps her fist on the water to demonstrate, spraying us both. 'Like a great big poo hitting the toilet. Splash!'

She says it so seriously that both Luca and I burst out laughing. Ella giggles, then splutters, then starts to sink. Luca hooks one hand under her armpit and helps her to the edge of the pool.

'She's not much of a floater,' he says, and that starts us all off again.

'Would you rather poo all day or be a poo for a day?' asks Ella.

We laugh so much we have to stay by the side of the pool because it's too hard to swim when you are having hysterics.

> *Kute Magazine. July 1982*
> *Laughter is the best medicine, Doctor Love*
> *says.*
> *Have some fun in the sun and find your*
> *summer haze.*

We stumble around the shallow end playing Marco Polo. Ella and I are squealing as Luca, his eyes shut, is reaching out blindly, hands grabbing and splashing. We play all our favourite games. It could be last year's holiday, or the year before, or next year even. Luca and I swim races. He beats me at front crawl but we draw at breaststroke. Ella times us, counting out loud. I know she's counting faster when Luca is in the lead, but I don't mind. Luca finds some water pistols abandoned by the side of the pool. I shriek as a jet hits me between the shoulder blades. Ella and I gang up until he's cornered and screaming.

The pool gets quieter. I float on the surface, arms spread, sun on my eyelids, cool water lapping my ears. The rest of the world seems a long way away. The three of us float around each other, gently bumping then drifting away, to entangle again moments later. I don't know whose arm or leg is whose.

We are the last ones to leave the pool. The lifeguard closes the gate. My legs are heavy as I haul myself out of the pool. The ground feels hard underfoot as I take my first step. Luca is standing on the side drying himself quickly. His stomach is toned and brown. I look so pale next to him. I hate my white skin. I have tried fake tan but the colours never look right on me, like I'm wearing someone else's legs. I feel self-conscious so I quickly wrap myself in a towel. My bikini clings and I pull my T-shirt over my head. I hurry but he's not looking at me.

'I'm starving,' shouts Ella. 'I've got the swimming hunger!'

*

I am queuing in the shop. Swimming was fun but now my stomach feels more than empty and my head aches. The low sun catches my eyes through the shop window and I wince. The queue moves slowly and I take a step closer to the till. Suddenly my phone comes alive. The clubhouse bar is next to the shop and I must be picking up the WiFi. I ran out of data before we even started the holiday so I can't use my phone in our caravan. I scroll through posts and messages hungrily but it's the same stuff as usual. My form WhatsApp group is a long stream of people saying everything about nothing. Weirdly none of it seems important here. Of course, everyone I'm friends with is on holiday in amazing places, looking amazing. Sophie says she is going to a party but I'm not sure I believe her. There are several messages from Sophie. 'How's it going?' 'Luca-Chloe. Chloe-Luca.' 'Send me pics.' 'Did he like the bikini?' There is a mirror next to the till for people to try on sunglasses. I catch my reflection and am shocked at how terrible I look. Hair flat and dripping, panda eyes, pink skin, a million more freckles. I quickly rub at the smudged mascara. I can see Luca waiting outside the shop. *Ping.* Another message from Sophie: 'Spill the tea?' She means gossip. What does she expect? We've only been here a few hours. I drop my phone in to my bag with the wet towel.

'Can I eat my ice cream now?' Ella whines.

'Shut up,' I snap. 'I've got to pay.'

She's so annoying. She hasn't dried herself properly and a puddle is forming around her feet. I get the change and push her towards the door.

> *Walk. Slap. Walk. Lick.*
> *Walk. Slap. Walk. Lick. Walk.*
> *Drip. Lick. Lick-lick. Walk. Slap. Lick.*

Ella is dawdling, flip-flops slapping against the path, stopping every other step to lick her melting ice cream. Her little pink tongue traces the dribbles of ice cream back up the cone.

'Can't you walk and lick?' I grumble.

She's so slow. I want to get back to the caravan so that I can shower and blow-dry my hair for the barbeque tonight. I look and feel a mess. Luca, walks ahead, one hand holding his ice cream, the other checking the football scores on his phone. He says his team are playing. I turn around to glare at Ella again. The ice cream has started to run down her hand. She pokes her tongue in and out of her fingers trying to catch the drips before they fall. Luca stops every now and again to take a picture of 'cute' Ella with ice cream running down her chin. He doesn't take any photos of me. Anyway,

I finished my ice cream ages ago. My lips still feel cool and sweet. The rest of me feels hot and swollen. I don't really like the heat so the slow walk back in the late afternoon sun is torture. My body feels heavy as though I am dragging the swimming pool back with me.

'Hurry UP!' I shout at Ella. The last word bounces back angrily from the hot tarmac.

Luca turns around and I look down at my feet, pretending that the sound didn't come from me. I hate it when I shout but I can't help it. One minute I feel okay and the next moment the words come out of me at a hundred miles an hour. For a millisecond Ella miraculously starts to walk faster, then her feet gradually slow as though she were walking into jelly. *Walk, slap, lick.* Her hand is now painted completely white with creamy ice cream. I stop to let her catch up and put down the plastic bag full of shopping. I stretch out my fingers. The bag has moulded my skin into new shapes like playdough, weird little red and white bumps and lines. I sigh loudly. It feels good to let out some air.

'Hey, Ella,' says Luca suddenly, 'Can you march like a soldier?'

He marches on ahead lifting his knees high, looking back to see if Ella will copy him. Ella perks up at the idea of a game. She starts lifting her legs high and quickens her pace to overtake him. Her tongue pokes even faster to catch her ice cream drips but her eyes are on the race. Every time she starts to slow, Luca moves slightly faster. Just as Ella finally overtakes him, Luca looks over his shoulder at me. He mock salutes, pulls a goofy face and grins. He's got nice teeth. I smile back but he has already turned ahead to march in front of Ella. He barks, *One, Two, Three, Four,* in a comedy soldier voice to her moving in time. A warm flush starts at the base of my stomach and spreads upwards over my chest and neck until it meets the tips of the smile still lingering on my face. For once I don't care that I am blushing.

> *Kute Magazine. November 1983*
> *Movie moments! That first glance, the funny*
> *joke, something he did that was kind.*
> *Look out for the moment you'll always*
> *replay in your mind!*

*

I drop the bag of shopping on the floor of our caravan's tiny kitchen.

'Did you have a good swim?' asks Mum.

She is chopping; the knife flies up and down so quickly the vegetables look like they are alive and trying to jump out of the way. She sweeps a waterfall of colourful veg from the chopping board into a bowl without spilling one. Her Dad, Grandad JJ, was a chef and he taught her some moves.

'I'm going in the shower,' I say.

The heat walking home was bad enough, but the caravan feels worse even with all the windows open. I don't know whether the wet feeling on my back under my T-shirt is sweat or my still-damp bikini.

'Swimming was BRILLIANT!' says Ella. 'Luca bombed in the deep end and Chloe got all… wet… then…'

She trails offs mid-sentence and stares puzzled at the wall behind Mum. 'What's happened to the mirror?'

I'm about to push past Ella to get to the bathroom but I stop and follow her gaze. Something's different.

The wall that divides the kitchen/living room part of our caravan from the bedrooms and bathroom is covered by an enormous mirror. It makes the caravan look twice as big as though we have another room exactly like this one. It reflects everything back at us, good or bad, including the identical family we see in the mirror who copy everything we do. According to Mum, the 'other family' are just as messy as we are and the 'other Mum' agrees with her. Ella likes to balance on a stool at the little kitchen counter watching our other family carefully. She will ask the 'other us' questions and then turn around and ask the same questions to the real us. I pull faces at her in the mirror and when she turns around to glare at me, I smile sweetly. It's stupid but it cracks us up every time.

If we are arguing Mum points to the mirror and asks if the 'other Ella' or 'other Chloe' are behaving better than us. Ella can get really angry and goes red in the face like a tomato when she is mad about something. Dad says that I got the red hair but Ella got the temper that red-heads are supposed to have. When 'our Ella' first saw the 'other Ella' having a tantrum in the mirror they both ran crying to their bedrooms. I found 'our Ella' face down on the bed, sniffling into her pillow, arms wrapped around her big fluffy lion, Leo. She said that she hated the 'other Ella' and never wanted to see her 'ugly angry face' ever again. Now she's a bit older, they get on better. Ella's more likely to high-five the 'other Ella' if they are playing a good prank or perfecting their dance moves. Mum tells her off though if she smacks the glass.

We've done a lot of posing and dancing in this mirror. Mum loved the Spice Girls when she was our age. She has made us watch all the old videos on YouTube. She knows all the words. She will grab a spoon as a pretend microphone and get us dancing until the floor of the caravan shakes. She also loves Madonna's 'Vogue' and taught us how to 'strike a pose' like in the video. When we were little Ella and I would get our arms tangled over our heads as we tried to copy the moves. Mum only has to shout out 'Vogue' and we all automatically 'strike a pose' in the mirror, even Dad.

We learnt to 'model walk' here as well. It is a short runway across the caravan but Mum showed us how to 'work it', hand on hip, swinging side to side, strutting up to the sofas at one end of the caravan and back to the mirror. Mum likes to finish her turn by blowing a kiss at herself in the mirror and shouting, *Darling, you look fabulous!* Not today though. This morning, before Luca and the others got here, Ella and I were messing around in front of the mirror. Mum was unpacking in the kitchen, surrounded by a wall of boxes and shopping bags lined up on the kitchen counter.

'Mum', shouted Ella, 'the other Ella is waving at you.'

Mum waved briefly looking at the real Ella but not into the mirror behind her. Then she carried on stacking boxes of cereal into a cupboard, lining them up perfectly before closing the door.

'Hey, what do you think, Mum?' I was pouting over my shoulder into the mirror. 'I think the other Chloe is looking go-o-od…' I pushed both hands up through my hair and wiggled my bum. Ella had hysterics.

Mum laughed and looked over for just a second. Normally she would start posing herself.

'Mum,' Ella pleaded. 'Come and strike a pose with us. Let's dance!'

Ella started doing a Tik Tok dance that all the kids in her year are crazy about. Her feet got faster and faster until the caravan floor wobbled and I felt like it would force me to join in as well. Mum watched properly this time and applauded with big hand claps and a small smile. Out of habit, she glanced at the mirror to check her make-up and hair. However, when she saw the 'other Mum' in the mirror, the hand that was half-raised to smooth back copper strands from her forehead, dropped to her side and she quickly turned away.

That was this morning. Now, Ella stares confused at the mirror, her face scrunched up like an empty bag of crisps. She did some drawings on the car journey and they are now stuck to the mirror behind Mum in the kitchen. We're not usually allowed to stick anything on the mirror and Mum polishes the glass every day to remove smudges and finger prints. She doesn't like clutter but there are lots of things stuck to the mirror now. There's a map of the coastline on which someone has written 'We are here' in a thick black pen next to an even thicker arrow. Next to the map, are some old postcards of the beach and local town which we probably bought to send to people at home last year but never did. There's also a couple of photos of us which must belong to Gran and Grandad unless Mum brought them from home.

'Thought I'd brighten the place up,' says Mum seeing us staring at the wall. 'That map shows all the local walks.'

Boring, I think.

'But how will I see the 'other Ella''? whines Ella.

'I think you will find that she is eating a biscuit at the end of the counter,' replies Mum.

She pushes a packet of biscuits towards the end of the kitchen worktop next to Ella's usual stool. Ella slides up on to it. She watches the 'other Ella' take a nibble of a biscuit. They pull a face at each other then chuckle, spraying biscuit crumbs.

'But, Mum, how are you going to look at yourself 'ten times a day', says Ella giggling.

Ella deepens her voice to say 'ten times a day' and I know she is pretending to be Dad who normally teases Mum about how often she looks in the mirror. I nudge Ella sharply with my elbow to get her to stop talking but she doesn't get the hint.

'Ow,' she says glaring at me and rubbing her arm.

Dad said we must all be more careful around Mum since her operation, whilst she's 'getting used to things'. The doctor told Dad that having something wrong with your face, even if it was only a small thing, was a million times worse than your arm or leg or somewhere else more hidden on your body. It's true, who cares about a zit on your back but one on your nose can ruin your day.

'But Mum,' continued Ella not seeing my hard stare. 'With all these pictures in the way, how are you going to check your hair?'

'There's plenty of room', says Mum rinsing a cloth under the running tap.

No, Ella's right, there isn't room for Mum to see her hair or anything from the kitchen. We can see ourselves on this side of the caravan but the space on the mirror behind Mum is camouflaged with pictures, maps and photos. There is no 'other Mum' reflected in the mirror cleaning the 'other kitchen' with our 'other family'. Just our Mum, with her back to the mirror, wiping down the already clean surfaces.

I want to get in the shower and wash off the sticky feeling of chlorine but my feet feel rooted to the spot. Mum's lost in cleaning but I'm worried that Ella will say something even more stupid. *What is Ella doing?* She has slipped off the stool and is standing so close to the mirror now that her breath creates a mist on the glass around one of the photos. It's a picture taken on holiday last year of the four of us on the beach. I know it's last year because I had that stupid bob – so glad I've grown it out. In the photo, Mum, Dad, Ella and I are kneeling in the sand, arms linked together, grinning. Hair whipped up in all directions by the wind, our faces squint into the sun. We've swapped shorts for jeans so it must have been taken at the end of the week when it's started to get chilly. The thought makes me shiver despite the oppressive heat of the caravan. In front of us, etched into wet sand, are drawings of four faces. At first glance they all look the same; skin the colour of sand and hair speckled with grit, ground up seashells and the dark trails of seaweed that are thrown up near the water's edge. The faces are just lines drawn in the wet sand but you can tell it's us; Ella's wild hair, Dad's big nose, dots for freckles for Mum and me.

Ella's nose almost touches the shiny paper. The tip of her tongue pokes out the corner of her mouth as she concentrates on tapping the picture carefully with her little finger.

'What are you doing?' I ask.

'I'm patting Salty Dog,' she says as if it's obvious.

Next to our beach portraits, there is another shape sketched into the sand, a rough drawing of a dog that we've never met. In the photo, Ella's right-hand hovers mid-air in the space she imagines Salty Dog is standing next to us. Her fingers ruffle his invisible shaggy mane.

'I can't wait to get to the beach,' says Ella. 'Do you think our sand pictures are still there?'

'No, idiot,' I say, 'the sea will have washed them away.'

'I knew that,' says Ella quickly. Her finger gently strokes the photo now.

'I want to do everything the same as last year,' she says dreamily. 'The beach, swimming, the fun fair, a barbeque, shopping…'

'I don't,' I mutter irritated, not listening to whatever she says next. I push past her through the door that leads to the bathroom. *I want this holiday to be different.* This holiday is *going* to be different.

*

Barbeque. Uncle Toni and Dad are making a lot of 'man noise' as Mum calls it. They are in their element shouting instructions to each other and whooping at anything that sizzles or pops. The mouth-watering smell of burgers, ribs and sausages fills the air. My stomach rolls like a tumble dryer. Luca, Ella and I stand in a line watching them cook like starving dogs waiting to be fed. I can hear Mum behind us talking to Auntie Helen about the award that I won at school for helping with reading at our local primary school. I mean it was good and everything, but does she have to keep telling everyone the boring stuff about me? I know she's going to talk about the charity thing with the Guides next. I'm hoping Luca can't hear her. I start telling him about a hilarious video that a friend had shared where a rapper raps with this cat. Ella is following every word of my story, laughing hysterically even though she hasn't seen the video and I haven't even got to the funny bit yet. I try to turn my back on her and concentrate on Luca but she squeezes between us.

What is strange about the holiday this year is not having Marco, Luca's older brother, with us. Marco is crazy and funny. I notice that Luca is quiet even though Marco isn't here. I always thought Luca seemed quiet because Marco was loud, but maybe not.

Toni grips a blackened rib in the barbeque tongs and waves it under Luca's nose. Luca ducks back irritated.

'Dad!'

'Luca, you are breaking my heart,' pleads Toni. 'You used to love Papa's special ribs.'

Auntie Helen's quiet voice drifts over. 'Toni, leave him alone.'

'Look at Chloe,' continues Toni, waving the tongs at me now. 'That's a beautiful appetite.'

I sink my teeth into the tender flesh of the ribs. I am starving. Luca is watching me with no expression.

'So good,' I mumble, trying to grin through a mouthful of sauce. 'Mmm.'

'Dad,' says Luca, 'I'm a vegetarian now, get over it.'

He walks off towards the food table. I stare after him hungrily and pick bits of meat out of my teeth while he has his back to me. *Should I eat any more?* Auntie Helen is putting a veggie burger on Luca's plate and balancing some fresh lettuce and tomato on top. It looks so neat and fresh compared to the sticky mess of ribs and sweet sauce on my plate. Everything about Luca looks neat and clean. His white T-shirt fits his square shoulders perfectly. The white lines down the sides of his perfect-fitting tracksuit bottoms end at his white box-fresh trainers. I bite into another rib without thinking. The sweet sauce oozes and I lick my lips. A blob of sauce drips onto my crop top. I rub the stain making it worse. I'll have to get changed before he sees it.

> *Kute Magazine. December 1982*
> *You can't be anyone but you.*
> *Cinderella wears a ragged dress, but the*
> *Prince wants the girl that fits the shoe.*

I hope so.

2

SUNDAY

We have lots of traditions on holiday and yesterday was no different. When we arrive on the first day Ella and I must do our 'tour of the town' as Mum calls it, which is just a walk around the whole campsite to see if anything has changed. Answer: not much. Occasionally one of the caravans gets sold, or someone builds a posh veranda, which is code for 'new steps'. Everything was just the same as normal this year, except, it was weird, but when Ella and I walked around yesterday the field seemed smaller than I remembered it. We were soon back at the caravan with Mum looking disappointed at us being back so soon as she was still unpacking. The next tradition of our first day is that we have a big barbeque on the first night and Uncle Toni has to make his special sticky ribs. Well, we did both of those. Check, and check.

On our second day, that's today, if the weather is okay, it's our holiday tradition to spend the whole day at the beach. The beach is really pretty and we always swim in the sea. Dad throws himself in, does a few strokes, and then shakes himself like a big dog. Ella and I chase each other in then splash around screaming at the cold. Mum won't go in the water unless it's a very, very, *very* hot day. She makes up excuses not to swim, like 'I've just washed my hair', or 'I just want to relax', but we all know she hates the cold. If she goes in the water at all, she submerges herself slowly, stopping every few minutes to acclimatise. She does this quietly as though she doesn't want to alert the water that she's here. Then a wave will splash up her bum and she gives a little scream which is funny. She gets *very* cross if you splash her. Once she's in the water, her pale skin reflects the grey-blue around her. If she's too cold her lips turn purple. Dad says that's when we know she's ready to come out. Dad says Mum can't hide anything. Her skin is like mine, pink when she's hot, blue or purple when she's cold. Of course, the worst thing is the blushing, the red wave that washes over our faces when we're embarrassed. Not that Mum is ever embarrassed, that's usually me. Especially in class at school, knowing everyone is wondering why the ginger kid looks like a tomato when she's reading out loud in class.

It's even hotter today than yesterday. The weather is never this good normally. We could be in Greece where my friend Millie is this week. Well, maybe not, Dorset doesn't look like Greece. Millie posted these amazing pictures of the island where she is staying with her family. Their villa looked like it was hanging off the side of a cliff but in a good way. The sea below was such a deep green it didn't look real. I wish we could go somewhere like that, or France, or Spain, or Disney World, or anywhere. It's so boring going to the same place every year and we never go abroad. We do always have a nice time though at the caravan, and the Rossis are fun. And of course now I like Luca, I suppose I wouldn't want to do anything else. I sneak a look at Luca and follow his long shape all the way down to his toned legs. He's really fit. He wants to be a professional footballer. He's helping Ella bury his Dad, packing the sand around Toni's hairy waist. They're all laughing like they're drunk on the sun.

'Chloe, have you put sunscreen on?'

Mum's voice breaks into the fun. She is probably still cross with me because, apparently, I took too long in the bathroom this morning and 'held everyone up'. Excuse me for wanting to look good. I try not to look at her. Mum is so pale that sometimes you know exactly what she is thinking by the colours moving under her skin. Red dots on her cheeks when she's cross, deep flush all over when she's busy and stressed. They could have gone down to the beach without me, but no, we had to go as a family. Same traditions, same routine every year. I just wanted to finish my makeup. What's wrong with that?

> *Kute Magazine. July 1985*
> *Summer Splash! Lush Lips and Sparkle*
> *Eyes: Let your summer make-up shimmer*
> *not shame-yer!*

'Chloe, did you hear your mum?' Dad shouts over from where he is setting up the cricket stumps, struggling to get them to stay upright in the soft sand. 'We don't want you fried like an egg. It's bloody hot today.'

Dad has pulled off his shirt and his stomach hangs over his shorts like a second smile. I nod to shut him up. Dad says that I'm lucky to have Mum's complexion. He calls us his 'English roses'. I just think it's a pain. Pale skin, red hair, freckles. Every summer they nag me to cover up and put on more sunscreen, but it really clogs up your pores. They are going to make me get spots. I look over at Luca enviously. He is always naturally tanned, I bet he never burns.

Mum and Auntie Helen are sitting under the beach umbrella leaning against the cool-boxes, hands wrapped around brightly coloured paperbacks. Mum never sits in the sun. It was a shock to everyone when she got skin cancer. Cancer. Dad told us not to call it that because it was too scary, and he didn't want anyone to get upset. I presume he means Ella. He said Mum didn't have 'cancer', but a 'form' of cancer. It's called a BCC, basal cell carcinoma. It is a type of cancer but not the sort that kills you. They cut it out and that should be it. Mum is waiting for the test results to make sure they removed all the affected skin around it. That's why her scar is so much bigger than what was there before. If the test results are clear, then everything will be alright. Dad says that the doctors are 95% sure it will be. Dad says that Mum is *not* going to die. Mum should have seen the doctors sooner, but she didn't think there was anything wrong. It was something she had had for ages, growing very slowly. You think moles are big and black and hairy, but this was skin-coloured, a small, pale, flat circle sitting on the edge of her lips. It wasn't very noticeable from a distance, but I could feel it sometimes when she brushed my cheek with a kiss. It was only when it changed that she got worried. Now we're all worried but we're pretending we're not. For Ella, of course. We should know next week about the other 5%. Dad said the hospital would have rung us if there was anything wrong. And it is only 5%. If I only got 5% wrong on a test at school then everyone would think I was a genius.

'Chloe?!' Mum's voice is firm. She points at the beach bag next to me.

I roll my eyes to show her how stupid this is and grab the sunscreen bottle. It is poking out of the beach bag from amongst the squash of towels and snacks. I squirt a white blob into my hand. It runs across my palm like paint. If Gran was here she would be telling me which lines it was crossing. Apparently one of the lines on my palm is my life line and one is my love line. I can't remember which is which. I dot a tiny bit of sun cream on each cheek and rub gently. It's so annoying. I don't want to put this gunk over my foundation. It took me ages to get the colour right. I love it because it helps me not look like me. I don't have to be pale with pink cheeks and freckles. I can be normal for a change. People at school go on about how they wish they could have red hair like mine, but they don't get it. They don't know what it's like for everyone to call you 'ginger ninja', 'ginger whinger', and worse, and then expect you to laugh about it. They also moan about how pale they are, but my legs are almost blue-white, and the veins show through my skin like a map. I wish I could tan like the other girls. When I started secondary school last year, it was baking hot at the beginning of term. It was torture wearing the new blazer and thick skirt and I wore ankle socks rather than the grey knee-high socks. One lunchtime I was sitting with some girls from my form. None of us knew each other very well then, apart from the few who went to primary school together. They were talking about where everyone had been on holiday in the summer. Someone asked me where I'd been, but before I could answer a girl called Mia pointed at my legs and said the 'Isle of Wight'. Everyone laughed, especially Mia, loving the attention. I hate her now and so does Sophie. I don't wear ankle socks to school no matter how hot it is.

I don't know if Mum is still looking at me but I keep my head down and message Sophie. It's mainly emojis. Sun. Ice cream. Love hearts.

'Chloe, phone,' Mum's warning carries across the beach.

I sigh. Mum insists that we don't look at our phones when we are having 'family' time. Dad as well, even though he will be dying to check the football scores because the season has started. I see a string of emojis on the screen from Sophie before I turn off my phone. Sun. Kiss. King. Some bricks – that must be for crush – *nice*. Mistletoe. Bikini.

Dad has finished setting up the cricket stumps.

'Come on, Chloe. We're going to start the game.'

'It's okay, Dad, I'll just watch.'

I'm still messaging Sophie with my hand hidden in my bag.

'Don't be silly, Chloe-Bear, get over here, you're in my team – the-e-e winners!'

He flexes his arms like a body builder and shakes his fists in Uncle Toni's face who rises from his beach grave, sand clinging stubbornly to his thick chest hair.

'Forget it, John-boy,' says Toni in a fake American accent. 'Me and my boy are taking you down.'

Luca stands next to Toni. How different they look. Luca is a head taller than his father, and he has blue eyes like Auntie Helen. The only thing Toni and Luca share is their tanned skin. What all the Rossi boys share though is a competitive streak. They scan our group for potential teammates narrowing their eyes as they weigh up who to pick first.

Ella is chanting, 'Chloe-Bear, Chloe-Bear', grinding her feet into the sand.

'I'm not playing,' I say. *Shut up*, I think. If I play, I'll get hot and sweaty and ruin my makeup.

'Chloe... phone,' Mum's quiet voice sounds more dangerous. She's already told me this about a million times today. I can feel her cool glance from the shade and my cheeks burn.

Then Luca starts waving me over. 'Chloe, come on. We haven't got enough people without you.'

'Coming!' I shout and scramble to my feet.

I stuff my phone into my rucksack. I'm wearing another new bikini and matching shorts. They are all deep blue with tiny silver fish darting along the edges. Mum gave me the money to get everything.

Dad is mucking about jogging on the spot, bending and stretching, pretending to line up the perfect bowl. I'm hot from running and the handle of the cricket bat is slippery. I puff air up into my fringe and the sweat on my forehead cools a bit. I grip the bat tighter and try to concentrate, but Toni, who is wicket keeper, keeps singing and dancing around the corners of my eyes.

'Stop it,' I shout, trying to be stern. 'You're putting me off. Just 'cos we're winning.' We are too. Me and Luca.

Luca and Chloe. I usually play with Dad so he looked a bit weird when I said that I would be in Luca's team.

The ball comes sailing high straight at my chest. I twist and flip it over my shoulder. 'Catch, catch, catch,' screams Ella but Toni, who is too far over to the right, dives and stumbles in the sand, falling with a 'flump' sound as though he's landed on a pile of cushions. I run for it. Arms flying out, my fingers feel the rush of air as Luca tears past me in the other direction. It's like dipping them in warm water. We only need one run.

'Yes-s-s-s-s!' Both hands in the air, Luca charges back towards me yelling like he's just scored a goal at Wembley. I reach out my arms to meet him, but instead of the hug I'm expecting, he high-fives the space where my arms should be, and accidentally hits me in the eye.

*

Chips. So good. I breathe in steam and vinegar, chomping quickly at chips too hot to eat, each bite agony as they scald my gums. Ella is mashing them with her mouth open, sucking and blowing air over her burning tongue. It's disgusting. I want to stuff the chips in her mouth and tell her to get lost. I wish Ella would stop hanging around us. I know I used to do everything with her but things are different now. I'm older and she's just a kid. I thought Luca and I could be alone tonight but Mum makes me take her everywhere. Sophie keeps messaging me to see how I am getting on with 'Operation King Krush' as she calls it, but I haven't got anything to tell her.

When I suggested that we share a bag of chips, Luca looked at me as though I was crazy and said he was starving. He bought three portions, one each for him, me and Ella. We'd have to walk close if we were sharing a bag. If I reached for a chip, my arm would brush his. He has dark hairs growing on his forearms. Perhaps if it gets cold he might put his arm around my shoulder. I wonder how soft the hairs would feel against my skin. Instead, Ella walks between us chatting about how much she loves chips.

'I love fat chips, but I love thin chips too,' says Ella. 'If you could only eat one type of chip for the rest of your life, would it be one of these…' She holds up a big fat chip for us to admire. '... Or a skinny one?'

Why is she always here?

> *Kute Magazine. February 1982*
> *Valentine's Day. Turn off the TV, put down*
> *the phone. It's that special time for you two*
> *to be alone.*

I look at the top of Ella's blonde head resentfully. Being alone is not as easy as you think.

It's late and the sea and sky are one black strip. The lights of the caravan site are behind us and we're following the path back from the chip shop to the field. Luca is talking about his football trials coming up in September. It's the same team that Marco plays for. Luca's always talking about sport. I really like Luca, obviously, but sport is pretty boring. I watch his mouth moving. He has thin lips and very white teeth. As we get near to the caravan park, the lamps in the lane pick up the tiny line of hair across his top lip, making it glow.

Kiss me, I think.

'Harry Kane.'

Please. Now.

'The England player'.

'What?' I realise Luca's saying something to me outside my head.

'I want to be the next Harry Kane or Ronaldo.'

> *Kute Magazine. October 1985*
> *Take an interest in his hobbies. Girls can*
> *like football too!*

That's not as easy as you think either.

*

It's so stuffy, I can't sleep. The window is open but our tiny bedroom is hotter than an oven. The air is so thick and stale I think someone has stuffed an old sock into my mouth and nose. I sit up and shuffle down the bed so that I can push the door open wider. You don't have to get out of bed to do this. Our room is exactly the length of the beds and between them there is a narrow gap that is barely wide enough to stand in. It's currently filled with all the cuddly toys that have slipped off Ella's bed on to the floor. She has also kicked off her duvet and she is half-sprawled out of bed, one leg and arm invading the space between our beds. She shifts position and her leg presses hotly against mine. I shunt it away feeling her damp skin slide away. *Yuck*. She is covered in a thin layer of sweat like see-through pyjamas.

The walls of the caravan are thin. In fact, the caravan walls are literally made of plastic and if you bump against our bedroom walls they bend slightly. It's like fighting in a massive packed lunch box which can be good fun if Mum and Dad don't catch us. At night, when the caravan site is quiet and still, you can just about make out what Mum and Dad are saying through the thin walls. Luckily, they usually just mumble about nothing important. Occasionally we hear the bed creaking heavily but you know Mum will quickly whisper, 'John, no . . . the girls will hear.' She never sounds that cross though. It's the same voice she uses when she's not going to have another slice of chocolate cake but does anyway. *Ew*. I don't want to think about it. Tonight their voices are clearer, they must have left their bedroom door open too.

I hear the familiar squeak of Mum and Dad's bed and then the low rumble of Dad's voice.

'Love. You awake?'

'Hmm.' Mum's sleepy voice has kittens curled up in it.

'Is everything okay?' he asks. He's trying not to sound worried. He's getting better at it, but I can still tell.

'Mmm. Bit hot in here. Is the window open?'

'No, I mean, are you enjoying the holiday?'

'Of course.'

'I'm just checking.' Dad's voice is careful. I can tell that he wants to say more but doesn't want to upset Mum. We didn't even know if we would be able to come on holiday this year until a couple of weeks ago. There is a long pause as though they are waiting for a big sleepy cat to cross the room.

He tries again. 'You only have to say if you're not feeling well. Or stressed. Or tired.'

'I will. Go to sleep, love.'

Another pause. I don't expect to hear anything else.

'Do you think Chloe is okay?' says Dad.

My name stands out like a thunderclap. Goosebumps cover my arms and legs. I lie as still as possible listening.

'She seems so distant these days.'

His words sink helplessly at the end like the 'Oh well' he mutters after not winning the lottery every week.

'In what way?' says Mum, sounding a little more awake.

'I don't know. She doesn't seem to want to do anything. She's always on her phone...'

'All the kids are,' says Mum. 'And some grownups too.'

Dad ignores that one.

'Do you think the girls would prefer to do something else?' he asks.

My ears prick up. *Er, yes.* Maybe we might get to go on holiday somewhere else. Somewhere with WiFi. Somewhere interesting.

'They're fine,' says Mum. 'Chloe's just at that age.'

'Is that code for *they're growing up*?' he says flatly.

'I'm afraid we're the 'rents now,' said Mum.

'What?!'

'Parents,' she explains. 'We're old news. She doesn't want to do everything with us now. Ella will be the same. It's normal.'

43

'I know,' says Dad. 'I just… sometimes… miss how it was when they were both little…' Dad sighs loudly.

'I know. Me too. Go to sleep, you old softy.'

I hear them kiss quickly and the bed creaks again under their double weight. The sound makes me feel lonely. I think that they have gone to sleep then suddenly Dad's voice sounds out of the darkness.

'But, she seems so different…'

'John! She's just the same Chloe, no different, and no different to any kid her age.'

A hot splash of anger drenches my body. I am *not* a kid. I *am* different. Neither Dad nor Mum can ever understand. I hate it when they pretend to. And I hate them talking about me. I blow a rough blanket of air across my face but the fire in my cheeks rages. Ella gives a little moan as though the flames are licking at her dreams.

3

MONDAY

I am trying to talk to Mum about Ella but she's not listening – *as usual*. Mum is filling the kitchen sink with hot water and adds a green squirt of washing up liquid. She drops the breakfast bowls and spoons one by one into the water and they disappear under the expanding bubbles.

'She's not following you around,' says Mum. She is using her 'I'm trying to be patient with you' voice.

'She is. She's everywhere,' I complain. 'I can't do anything without her.'

I can hear the whirr of Ella's electric toothbrush from the bathroom. She never closes the door. I am trying to keep my voice low. Mum dips her fingertips to test the temperature and then adds some cold water stirring it around. The china bowls bump together under the water like an uncomfortable soup.

'Chloe, love, we are on holiday in a caravan,' says Mum. 'The whole idea is to spend time together and Ella is your little sister who wants to do everything with you because that's what you've always done.'

'Exactly!' I huff.

'And what exactly is it you want to do without her?' asks Mum.

I shrink a little at the unexpected question. I look down and pick at a loose thread on the hem of my T-shirt. I can feel my cheeks reddening.

'Just my *own* stuff,' I reply.

That's my business, I think, defiant. *What if she suspects something?* I panic.

'Well, you tell me when you want to do 'stuff' and I will try to make sure Ella gives you some space. Okay?'

Mum tries to catch my eye but I look away and just nod. What else can I do? Mum turns away satisfied, finds a missed teaspoon and drops it into the washing-up water with a little plop.

'It's just,' I blurt, 'she just gets under my skin.'

I scratch at my arm as though to prove a point that there really is something irritating under there. I scratch harder as though trying to pick off all my freckles in one go. Mum gives a little snort of laughter. I don't know what's so funny.

'If she's getting under your skin then, take it as a compliment,' said Mum. 'The ones who know you and love you will always find the best ways to wind you up, and Ella loves you very much.'

'Well, I don't love her.'

'Oh, Chloe…' Mum tuts half-reproachfully, half-amused. 'Don't be silly. Now, you have some *alone time* by doing the washing up.'

She slips her arm around my waist and tries to give a kiss on the cheek. I flinch and her lips brush my ear instead.

Annoyed, I thrust my hands deep into the hot water elbow deep in suds and wincing at the heat. The sting feels good.

'I'll dry!' announces Ella next to me.

I jump. Why did she have to creep up on us like that? *Did she hear?* I sneak a look at her but she's as chirpy as ever swinging the tea towel around above her head like a helicopter.

'Come on, slow coach' she says cheerfully and flicks the tea towel at me.

I duck away annoyed. 'Stop it,' I hiss. Under the water I try to grip my hands together in frustration but they feel strange, soft and slippery, as though I can't hang on to the angry feeling.

*

Ella looks like someone has just asked her to multiply 143 by 2,082 or something. She squints and screws up her nose and stares at me in deep concentration before giving up.

'I don't *understand*,' she says with a hint of whine.

I knew she'd make a fuss.

'Why are you playing golf and not coming shopping with us?' says Ella.

'Because I am,' I reply.

I fold my arms and lean back against the sofa hoping this isn't going to take too long. I need to get ready to go out. I'm dressed but I want to finish my makeup. I need to check that my eyebrows are even. They frame your face and mine are so pale it takes me a long time to get the colour right. Ella turns to Mum, confusion smeared across her face like jam.

'Mum, why isn't Chloe coming shopping with us? We always go shopping together on holiday.'

'She's playing golf today,' says Mum. She is keeping her tone neutral, trying not to take sides.

'But she doesn't like golf,' says Ella.

'I am here you know,' I snap. 'And how do you know I don't like golf?'

'You say it all the time,' says Ella indignant. 'You say it every year when Dad asks us to go.'

I sigh.

'Well, I can change my mind, can't I? I don't have to do the same things every year.'

There's a pause before Ella begins another assault.

'Mum, tell her she has to come,' says Ella. 'I *want* her to come. We always go shopping together.'

Her big blue eyes are bigger and bluer and pleading. I hope she's not going to cry. I almost feel sorry for her but not quite.

'No.' My tone is flat. *Final*.

'Okay', says Ella more cheerfully, 'I'll play golf as well.'

I sigh. Mum sighs. Dad looks less than keen but studies the newspaper to avoid any revealing eye contact with anyone. I don't know what the big deal is, at home I hardly ever go shopping with Mum and her. I go with my friends from school instead. I only go with Mum for boring stuff like school uniform and shoes. I had a great time with Mum picking out my holiday clothes but that doesn't count because I needed those.

Mum is still standing in the kitchen, the counter between us and her. She walks around and sits down opposite Ella at the table with the rest of us. Mum reaches over and covers one of Ella's little hands in hers and looks directly at her. She speaks in a soft voice. It's like watching one of those hypnotists on TV.

'Ella,' says Mum. 'Chloe can go shopping with us anytime. She's older now and sometimes wants to do different things. It's good to try new things.'

'But…' says Ella. Mum shushes her.

'Ella, you and I, and Auntie Helen, are going to have the best, most fantastic, super-special-sparkly…'

Wow, Mum's bringing out the big guns to impress Ella if she's using the word 'sparkly'.

'…ultra-girly-ultra-pamper shopping trip. You get Auntie Helen and I all to yourself all day, and you can choose the shops we go in. We will be your shopping slaves.'

Mum bows her head and says very seriously, 'At your service, Princess Ella.'

Ella giggles. Dad and I exchange a look, impressed with Mum's ability to turn this situation around. Dad, in particular, looks like he wants to applaud as Mum has just saved his beloved annual golfing trip. Dad is not a big golfer but he likes to pretend he is on holiday because Uncle Toni plays all the time and takes it very seriously.

'Can we get ice cream?' says Ella suddenly back to her default position which is 100% excited.

'Yes,' Mum nods. 'Two scoops.'

Ella gives a little gasp.

'And pretzels?'

'Of course,' says Mum.

'Woo-hoo!' shouts Ella. She lets go of Mum's hand and points at me. 'In your face! Enjoy your boring old golf.'

She jumps up and catwalks up and down the caravan, swaying her hips and snapping her fingers, sassy-style.

'I don't care,' I say, trying not to show how irritating she was being.

Ella stops and puts her hands to her face like she's the kid from Home Alone. Her blue eyes blink with excitement.

'I can't wait to go to Mirabelle's! Mum, can we have our ice creams there?'

Oh. I had forgotten about Mirabelle's, the gorgeous vintage boutique just outside of the village. We always stop off there either on the way to the shopping centre or on the way back. A pang of regret chimes in my chest like a flat bell. I love Mirabelle's but I won't get to go if I am playing golf. It has an old-fashioned ice cream bar in the window where you can sit up high on pale blue leather stools, like a 1950s diner. Mirabelle's sells a mix of vintage and new clothes but the whole place feels like you've gone back in time. The shop assistants dress up too. Madame Mirabelle wears red lipstick and those full skirts with a frilly petticoat underneath that make her look like a walking cupcake. Her hair is amazing, coiled around her head and clipped up with tiny butterflies or cats and all sorts of crazy things. She always remembers us. There is a large changing room at the back with red velvet curtains where you can try things on in a group. Madame Mirabelle will reserve it for us, stretching the gold rope across with the sign that says 'Reserved for VIPs only'. She encourages you to try anything on, even if you don't think it will suit you, and we all find something to come home with, even if it's just a little top or earrings.

Auntie Helen spends hours standing by the colourful jewellery racks trying on necklaces, bracelets, holding up beautiful earrings and sighing with indecision.

It's fun, all of us in the changing room together. Mum's not shy, she will strip off in front of you. She's slim, with a bit of a tummy like most mums, and although she's not tall, she has long legs like me, and a short body which she jokes about. She's quite pretty for a mum and she's not that old. Sophie is always complaining that her Mum is really old. However, she used to be a model and you can tell, her face is really striking and she's very thin. Apparently, all Sophie's brother's friends go a bit weird when they come around and meet her mum. Eva J's mum is probably the oldest mum I've seen. She has grey frizzy hair. When I was in primary school last year, Eva J had a party and someone thought her mum was her gran. Eva J said her mum thought it was funny. My mum would have hated that.

I get up and look at myself in the caravan mirror. I am pleased with my outfit; I think it works – plain white T-shirt and jeans shorts with a white trim down the sides, and trainers. I turn and look at myself side on. My legs are long at least but my skin is lily-white, I never tan. I should have tried the fake tan again. Thing is, last time it gave me a rash because I've got stupid sensitive skin, so not only did I have wrong-looking legs – the colour is never right – they had spots all over them.

I have to stand on the other side of the caravan, near the door, to see myself full length in the mirror. Half the caravan mirror has disappeared under a creeping paper ivy of drawings, maps and postcards.

Mirror, mirror, on the wall.

Not for much longer. If Mum keeps sticking things on the wall there will be no mirror left.

When we were little, Mum would sit in front of her dressing table mirror and cackle in her best Wicked Queen voice, '*Mirror, mirror, on the wall, who is the fairest of them all?*' Ella and I would be hiding behind the mirror, crouched on the floor giggling. When we heard her ask the question we would jump out shouting, 'Mummy!' or 'Me!' or 'Snow White!' depending on how true to the fairy tale we were being. As I got older I was better at remembering the story and would reply, 'Not you, your majesty, as long as Snow White lives.' Mum would cackle, '*NO!*' and threaten to lock us in her dungeon while we ran around her bedroom screaming.

Mum's dressing table has three mirrors, a large one in the middle and two narrower ones on either side that you can move to see yourself at different angles. The glass has black marks around the edge and is chipped in places. The dressing-table is old-fashioned and doesn't go with any of the other furniture in Mum and Dad's bedroom which is mostly white and modern. It's made of polished peachy-coloured wood. The grain of the wood has swirly patterns in it. Once Ella tried to trace them with a felt tip but luckily Mum managed to clean it off. Mum says that was me but that can't be right, she must have forgotten.

The dressing table has curved drawers on both sides and a long flat one in the middle. Under this is something that doesn't look like a drawer. It's a secret slide out tray where mum keeps her precious earrings. *Shh*, she always said when opening it, fingers to her lips, sharing a furtive look with us. Ella and I would take turns sitting on the floor at her feet, tucked up against the footrest, one sliding out the drawer, while the other said, *Shh*. We must have been very small to fit.

The dressing table also has a little matching stool covered in a dark pink velvet and there is a matching piece of padded velvet at the base of the dressing table for you to put your feet on. The fabric is stained and Mum often talks about re-covering it. It's on her list of things to do. She saved the dressing table from her grandmother's house when she died. Mum has three aunts and they used to share a room and this was their dressing-table. Mum remembers it covered in makeup and her aunts arguing over whose turn it was to sit down and use the mirror. Mum said she used to escape upstairs and sit in the corner of her aunts' room watching them get ready to go out for the evening. She would watch them try on outfits and curl their hair, singing along to the radio. The floor was a tangle of tights and shoes and discarded clothes. Mum says that the dressing table still reminds her of hairspray, disco music, and laughter.

I used to like to watch Mum do her makeup at the dressing-table, shading her eyes, spreading out her eyelashes like delicate spider's legs. Without mascara Mum doesn't have any eyelashes, her lashes are blonde and invisible. I keep offering to do her makeup but she won't let me. I could at least give her some eyebrows. I told her it would make her look a lot younger, but she just laughed and said it would take more than makeup to do that. I always liked to watch her draw around the shape of her mouth with a dark lipstick, or sometimes even changing the shape of her mouth slightly, making more of her cupid's bow. I haven't seen her do this for a while, I don't know when she will start wearing lipstick again. Since the operation, the shape of her mouth is slightly different, although from a distance it's not so noticeable. The doctor said it would improve but the scar tissue needed to soften first. She has to massage it with a special oil every day.

I look at the freckles on my arm. Mum used to tell us they were kisses from the sun. When she went to the hospital they called her freckles skin damage. She said she suddenly saw them as something very different whereas they had always made her think of summer, one freckle for every summer she'd ever enjoyed. Mum said it was like when she discovered that the moon didn't glow and that it was just a rock in the sky that reflected the Earth's light.

'It's still pretty,' I said.

'Yes,' she replied. 'I'll always love the moon but it will never be quite the same.'

'Chloe.' Ella's hand is on my arm. I snap back into the room aware that I hadn't heard the last thing that was said. Ella is looking at me very concerned.

'Chloe, I can bring you back an ice cream if you like. I don't know if they sell them at the golf course.'

'It will melt, idiot,' I laughed. 'Maybe a pretzel instead.' Ella nods.

'I'm going to miss you,' she says snaking her arm through mine and leaning into me. Her hair is silky against my bare arm. It tickles. I push her off, but not too roughly.

'I won't miss you at all,' I say sweetly. Then I slip my arm around her waist and go for a full tickle-grab to the back ribs. I manage to hold her squirming body on the sofa for a few moments until she pulls away panting and giggling. Her eyes are bright and keen, ready for another attack. I used to be able to hold her longer. She's getting stronger.

*

It's peaceful in the car. Dad is driving, Uncle Toni next to him. Toni is leaning against the side window, his stocky body turned towards Dad. He rests one hairy arm across the back of his seat. They chat a little, about golf, the route (of course), and the weather. They squint out of the windows at the bright sunshine occasionally saying things like, 'Couldn't ask for a better day, mate.'

It feels like we are escaping. We've only been staying at the field for a couple of days but my eyes and ears are having to adjust to seeing not caravans, but village streets and houses, and then country lanes and less familiar fields. I watch sky, trees and rooftops roll across the car windows on a continuous loop.

Luca and I are slumped down low at opposite ends of the back seat. I can feel the space between us as though it were something touching us both. It makes me feel nervous. Luca's long limbs look like they have been folded several times to make him fit in the seat. His knees are pressed up against the seat in front. I'm careful not to stare at him too much. Got to keep things casual. We look at our phones mainly, occasionally commenting on something funny, or glancing outside to see where we are. Luca sometimes shows me stupid memes on his phone which have us cry-laughing at one point. Toni and Dad glance back at us asking what it is. They wouldn't understand.

The car turns sharply to the right. The road is bumpier, and we slow down, rocking gently in all directions. I shuffle upright in my seat so that I can see properly out of the window. There is an old house at the end of a curving, gravel drive. There's a lot of people milling around the entrance, some holding take-away coffee cups in that weird way people do, arm stiff and slightly higher than normal, as though someone is about to clink glasses and shout 'Cheers!' There are a few tables and benches scattered on the fresh lawn in front of the house. We park the car at the side of the building. Dad twists around in his seat to face me. He looks like an excited puppy.

'We're here!' he announces. 'Ready for your first game, Chloe?'

'Ok,' I mumble, alarmed at his enthusiasm. I hope he's not going to be like this all day. It's just a game.

Golf. It is good at first, but then it isn't.

The golf course is pretty, rolling greens separated by clusters of trees and shrubs, the smell of cut grass and scented hedgerows everywhere. There is a lake in the middle and several ponds connected by arched bridges like something from a fairy tale. We cross some of these to reach different parts of the golf course. This is fun at first, Luca and I striding ahead of the others, an adventure. However, every bridge leads to the same thing, another long field with a hole at the end which everyone else can get the ball close to except me. It feels like a cross country lesson at school with our evil PE teacher, Mrs Brandt. Just because you ask where the finish line is she adds another mile. Then says it's 'just over this hill' or 'just beyond those trees' but it never is. Cross country lessons are like a bad dream where you are running but never getting anywhere. This golf course also never ends – bridge upon bridge, green upon green, and one humiliation after another. Dad has turned the whole morning into a very long boring golf lesson for me. *Stand like this, straighten your arms, loosen your legs, watch your swing, eye on the ball, keep the line, relax, grip tighter.* How am I supposed to remember all those things at the same time? He wouldn't let me team up with Luca – apparently, they don't do that. I made a face at Luca when Dad wasn't looking but Luca just shrugged.

Mum made Dad bring a hat for me to wear which was embarrassing. At first I refused, but it was a baseball cap and not totally uncool. Now I am glad to have something to keep the sharp sun out of my eyes. I can also pull it down to cover my scowl as Dad keeps giving me instructions. If I try to ask Luca for advice, Dad just interrupts. I didn't think golf would be so hard. I've played crazy golf on the sea front and pitch and putt. They are fun but this is not fun.

It feels like we have walked for miles and my feet are throbbing. My arms are starting to ache as much as my feet. You have to hit the ball miles to get to the hole and so far, if I have hit the ball at all, it has travelled no more than a metre if I'm lucky. Dad is being very patient, and he is patient generally. He taught Ella and I to swim, ride a bike and bake a mean sponge cake. Not like Mum who if a recipe has more than three ingredients, she slams the book shut in frustration and says she will just 'make it up as she goes along'. Dad and Toni are encouraging me to keep trying but I am sick of being such a loser. I didn't want

Luca to see me like this. I thought he and I would hang out and chat but all he does is talk about golf. Luca, Dad and Uncle Toni endlessly debate every shot, discuss tactics and approach each hole like it's a military campaign. They also keep checking the scores. They are trying not to be competitive as I am doing so badly, but I can tell from the little looks and glances that Toni is enjoying beating Dad.

I am so bored. Toni is pointing something out to Luca towards the next hole. I follow their gaze without interest but feeling left out. I imagined that Luca would help me learn to play golf. He would stand behind me with his arms wrapped around mine. I've seen couples in movies like this. His warm hands would cover mine on the golf club helping me line up my shot. It would just be an excuse, of course, we both would know that.

> *Kute Magazine. November 1985*
> *The first touch is the sweetest whether...*

'Chloe!' Dad's voice. 'Earth to Chloe. You're miles away.'

I wish I was, I thought. *Miles away from this golf course*.

'Sorry,' I mutter.

'Your shot, love,' says Dad.

The sun is burning the back of my neck. The club feels heavy and slippery in my hands. I try to remember everything that Dad has told me. I swing. Up comes the turf.

'Good girl, Chloe,' claps Dad. 'Try again.'

I swing again sending more grass flying. I can feel a trickle of sweat starting to run down my back into my shorts. I hope no one can see.

'Chloe…' says Dad.

'I'm fine,' I say through gritted teeth.

I hack the turf another couple of times. I can feel the frustration flowing faster like lava under my skin. I grip the club but my hands are so swollen with the heat it feels like I am wearing thick rubber gloves. Dad can't hold back anymore. He steps forward and starts to put an arm around my shoulder. I am sweating and I don't want anyone touching me *or* helping me.

'Back off!' I grunt. 'Just let me concentrate!'

'Oh-oh!' Dad puts his hand up in mock terror and takes a step back. 'Redhead alert!'

I hate it when he blames everything on my red hair. I'm angry because he's treating me like a child, you don't have to have red hair to be annoyed about that. My next swing kicks up the turf again. I glance quickly at Luca but he is staring at the ground, prodding the grass with his club.

'Chloe…' says Dad.

'Dad, SHUT UP!'

I swing the club up high following the words that I yelled over my shoulder at Dad, and without thinking about *my grip* or *loosening up* or *being in line*, I whack the ball as hard as I can. My hands feel bruised from the impact and it's all I can do not to burst into tears from the pain. Unbelievably the ball soars into the air and Dad, Toni and Luca whoop with delight. Dad squeezes my shoulders; Toni grabs the peak of my hat and twists it around.

'Brilliant, Chloe. That's my girl,' says Dad.

'Good carry,' says Uncle Toni. He shields his eyes from the sun and watches the ball land half-way between us and the hole.

'Nice,' says Luca. It's the first thing he's said to me in ages.

'You see, Luca,' Toni gestures to me. 'Women are the ones to watch. This is only her first game and she will soon be beating us all.'

Dad and Toni move off across the green. Luca walks close by me and whispers, 'Not a total loser then.' I instinctively try to punch him in the ribs but he jumps away from me grinning. The fingers of one hand shape into an 'L' which he sticks on his forehead doing a little dance. I wanted to cry a few minutes ago but now I'm laughing.

We are having a late lunch in the golf club bar. I am absolutely starving and completely exhausted. We are sitting outside in the shade of a tree but it is not exactly cool. I slump at the table, drained, chin in hands, fingers pushed into the sweaty roots of my hair. *Urgh.* I don't care what I look like. Well, maybe I do, but I don't want to get up and walk to the loos and see my disgusting red face.

I am too tired to follow the conversation. I am even too tired to look at the menu. The others are choosing food and going on and on about the game. They work out the scores and I am, of course, last. Dad is telling me how proud he is of me and how well I did for my first game. I smile along with it all. I ask if there is steak on the menu and he lets me order it as a treat. Dad and Toni are being nice about my score, Luca keeps making an 'L' sign near his leg where they can't see. I smile and laugh along but it's an effort. Dad is going on and on about how he now has a golf buddy for holidays. I didn't realise what a big deal it was for me to play with him. I suppose Uncle Toni always has Luca and Luca's brother, Marco, with him. However, one good whack does not make me a golfer. There is no way I am ever playing golf again. Well, maybe not. I could ask Luca to give me lessons. I wonder whether Mum and Ella have been to Mirabelle's Boutique yet. The thought makes me feel sad.

After steak and chips, I am starting to feel human again. Luca is eating veggie lasagne but I don't care, I needed that steak. Uncle Toni arrives back from the bar with more drinks. He puts two Cokes down in front of us then heads back to the bar. I don't know where Dad is, paying at the bar maybe, or in the toilet. I don't care really, it's a break from him telling me how great I am which I'm not.

Luca passes the drink to me. The icy glass is slippery with condensation. I cannot grip it, I am tired and my fingers aren't working properly. Luca's fingers press over mine steadying the glass so it doesn't slip. The combination of his warm hand and the cold glass is perfect.

'Got it?' he asks.

I nod. I'm gripping the glass with my hand, but I feel the tightness in my chest. He removes his hand but the feeling of warmth stays with me. I take a gulp of my drink and then cough. My cheeks flush.

> *Kute Magazine. November 1985*
> *The first touch is the sweetest.*
> *Whether it's your hand or your heart, it*
> *could be a start.*

'Do you want to go for a walk?' I blurt. 'Just us.'

'Sure,' says Luca. 'Where?'

I don't have a plan. I look around me at the tables with people drinking coffee and beer on the lawn. There are trees beyond the lawn, and little paths beyond that into the woods. I don't know where they might lead. Dad and Toni saunter back from the bar carrying their drinks. Dad is using a paper serviette to wipe his sweaty forehead.

'Drink up, kids,' said Dad. 'We're going to head back after this.'

The 'kids' reference annoys me.

'We're going for a walk,' said Luca standing up.

I'm surprised at how determined he sounds. Dad looks surprised too. He glances at his watch.

'I suppose there's time, we've got to finish these…' He gestures with his glass. He only has a lemonade but Toni has a pint.

'It's fine,' I say quickly. I am suddenly nervous. 'Don't worry, I'm tired.'

Luca shrugs and sits down again. I haven't moved but my heart is beating faster than when we were walking for miles.

In the car on the way back, Luca is sprawled at one end of the back seat again and me at the other. His long legs are bent even more awkwardly. He lets one knee relax to the side crossing the space between us. His knee is touching mine. Warm skin, soft hair, hard bone. He is head down engrossed in a game he is playing on his phone. *Does he know he is touching me?* Can he feel *it* too? I can hardly breathe. Why is it we can joke around like we've done for years, and then at times like this I don't know what to do or say. He's one of my oldest friends and yet sometimes I feel like I don't know him at all.

*

I must have nodded off for a few minutes in the car because I don't remember us turning into the field. I am a little groggy when I get out of the car and my legs feel as heavy as the end of afternoon heat. Toni and Luca have disappeared next door to their caravan. Dad is getting something out of the boot of the car. The door to our caravan stands open, and most of the windows, so the others must be back too. I hear them before I see them. The caravan steps feel as wobbly as I do. There is laughter and chatter coming from inside as I slowly approach the door. Mum, Auntie Helen and Ella are arranged around the sofas with lots of exciting-looking shopping bags between them. They all look snug and happy. Ella bounces up and runs to me with a crinkly paper bag like an excited dog who is returning a ball.

'Pretzel,' she says. 'Cinnamon.'

I take it and breathe in the delicious contents of the bag. Watching my face, Ella beams.

'Thanks,' I manage to say worried that I am going to cry. I quickly blink back the feeling. *What's wrong with me?* It's just a pretzel. I know Mum is watching me closely. She gets up and gives me a quick hug on her way to the kitchen. I try to brush her off.

'Had a good day, love?' she says. 'Sit down and I'll get you a cold juice unless you want a tea.'

'I'll have a tea,' says Dad.

He, Uncle Toni and Luca pile noisily into the caravan shrinking the space inside. They are all talking about the golf. I hear my name mentioned. Mum is trying to listen to them while taking drinks orders from the kitchen. I sit between Ella and Auntie Helen who start taking things out of plastic bags to show me. *A good haul*, Auntie Helen calls it. I am trying not to feel jealous. Ella wants me to comment on everything that they have bought. She is telling me in great detail which shops they went to, what they tried on but didn't buy, and how they chose the things they came home with. I don't know whether she is torturing me or making sure I don't feel left out but it feels the same. Ella tells me about Mirabelle's Boutique and shows me the dress Mum bought her from there. They have bought me two vest tops. I like them both.

Ella is proudly telling me how she picked them out for me. I give her a little hug and she hugs me back twice as hard. She is too hot as usual and her hair is sweaty. I have to push her away. Auntie Helen hands me a small delicate cloth bag. I take it, surprised at the gift. The bag is made from a grey, silky fabric which slips between my fingers. Inside there is a silver bracelet that she picked out for me from Mirabelle's. Instead of the usual charms it has tiny seagulls dangling from the chain. The metal has a rainbow sheen and the colours change as the seagulls move.

'I missed looking at the jewellery with you,' Auntie Helen says.

'Thank you,' I whisper still looking at my bracelet. Helen pats my hand.

'I have one too,' says Ella loudly even though she is sitting right next to me.

She lifts her wrist up to my face. Pink llamas with silver feet dance from the chain encircling her arm. Mum hands me a cold orange juice. I sip it gratefully. *You okay?* she mouths. I give a small nod.

Ella and Luca are now sitting on opposite sides of the table playing 'thumb war'. *1, 2, 3, 4, I declare a thumb war!* They hold hands and their thumbs cross several times like swords in a duel. The aim is to hold down the other person's thumb for three seconds. Luca was clearly letting Ella win, her thumbs are tiny compared to his. The thumb wrestling also involves lots of rolling about on the sofa shrieking and laughing. I watch them enviously. Luca hardly said a word to me on the way home in the car. *Why is it so difficult to get him to notice me?*

*

I am sitting on my bed in our tiny bedroom trying to Facetime Sophie. Dad has taken pity on me and given me some of his data. If I'd known that hitting a golf ball would get me data then I might have tried harder. Jealous of all the attention I got about playing golf, Ella has made Dad take her to the little crazy golf course in the caravan site next door. I have the bedroom to myself for a change. I have my new tops laid out on the bed to show Sophie and I am wearing the silver bracelet. The seagulls tinkle as they fall against each other on my wrist which is very different to the screeching sound that the real ones make above our caravan first thing in the morning. 'Hi!' Sophie's blurred face appears on my phone screen. I am so happy to see her. Then

I realise someone else is there. They are both in Sophie's bedroom lying on the bean bags.

'Hi Chloe!' Sophie waves. 'Hannah's here too.'

Hannah waves and says hello. Hannah is in our maths group. I've hung out with her a little bit at school but I don't know her very well. There are Primark bags on the floor next to them.

'Hiya,' I say forcing a smile. I wanted to talk to Sophie alone. 'Have you been shopping?'

Sophie and Hannah look at each other, pause and then burst out laughing.

'What?' I say, feeling uncomfortable.

They start telling me how they went into town today. They saw some boys from school in the shopping centre but they didn't talk to them at first. Then one of the boys said 'Hi' and started doing tricks on his skateboard but fell off. They talk over each other and keep collapsing into hysterics, but I don't understand why it's so funny. I pretend to laugh along with them. I try asking questions but they just giggle and glance at each other as though there is more but they don't want to say.

'What about you?' said Sophie. 'How's *King Krush*?'

'Ooh, yeah, what's happened?' said Hannah. 'Have you got a picture of him?'

Why did Sophie tell Hannah about Luca? I don't want to say anything now.

'Fine,' I say. 'Really good. Oh, you know what.' I pretend to look behind me. 'I think I can hear Mum calling. Will have to talk to you later. Bye.'

'Bye!' they shout in unison. I cut them off just as the giggling starts again.

I stare at my phone for a minute or so. It feels heavy in my hand. Then I message my friend, Maddie who I went to primary school with. She's gone to another secondary school so I haven't seen her for a few months. She doesn't reply. I miss her. Maybe I can arrange a sleepover when I get back.

*

SLAP!

I'm surprised at how much my hand stings. I want to rub it better but I let it hang at my side. The throb is like a pulse. My heart beats in time. I remain standing over Ella although I don't feel so angry anymore. I seem to have transferred the rage into her. Ella is screaming, crying with shock and pain and outrage. She is wearing one of my new tops that they bought me from Mirabelle's. It is too big for her: the back sags and the straps slip off her shoulders. There is a red mark between her shoulder blades where I hit her. Almost blind with tears, her arms flail as she pushes past me and runs out of our bedroom. I follow her into the sitting room where I know she will be telling Mum that it's all my fault.

'She – hit – me!' Ella gulps out between sobs.

'What?!' Mum looks at me horrified.

'She was in my stuff. She's wearing my top,' I explain.

'That is NO reason to hit your sister!' says Mum.

'She's always in my things!' I shout.

'Give me your phone,' says Mum. Her voice is dangerously calm.

'No!' My words hit back. 'That's NOT fair.'

Mum wraps her arms around Ella who has buried her face in Mum's chest. Typical, Mum always takes her side.

'She won't leave my things alone!' I say louder.

I glance at the caravan mirror. The 'other Chloe' is bent forward, stiff with rage. Mum kisses Ella's head and strokes her hair saying: 'There, there, we'll get you something cold to soothe your back.'

My hand hurts too. I follow them to the kitchen holding my palm stiffly. Mum rummages in the freezer looking for an ice pack. Ella blubs and rubs her stupid streaky face. She sees me watching her and sticks her tongue out angrily. The caravan mirror behind her is now completely covered in pictures so it's just her pulling faces at me. There is no 'other Ella' and no 'other Chloe' here. Just us. Are we the good Chloe and Ella or the bad ones? It doesn't feel so simple anymore. Mum fusses over Ella then realises I am standing there. Her expression is hard.

'Chloe, go to your room and leave your phone.'

'I don't have a room here, do I?!' I yell. 'I have to share with her!' I point at Ella whose eyes are as wide as saucers. 'And she won't leave me alone!'

I throw my phone down on the kitchen worktop. It bounces and skids across the slippery surface, just stopping at the edge. I want to check it's okay but I'm already pushing past them out of the kitchen, ignoring the 'other Chloe' who appears briefly as I pull open the door that leads back to the bedrooms. *Don't know why she's crying.* I slam the sitting room door behind me but because it's made of plastic it doesn't make much noise. When I get inside our bedroom, I slam the door twice instead, once for me and once for the 'other Chloe'.

4

TUESDAY

Mum and Auntie Helen have gone to the supermarket to 'stock up'. They have taken Ella with them to buy flip flops because hers have snapped. Luckily no one asked me to go. Ella's been hamming it up about her back still hurting but I just ignore her. Mum seems less cross with me this morning. She just seems tired of the whole thing like those swimming teachers who've had all the fun washed off from years of telling kids not to splash and muck about in lessons. It is only 10.30am but Dad and Uncle Toni have announced that it is too hot to do anything. They collapse into shady deck chairs, unbuttoning their shirts, muttering promises of swimming and the beach and something… later… just a little bit later. Eyes closed, their round stomachs rise and fall.

It is the hottest, sunniest day so far. It is also the best day so far. Luca and I are fossil hunting. Luca and I are *alone*. Finally, *finally* we are alone. *Luca and Chloe. Chloe and Luca.*

'I've got this project to do for science.'

Luca's words float behind him like a kite string. I follow him as he jogs down our secret path towards the sea.

'If I can get some samples then I won't have to write as much,' he says.

> *Kute Magazine. June 1982*
> *Enjoy a shared hobby, share a dream.*
> *You'll soon find someone to join your team.*

It takes about five minutes, maybe more, to walk down the beach path to the sea. We pass a few people and occasionally have to stand to one side against the rock and scratchy shrubs to let families pass with pushchairs. I nod shyly if they say hello and look at my feet. I wonder if they think Luca is my boyfriend.

On the beach we kick off our shoes then find the sand is scorching on our bare feet. We hop from one foot to another laughing and trying to get used to the heat. Luca throws the picnic bag next to our shoes. I managed to grab some food before we left. A makeshift picnic: a bit of cheese, the end of a French stick, crisps, biscuits, drinks. Not the most healthy lunch. *All the good stuff containing none of the good stuff*, as Mum would say. I shake my head as if to get her out of my mind. I don't want to think about anyone today. It's just Luca and me. I haven't even told Sophie what is happening, not that I could, as Mum still has my phone. I want to scream and jump, and I do, shrieking as I skip over a piece of driftwood. I always feel like this at the beach. Luca looks over his shoulder grinning. I slow down and try to look cool but he's turned again to face the sea. He lets out a whoop of his own both hands held up to his face.

71

We run towards the water's edge pushing each other and mucking around. All the awkwardness of yesterday has gone, the silence in the car forgotten.

We trawl the beach for fossils. Every now and then Luca dives excited into the sand, then holds out a flat stone, stained blue. His tanned fingers trace the dark squiggles.

'See these lines? These were creatures living millions of years ago. Amazing.'

'Great.' I blink, wondering why the markings don't seem so alive to me.

'Here, this is a fantastic one,' says Luca.

He grabs my hand and places a large pebble in my outstretched palm. It feels warm and heavy as though you could measure its age by its weight. Luca's fingers are dry and dusty, prematurely aged by the fossils. They bring me to life. At his touch, a charge of energy seems to erupt from my stomach and run up and down my thighs. I press my legs together, feeling the nip of denim where my shorts catch my skin.

By lunchtime it is scorching and the morning feels as tired as the longest summer sports day. There's no shade in this part of the beach, the sun shines directly at the cliffs. I realise I've left my hat back at the caravan. Who cares? It would only flatten my hair. We finally sit down and unpack the picnic. Luca digs his teeth into cheese and bread, staring out across the beach, his jaw works hard on the chewy bread. I watch his cheek bones and nibble at some crisps. After eating, he lies down and closes his eyes.

'So hot,' sighs Luca.

He sits up again quickly to pull off his T-shirt and tucks it under his head. Then he wriggles back into the sand, sighing, and shuts his eyes against the light. After a moment, he opens one eye, squinting against the sun. I am staring at his stomach, it's smooth and flat like the pebble I held in my hand. I screw my face into a frown and pretend that I am not staring but am lost in some important thought. I must look awful from his angle, like when you see yourself reflected in your phone screen, all chin and scowl.

'Chill, Chloe,' says Luca. 'Might as well enjoy the sun. I reckon I've got enough samples.'

Gently I lower myself into the sand next to him. The grains, velvety under my feet, graze my bare shoulders and elbows. I look up at the sky, partly obscured by the cliff behind us. You would think the cliff would give us some shade but we are completely exposed. The light is sharp as stone. Feathery threads of cloud hang lazily above us. They look like they don't have the energy to move. I don't know how long we've been lying here. Is it a minute, five minutes, an hour even? The sky is still, there is no breeze, maybe time has stopped as well. Luca's breathing is slow and even. He could be asleep. My heart is beating so hard I am afraid he can hear it. I turn my head slightly and see his dark silky lashes spread across his cheeks. He murmurs and shifts a little so that one arm lies full length against me. The warmth and stickiness of his skin soaks into mine. The sun is higher and hotter than ever. The heat on my face and arms is heavy as though the whole sky is lying on top of me.

Just wait, I think. Be patient. I think I've stopped breathing. *This is it*, I tell myself. *Relax and wait. He will kiss you.*

Kute Magazine. February 1983
You've sent out the signs, now sit back and
relax.
Cupid has a way of getting on the right
tracks.

Luca coughs. Or maybe I cough. I open my eyes from sleep or not sleeping, I'm not sure. I don't know what time it is. My face moves stiffly like a towel left to dry too quickly in the sun. The sun is piercing, I squint and turn my head sideways to find myself looking straight into his sleep-creased eyes. A blush springs from my cheeks and spreads quickly down my body like warm red paint. It gathers in a damp pool between my legs.

'Hey,' he mumbles, eyes still unfocused. 'What time is it?'

Not time to go. Not time to go. His lips are centimetres away. My tongue creeps to the edge of mine to soothe the dry cracks. Luca yawns and starts to sit up. *No, no. Wait. Not yet.* I panic and, scrunching my eyes shut, I dive forward. I find... skin… lips, I think. Yes. His head falls back and I am above him, our mouths pressed together. I reach out a hand to steady myself and feel his shoulder. The movement pulls us closer together.

I don't know what to do. Sophie and I practised this on the backs of our hands but it doesn't feel the same. It's fleshy and close and dry. I desperately want to lick my lips but am worried that this is wrong. Luca feels lifeless below me. I only know he is there by the quick breathing that floods my face in short blasts. He must be able to feel my heart pounding against his chest because it is almost killing me. Seconds, hours maybe, go by. Surely we are supposed to do more than this? He must think I'm an idiot. I untighten my eyes to take a quick look at Luca who I find is staring straight back at me. It is like being pressed against a distorting mirror. I squish my eyes shut again, frightened.

> *Kute magazine. October 1984*
> *Fellas get the fear too. There's nothing to*
> *prove.*
> *Help him out, you can make the first move.*

I lift my mouth away a little and quickly wet my lips before putting them back on Luca's, looser this time. It is better, a bit sticky but softer. I feel the tickle of hair across his top lip. I move my lips open and shut against Luca's, just a little, then more as I feel him respond. It's amazing. Luca is kissing me! I think he is. I'm sure he is. Just to be sure, I stop moving my mouth for a few moments and lift my lips away from his creating a tiny gap. Luca's lips reach out for mine and he carries on moving them over mine. I knew he would. I don't know whether I want to cheer or cry.

I wish we'd sat in the shade because the afternoon heat is almost unbearable now, and funny waves are tingling up and down my body. I move my mouth harder against Luca's. I feel the bones in his jaw where our faces meet. Our mouths are open now and there is a cool moist gap inside his teeth. I don't know if I dare. Seagulls flapping inside me, I push my tongue forward, just the tip, then more, edging forward in the dark. The unexpected relief of nothing, then a blunt point, wet and rough. You'd think that

I'd hit an electric eel because Luca jerks, smacking his mouth against mine, teeth denting my face, then pulls away. He stares, all white eyeballs with shock. Then he seems to recover and looks embarrassed. He touches his lip where our mouths clashed. 'Sorry,' he mutters. Then he almost jumps out of his skin as Dad's deep voice rolls across the cliff above us like the warning growl of a bear.

'Chloe! Luca!... Chloe! Where are you?'

Dad has a booming voice. It makes it sound as though he could be closer than he is. Is he on the beach or the path or above us?

'Shit.' Luca looks freaked like someone is about to punch him. 'It's your dad. Shit.'

Luca jumps to his feet, grabs a couple of fossils and races across the beach away from me.

'Luca!' I call. 'Luca, wait!' I struggle to stand up in the soft sand. My head throbs with heat. I feel dizzy. I have to wait a minute swaying slightly before I can move. I watch Luca disappearing up the beach path heading towards the caravan site. *Why isn't he waiting for me?*

'Luca, wait!' I call with a voice not strong enough to carry across the beach. He doesn't hear me.

I gather up the picnic things stuffing them chaotically into the bag. My shoes in one hand I run as quickly as I can across to the path, the beach bag bumping against me and nearly tripping me up. My arms and legs are sluggish in the heat but I push myself to move faster. It's a slog running up the beach path as opposed to walking down it. I catch up with Luca at the field. I arrive panting at the top where the path comes out near our caravans. Luca is standing stiff like a statue with Mum, Ella, Toni and Helen forming a little half-circle around him.

'Here she is!' chimes Ella as she sees me.

Luca doesn't turn to look at me. It's as though he is pretending that he isn't there. His arms, as stiff as driftwood, dig into his pockets as he stares at his feet. I slump over slightly to get my breath and my forehead fills with a burning pain like molten lava pouring behind my eyes. I stagger and a hand, I don't know whose, grabs my arm to steady me. I think I am going to faint. I am suddenly surrounded by people. My face is on fire, it hurts even to wrinkle my nose, but they are all looking at me like *they've* been burned. Mum cries out in her angry voice but her face is upset.

'Oh, Chloe, you silly girl! Look at your skin!'

The last word is almost a shriek. Her fear makes me frightened for myself. Tears prick my eyes. Heavy footsteps behind us bring Dad.

'Here you are!' says Dad. 'I've been looking all over for you. We were going for a walk but we couldn't find you.'

He pauses, looking from Luca and me to Mum and the others. No one is saying anything. I feel sick. The ground is moving. The grass blurs at my feet.

'What's going on?' he says, and then when no one answers he asks again, 'What?!'

I don't know who he is asking. He is looking at Mum. She is looking at me.

'Why is Chloe's face so red?' asks Ella. 'She looks like a tomato.'

The more they all stare at me, the hotter I feel, and if they don't stop soon I think I might explode like an unpricked sausage on the barbeque. I'm swaying a bit now. In one hand I'm holding the empty picnic bag and in the other I tightly grip the T-shirt that Luca left behind on the beach. It hangs in my hand like a snakeskin he's left behind. The only person who isn't staring at me is Luca. His eyes haven't moved from his feet. Mine are lost in the cool grass, silver toenails shining like fairies. I envy them half-hidden in their beautiful green world. I want to shrink down and hide with them and let all the tiredness and pain and heat drain into the soil.

*

I am lying face down on Mum and Dad's bed, my head sandwiched between the pillows. The skin on my face is tender where it touches them. I could turn over but I prefer to be buried in the soft darkness. Anyway, moving my head is agony so I lie still like I'm dead, or at least I wish I were dead. The fabric is not as cool as the cotton pillowcases that we have at home and the smell of the fabric conditioner is too strong. I wish I were in my own bed at home far away from all of this. Dead or away, anything but this.

Mum is shouting but trying not to. Her voice goes up and down like someone is fiddling with the volume on the radio. *Such a stupid thing to do! You can make yourself ill! I am always telling you girls not to get sunburnt!* She places a cool flannel on the back of my neck, her voice softer. *Is that better? The painkillers will work soon, just try to relax.* Her tone is kind, a calm moment before the next crescendo of anger. *Why didn't you wear a hat? Or sunscreen! How many times do I need to tell you?!*

My head throbs like a bomb about to explode. Everything feels white hot. My thoughts are like jets of angry light. I wince as I try to control them. *What was I thinking? Where is Luca? Why didn't he try to speak to me? Why did I kiss him? I should have waited. This is awful. Do they know? Did someone see us? Why was everyone staring? Oh no, the T-shirt. Where is Luca now? Was the kiss rubbish? Did he like it? Why didn't he wait for me? I can't face him ever again.*

Mum's angry phrases run over the top like we're singing two clashing parts of a duet. *Why weren't you more careful?! Sun damage is for life! I tell you girls but you never listen.* It's too much. Pain stabs me in the forehead from all angles. I groan.

'Sshh,' she says, the storm abating again. 'It's okay. It's sunstroke, it will pass. Try to sleep.'

Mum places her hand gently on my back. Her fingers are delicate but firm. I want to cry but the sobs make the pain in my head throb more so I swallow them, washed down with a full glass of embarrassment as I remember again what happened. I hear someone open the door and then Dad's loud voice trying to whisper.

'How's she doing? Is she well done or medium rare?'

'It's not funny, John,' says Mum.

'I know,' he says. 'How are you, Chloe-bear?'

'I've covered her in after sun,' says Mum. Her voice is soft but business-like. 'She's had painkillers, luckily Helen had some strong ones for migraine although I only gave her half a dose. Now she just needs to stay cool and rest and hydrate. I'll fill up some more water bottles. We need to keep the curtains closed as the light hurts her eyes.'

I can hear Mum moving about the room, arranging things.

'Love, relax,' says Dad. 'She'll be as right as rain tomorrow. It's just a bit of sunburn.'

'How can you say that?!' Mum turns the full force of her anger on Dad as though swinging a torch into his eyes. 'There's no such thing as just a bit of sunburn! Look at her, she's in pain.'

I am and I wish they'd stop arguing but I can't say anything. I cannot move my head. I cannot move my eyes. I cannot let my thoughts race around my head like this. I need everything to be still and quiet. Nothing has ever hurt this much.

'Lizzie, why don't you take a break and I'll sit with Chloe.' Dad is choosing his words carefully.

'I don't need a break', Mum snaps. 'What I *did* need was for you to remind Chloe to take a hat to the beach, or make sure she'd put sun cream on. *Do I have to think of everything?* We should both be trying to protect her. *Do you want her to end up like… me?!*'

Shut up, I think. Then I try not to think. I keep my eyes closed and my head perfectly still. Every time I move it feels like someone is sticking a knife in my forehead. After Mum has left the room, Dad tries to explain the shouting. Since Mum's operation, Dad's had to do a lot of the explaining which is usually Mum's job in our family. He keeps his tone as quiet and even as he can so just a gentle thudding on my brain.

'You see, Chloe, the thing that's happened to your Mum, might be from having sunburn as a kid,' says Dad. 'I mean, no one really knows, of course.'

I know all this; the doctors told her. *Does this mean I am going to get cancer?* My stomach tightens in fear. My head throbs. No, I can't think about that right now. I concentrate on not thinking which of course just makes you think more. I let Dad's words wash over me lightly while I stay buried in the pillows trying to block out all light, sound, movement and feeling.

'That doesn't mean the same thing will happen to you, kiddo.'

He strokes my head gently. His hand feels too hot.

'I don't want you to be scared. You've just had a bit too much sun today. Happens to everyone. Sunstroke's a killer…No! I mean…'

Well done, Dad, I think. He'll be kicking himself for saying that. I imagine the panic on his face.

'I mean, sunstroke will give you a splitting headache, but you'll be okay. And your sunburn will fade, I don't think it's as bad as your Mum thinks.'

He pauses and pats my arm which makes me think that he doesn't know anything.

'Years ago, people didn't understand how dangerous sunburn could be. When your Mum and I were growing up people put anything on their skin to get a better tan. I once saw Gran put cooking oil on her legs!'

Dad pauses perhaps expecting me to laugh at this. I can't imagine Gran doing something so stupid, but she does have very wrinkly legs.

'Mum just doesn't want the same for you and Ella. This has probably scared her a bit and when people are scared they… *react*… sometimes that might seem like she's angry but she's not.'

He's choosing his words very carefully. I'd be impressed but I just want him to go away.

'Okay?' he says after a brief pause.

The only way I am going to get any peace is to say something. I lift my face slightly out of the pillows and mumble, 'Okay'.

'I'll leave you to it,' says Dad. 'Get some sleep.'

He kisses the top of my head. Even that slight pressure hurts.

*

I don't know what time it is. I open my eyes slightly and squint in the half-light of the bedroom. I lift my face from the pillow. My skin is sticky with sweat and the thick moisturiser Mum slathered on my face and neck before I lay down.

Mum is running a flannel under the tap in the tiny en-suite bathroom which is basically just a loo and basin. I had forgotten that I am in their bedroom. The drumming noise of the water hitting the sink doesn't hurt my head like it did before. It's more a dull ache now, not the 'red-hot poker stuck into my eyes pain' that I felt earlier. Mum places the wet cloth gently on my forehead. For a perfect moment, the cold takes the pain away.

'I've put some flannels in the freezer,' she says. 'That will feel even better. I'll bring you a lolly as well. *Yes please*, I think. I am not ready to speak though. My mouth is dry and sort of glued together. I look around for some water. Mum sits on the edge of the bed carefully trying not to rock me.

82

'How are you?' she says.

My head is thick with sleep and my body feels like it's made of lead. My cheeks are tight and dry and sore. It hurts to wrinkle my forehead. I remove the flannel and move my skin in all directions testing it out as though someone has given me a new face. I bet I look awful.

'What time is it?' I croak and reach for a water bottle. Mum has placed a line of them on the bedside table, a little queue of helpers waiting for me to wake up.

'You've been asleep for a couple of hours,' says Mum. 'Head any better?'

I nod but regret it. The pain tips from one side to the other like a burning metal ball rolling around inside my head. I want to ask if anyone has been in to see me, whether Luca has asked about me. A rush of embarrassment and longing overwhelms me and my head throbs.

'We redheads are rubbish in the heat,' she chats. 'The sun is too bright, too hot, it all gets too much. I'm just the same.'

'Where is everyone?' I whisper, taking longer and longer sips of water until my voice sounds semi-normal.

'Swimming,' says Mum. 'They are all worried about you. I said that you had just had a bit too much sun and needed a quiet afternoon. Dad keeps popping in and Nurse Ella is waiting to start her shift.'

Typical. Ella would definitely want in on the action, she loves a drama. No Luca then. I feel something inside between disappointment and relief. I drain the water bottle and open another one. Mum is watching me.

'Were you okay on the beach today, Chloe?' asks Mum. Her voice is light but there's an edge.

I panic and glug the water slightly making me cough. *She knows*. I keep taking sips of water and avoid eye contact.

'Yeah, why?'

'Well, it seemed like you and Luca were running from the beach,' continues Mum. 'Did something happen?'

I flush scarlet all over. I'm grateful for my sunburn as Mum might not notice. This is almost as embarrassing as what happened on the beach. *Almost*. I presume she's guessed we kissed, however, there is something else in her expression. It slowly dawns on me. I don't want her to blame Luca for anything.

'No, no, it was nothing,' I rush. 'We, we... just heard Dad shouting and when I ran I... I started to feel weird and sick and my head was hurting.'

'Why didn't Luca wait for you?' asked Mum, her eyes on me, gaze sharpened to a point.

I wish I knew, I think.

'He didn't realise,' I say.

'Are you sure?' says Mum looking at me meaningfully. 'I won't think anything is your fault. You can tell me anything.'

'There's nothing,' I say quickly. *Please don't think that*. Does she think Luca attacked me or something?

'I just want to make sure you are okay,' she says.

'I'm fine,' I lie.

Tears spring. Squeezing my eyes shut, I lower myself back against the pillows. The touch of the cotton is like a cool kiss on each burning cheek. A sob rises up but I swallow it. Neither Mum nor I say anything for what feels like a year. The silence in the room is deafening and alive. Secrets creep like spiders in the corners of the room.

'You like Luca, don't you?' says Mum suddenly.

Oh no, oh no. Don't ask me that. She's closed all the blinds in the caravan to keep the light out of my eyes, but my eyes are shut anyway to keep the tears in. I don't want to talk about this. Well, I sort of do, but I feel so stupid I can't.

> *Kute magazine. February 1984*
> *Don't break your heart if your crush don't*
> *wanna know.*
> *He's obviously not the one to make love*
> *flow.*

It doesn't feel obvious. *Stupid magazine.* Stupid everything. I'd knock all those *Kute* phrases out of my head if it wouldn't hurt so much. My fingers gently massage my temples.

'You don't have to tell me,' says Mum.

'We're just friends,' I whisper.

My voice is small as though I'm squeezing the words through a tiny crack.

'Of course,' she says.

I let my eyes flicker open for just a second. I see that the warmth in her voice has spread to her cheeks. Perhaps the conversation is not easy for her either. She smiles at me. She places the flannel back on my forehead. It's not as cold as it was but it still feels good. Anything to stop my head aching like my heart. At least, I think it's my heart, a dull tight sadness in the middle of my chest. It's something.

85

The bed bounces as Mum stands up. Her space next to my legs fills with cool air. As she closes the door, I move my fingers onto the bed where she has been sitting and let the warmth soak into my hand.

*

I don't know what time it is. I think I have been asleep again. My head feels better. The pain behind my eyes has eased. There's a movement at the door. It's Ella sliding hesitantly through the narrowest gap. When she sees I'm awake she bounces into the room like Tigger on a sugar rush.

'Mum sent me to see if you were dead,' she says.

'Well, I'm not,' I reply deadpan.

'Shame,' she says and pulls a face. She hasn't forgiven me for the slap. Or maybe she has. She lies down next to me and puts her head on my stomach. Her blonde hair fans out across my chest. Surprised, I put my arm around her shoulder and we lay like this for a few minutes.

'When are you getting up, dead person?' she asks.

'Never.'

'I'm bored,' she whines.

'I don't care,' I say amused.

'Your stomach is making weird noises,' she says.

'Well get off then.'

I use my stomach muscles to pull in my tummy and then push it out quickly several times bouncing her head like a ball. She laughs. When she doesn't get off I sit up and get my hands on her shoulders and push her off me. We wrestle a bit and then she's tumbling onto the floor laughing and screaming 'Ow' at the same time. The ache in my head creeps back in across my temples and into the back of my eyes. My arms feel suddenly weak and I lie down turning on my side. I have been asleep on and off all afternoon but I'm exhausted.

'You still look like a tomato,' says Ella.

She picks herself up off the floor and fake rubs a fake bump on her arm.

'At least I don't look like you,' I answer.

She looks furious but before she can think of a good reply, Mum is calling from the next room: 'Ella!'

*

I hear them all in the kitchen, the cosy sounds of a family making tea. I wonder which family it is, our family or the 'other family' in the mirror. I like that I can stay here and feel part of it all without having to join in. Ella has left all the doors open as usual so the familiar noises drift down the corridor. Pans clanking on the hob, the kettle boiling, cupboards and drawers opening and closing, the sharp sound of plates, and the rattle of the knives and forks. There are voices as well. Ella is complaining about having to lay the table because I'm in bed. I can hear her stomping backwards and forwards making the flimsy caravan floor shake all the way to my room. Of course, if I were up, she would be desperate to lay the table to show Mum and Dad that I was the lazy one. I don't know why they are not eating outside. The evening is as hot as the day and the stuffy air hangs around the caravan like warm fog.

There are familiar images to the sounds I hear. Outside Uncle Toni is calling to Auntie Helen. He is going to walk to the shop. *Does she want anything?* I imagine Toni's expressive hands waving around as he shouts. Some children are playing football with high pitched shouts. I recognise the bounce of a football hitting one of the caravans. There's a special 'thwack' noise that is different to hitting someone's car or disappearing into the bushes. I see all this activity as though I am outside watching. It's probably Mr and Mrs Lacey's grandchildren who are staying for a few days: two curly-haired little boys who constantly kick a football around the field. Mr Lacey keeps trying to get them to play at the other end of the field where there are fewer caravans. He shows them where to go but their game gradually moves closer and closer again until there's another whack of a ball hitting a window or roof. Mr Lacey rushes out to speak to them, running one hand through his grey hair, his face struggling between anger and patience. I can see all this in my mind while staying inside but not miss out on anything. It's nice. I don't have to see anyone or be embarrassed when I see Luca. I can hide my red face in the pillows and for once no one knows what I am feeling. Well, maybe. I haven't heard Luca's voice near the caravan. I check my phone, he hasn't texted me either, so I keep listening hoping I hear him asking how I am.

You can hear everything on our caravan site if you stop and listen. Inside the caravan, the plastic walls are thin and even if you can't see what's going on, you can hear it. The water from the shower in our bathroom thunders against the wall of our bedroom, the TV rumbles through the wall of the shower. Outside, people talk just as freely in the fresh air as though the field is another room. People do things outside that they would normally do inside. We cook outside, Dad even cleans his teeth outside if he gets fed up with waiting for the bathroom. Everything is back to front just like me. I feel as though my insides are outside. My face is as red as the flesh underneath. I'm glad my heart is buried so deep below skin, bone and muscle. *Was it a good kiss?* Did Luca notice how fast my heart was beating? Frozen in my mind like a photograph is the shocked expression on Luca's face as I lunged at him. He did kiss me back though. It's so confusing.

Listening to the sounds around me, seeing the world with my eyes closed, it makes me think of Mum in the hospital and the funny story she told us about how they removed the BCC – the weird pink mole thing that the doctors told her was a form of cancer – from her face. When she went to the hospital that day, she didn't realise they would cut it out there and then.

'It was a bit of a shock,' she told us, 'But there I was, on the bed. I had to wait a while for the doctor. They wanted to get a plastic surgeon to come in and do the procedure because they are the experts.'

'What's a plastic surgeon?' asked Ella. 'Surely you need a skin surgeon.'

'That's what they are,' said Mum, 'A special doctor who is good with skin, and has steady hands.'

She mimed someone with shaky hands slicing with a knife. Ella shrieked and clasped her hands to her mouth giggling.

'So there I was,' said Mum, 'Minding my own business, waiting for the special doctor to get a scalpel and cut into my face.'

'Urgh!' Ella and I cringed. Mum cackled.

'Were you scared? Did you want to run away?' we asked.

'No,' said Mum. 'Ok, yes. But I thought I would just close my eyes and keep them closed until it was over. They gave me an anaesthetic, a tiny little injection, so I wouldn't feel anything. However, I didn't want to watch them operating on my face, so I kept my eyes tight shut.'

'*A little cut*, the doctor said, but all I felt was a tug on my skin as though I'd scratched an itch. Then I felt something wet and I thought, gosh…' She paused dramatically. 'That must be my blood.'

'No!' Ella and I gasped. 'How did you know it was blood?'

'I just knew,' said Mum. She laughed at our shocked faces as though she were telling a funny horror story and the way she told it made it hilarious even though I suppose it wasn't.

'That is disgusting,' I said.

'Awesome,' said Ella. 'I can't wait to tell my friends at school.'

I don't think Dad liked Mum telling this story and there were lots more gory details. *Don't frighten the girls*, he would say, but Mum's mum, Grandma Di, was a nurse and they were always very practical about anything medical.

'It's better if they understand, John,' said Mum. 'There's nothing to be afraid of, it was just a little procedure and now it's all sorted. I'm fine.'

She smiled at us with her new smile, very slightly twisted above her top lip on one side. Her smile was not as wide as usual because she had to be careful not to stretch the wound while it was healing. She can smile more easily now. Dad says that Mum's smile was the first thing he noticed about her when they met. Mum says that can't be true because she had her back to him so it must have been her bottom. At first, it was hard not to stare at her mouth, even though Dad told us not to.

'Poor Mummy,' said Ella putting her arms around Mum's waist. I don't know whether the hug was reassurance for her or Mum. 'Nasty doctor.'

'No,' said Mum. 'Good doctor, who made me better. Look how beautiful I am.'

She stuck out her tongue and crossed her eyes. She was so funny and made us laugh so much, that we got her to tell us again. Ella acted along, *What's that wet stuff on my face? Oh, must be my blood!* Dad laughed at first but then went a bit quiet and said: 'That's enough now, Lizzie.' Mum didn't seem to notice. Eventually he said he was going to make some sandwiches. The door banged after him.

After she told us this story, later that night, I had to get out of bed to go to the loo. As I passed Mum and Dad's bedroom door, I heard Mum crying. At first, I assumed it was Ella but their door was ajar and peeking through the crack, I could see it was just them sitting on the edge of the bed. Mum's head hung over her lap and Dad was rubbing between her shoulder blades. I quickly took a step down the corridor and waited. I didn't want to hear or see what was going on but I couldn't move. *Why was Mum crying?* She didn't often cry. The sound chilled me as much as if I'd heard a ghost. Then I heard Dad's deep voice murmuring. I could only hear, 'Hey love, come on now'. There was more crying, a little louder. Maybe they had had a row. I felt angry with Dad. He shouldn't be arguing with Mum when she was recovering from her operation, or procedure, or whatever it was called. Maybe she was just tired. Nothing seems funny when you are tired.

*

I don't know what time it is. I don't know why there isn't a clock in here. Ella has appeared with the laptop. She settles down to watch a movie with me. There are a few old favourites downloaded on to the computer from when we were younger. We both slip under the duvet even though it's hot in the room. We curl up with the laptop balanced between us and watch *Toy Story*. I haven't seen it in years. We could watch it in the living room with Mum and Dad but I am worried about Toni, Helen or Luca knocking on the door. I'm not ready to see anyone yet. I have been in bed since this afternoon. I still feel a bit sick and my head feels as fragile as an egg. Any slight knock or noise could cause it to crack and bring back the pounding headache. No, I am happy tucked up here at the back of the caravan with Ella. Ella's been popping in and out for the last couple of hours. At first it was irritating but with every visit she brought a new bit of information from outside. I start to look forward to her updates like little treats from the shop. *Mum's doing this. Dad's gone here. Toni's fallen asleep outside. Mr Jones popped by and asked if we wanted eggs. There's a big dog tied up near the gate and no one knows who he belongs to*. Every time she mentions Luca, I feel like she is feeding me only kitchen scraps of information but I'm hungry for more. I want to ask her a million questions, but I don't want to give myself away. Ella doesn't seem to know what's happened or she's pretending not to. No, she couldn't keep anything to herself. Unless Luca's told someone, I don't think anyone knows. Even Mum was guessing. *I think. I hope*.

Ella is asleep. Head slumped onto my shoulder and chest. She is making me overheat but I don't want to move her. She always falls asleep before the end of a film. She gets that from Mum. I shuffle the laptop more over to my side and plug in my headphones. It's late but I'm not tired because I slept so much this afternoon. The next time I wake up, it will be tomorrow and I will have to see Luca. *Do I talk to him or just pretend it didn't happen?* I don't want to think about that now. I'll watch the film for a bit. I hope Mum brings me something for my head soon, it's really aching again.

I had a look at my face when I went to the loo earlier. My nose and forehead look pink and stretched and shiny. I have a red stripe in my hair where my parting is sunburnt too. I'm sore but I'm relieved that I don't look as bad as I thought. From Mum's reaction I thought my face was going to drop off. I touch my cheeks gently with the tips of my fingers. There's a heat coming off my skin as though it's still cooking in the sun. My shoulders, chest and back are burned too. The worst is the scarlet half circle above my boobs in the shape of my crop top. I hope it will be more pink tomorrow than red and then maybe I can cover most of it up with foundation. I've got one with a green base that is supposed to tone down red skin. Urgh! I hate this skin. Why couldn't I inherit Dad's more olive skin? He tans so easily and so does Ella. I glance at her resentfully. You don't get to choose what you inherit from your parents and I got all the rubbish stuff. Even my name came from someone else. Half the books in the caravan have 'Emma Chloe Carter' written inside in rounded unfamiliar handwriting. I'm named after Dad's sister who died before I was born. Chloe was her middle name. Mum's skin, my Aunt's name, I just want to be me. I can't wait until I'm grown up. I'm going to get a job, my own flat and do what I want. I'm also going to go on lots of holidays and choose where I want to go, and not share a bedroom with my stupid sister. All my holidays will be abroad in interesting places like Italy, Spain, America, Mexico, Thailand. Everyone at school will be jealous of me, not that I'll be at school, but they'll see me post amazing pictures. It will always be somewhere hot and sunny. I feel a stab of guilt. After Mum's operation, or 'procedure', she was told to keep her scar out of strong sunlight for at least a year. We were never going to have anything other than a holiday in England this year.

I wince as I rub after sun painfully into my forehead. This isn't fair. In the mirror, the reflection of my fingers moves in small circles massaging cream into my cheeks, as though I am watching someone else perform an operation. I try not to make eye contact with the 'other Ella'. She forgot the anaesthetic. *Ouch*.

5

WEDNESDAY

My headache has almost gone and I don't feel sick anymore. I don't feel much better though. I feel hollow like that disappointing bit at the bottom of the ice cream cone which is all wafer and no ice cream. I want to go home but we are here for three more days. Luca didn't try to see me yesterday or this morning, so he probably hates me or just thinks I'm embarrassing. I want to message Sophie, but Mum wouldn't give me my phone back yesterday. She said staring at the screen would make my headache worse. *What would I tell Sophie? Would any of it make sense?* I think about the heat, the sun burning my skin as I waited and waited for Luca to make the first move, the way our teeth bumped, and the run from the beach. I decide I don't want to message Sophie even if I could. I don't want to talk to Luca either. I am going to just ignore the whole thing. I'll laugh it off. Hopefully he'll be too embarrassed to mention it either.

I heard the others go, rather than see them, car doors opening and closing. Toni calling to Helen to lock the caravan. Helen calling to Toni that she's left her key inside. Dad calling to Ella to get her water bottle. Toni calling to Luca to pick up… the rest of the words are lost in the cough of a car engine starting. I stay in bed until I am sure they are gone. They've gone to the adventure park up the coast, the one with the massive log flume. I thought about how I'd planned to sit next to Luca on the rides, squished up tight. I try to shake the image out of my head. I don't even like rides that much. Mum puts her head around the door. She's staying behind with me but she doesn't have to, I'm not a baby.

'Time to get dressed,' she says brightly.

'I'm not going out,' I panic. 'My head hurts.'

'You're not ill. Fresh air will do you good, and you certainly can't hide in here for the rest of the holiday.'

'Stupid holiday,' I mutter.

'*Stupid holiday*,' she mocks.

I smile reluctantly. She does a good impersonation of me. Mum hasn't mentioned Luca again, thankfully. I know she thinks she knows, but she's being cool about it.

*

Mum is talking to the pharmacist. Her face is half covered by her huge floppy hat. She looks ridiculous wearing it in the shop. I glance around to see who is staring at us. We're in the massive Tesco. It is the only big supermarket around here so it's always busy. Mum wanted to take me to the doctors in the village but luckily Dad persuaded her to take me to the local chemist instead. The pharmacist has a tufty grey-brown beard that starts in his ears and finishes halfway down his neck. He is nodding as Mum describes what happened – my sunburn, the headaches. He glances over at me occasionally as they talk. I blush under his scrutiny and stare at my feet. I don't want anyone looking at me. Mum wouldn't let me put on any make-up until the pharmacist saw me. My face is awful, pink and shiny, and without mascara on my blonde eyelashes I look like one of those pink-eyed mice in a lab. The pharmacist studies me again whilst Mum points at my face and drones on about 'long-term skin damage'.

I want to get out of here. After my day in the caravan, the supermarket is too bright and noisy. There are too many different colours and shapes, and the constant shift of people around me is confusing. I miss the quiet half-darkness of Mum and Dad's bedroom. Mum is buying something from the pharmacy. That's good, we must be finished. She slots her card into her purse with the receipt. She nods without looking up as I tell her I'm going to the toilet. She is struggling to zip up her purse which is bulked out with too many reward cards. The toilets are at the back of the store. My trainers squeak against the rubber floor and I cringe hoping no one is watching me. In the toilets I take in my reflection in the smudged mirror. The harsh fluorescent light drains some of my colour, but I still see the bright pink nose and cheeks. My freckles stand out darkly behind my flushed complexion. There's only one thing to do – I'm going to wipe it all out. I rummage in my rucksack for my foundation and other makeup. I can get rid of the sunburn, and the freckles, I know I can. Mum's waiting for me outside the toilet. She tries not to react when she sees my face but her expression gives her away.

'What?' I snap.

The makeup feels tight on my sore skin. I don't care though. This is how I want to look.

When we leave the supermarket, the weather has changed so dramatically that it could be another day entirely. The sun has disappeared behind a cluster of clouds. A gust of wind surprises us. Mum's sun dress is whipped around her legs and the chains connecting the supermarket trolleys rattle as if haunted. Mum hovers outside the shop entrance staring across the street. Her thoughts are hidden under her huge sun hat. The bus stop is opposite the supermarket, but Mum is looking up and down the little high street slowly as though breathing in the busy atmosphere. She likes coming here during our normal holidays, but this is the first time she's been here this week. I wait impatiently, a chill wrapping itself around my bare legs like a wet cat.

'What are we doing?' I say.

I feel stupid standing here. I felt better after I put my makeup on, but my mood is changing as quickly as the weather. Mum doesn't answer. Her face twitches a little like a clock ticking away the seconds.

'Mum!' I snap.

'Tea,' she says finally, 'Let's have tea. And cake.'

Okay.

In the cafe, Mum studies my face.

'What?' I say, unable to hide my annoyance. I hate people staring at me. Mum doesn't react. She stirs her tea, eyes following the spoon.

'You should give me some makeup tips' she says. 'I hardly recognise you.'

'Maybe I don't want people to recognise me,' I reply.

'Well, your makeup is very…' Mum pauses while choosing her next word, 'professional.'

'I could do your makeup,' I say hopefully.

Mum smiles and gives a little shake of the head.

'Maybe later, sweetheart,' she says. 'You're good, but not that good, and I'm not really looking my best today.'

She laughs but there's no humour in it. Mum normally wouldn't leave the house without makeup, but she hasn't worn any since her 'procedure'. Her pale eyelashes and eyebrows blend into her skin, so the most noticeable features are her blue eyes and the reddened scar. She still has the leftover smile on her lips from her laugh, and I try not to look at the way the corner of her mouth twists slightly. I see people do this all the time, people that don't know, like the shop assistants in Tesco. They stare at her mouth, wondering what's wrong with it, what happened.

Mum is gazing across the room lost in thought. She smooths down her hair with one hand. It doesn't need it; her hair is always straight and perfect. At least she has taken that stupid sun hat off. It's tucked under the table between us on its own chair. The waitress offered to hang it up but Mum preferred to keep it with her. A bus rumbles past the window. We both watch it roll by. It should be fun having tea out, but I don't think either of us feels like talking. I sip my cola. It's not the real stuff but it's cold and syrupy and delicious. The cotton tablecloth keeps sticking to the bottom of my glass when I lift it up. There's a dark, wet ring on the sky-blue fabric as though I've drawn around it with a marker pen. I straighten the tablecloth and try to place the glass exactly back on the ring. Eventually Mum speaks again.

'I saw Luca earlier…'

Really? My stomach lurches. I concentrate on my glass in front of me trying to keep my face as still as possible so that it doesn't show any reaction.

'…with Auntie Helen.'

Oh no. My insides flutter in panic. *What did they talk about?*

'They told me that Marco is coming tomorrow.'

'Marco?'

I perk up, suddenly interested. We didn't think that Marco, Luca's brother, was coming on holiday this year.

'Yes, he's back earlier than expected from his football training and is coming down to spend the last couple of days with us,' explains Mum.

'Great,' I say really meaning it. Marco is fun.

'We'll have to give him a good welcome,' says Mum 'Maybe a little party. Nice to have all you kids back together.'

The atmosphere around our table feels brighter, a little sun breaking through the clouds. Mum chats about whether we should pick up some special cakes from the bakery. We could have them when Marco arrives tomorrow. He's going to get the train down tomorrow morning and Uncle Toni will pick him up from the station.

The waitress arrives at our table with our order. Mum has a carrot cake – her favourite. A cluster of walnuts nestle in the thick cream cheese topping. I have a scone; it's shiny and enormous and hardly fits on the plate. The little dishes of jam and cream are balanced around the edges. My mouth is watering. The waitress clatters the plates clumsily when she puts them on the table. It's just what I would have done. I would make a rubbish waitress. I think the waitress is a teenager, only a few years older than me. She is apologising to Mum who in return smiles and reassures her that 'it's fine'. The waitress's gaze sticks on Mum's scar and she stares a fraction too long. It's only a moment but it is long enough to burn an angry hole in me. Then she flicks her eyes away and is careful not to look at Mum's face while she is talking and arranging the plates and cake forks. She promises to come back with the two glasses of water that she has forgotten. Mum takes a sip of her tea, all her chattiness drained away. We eat in silence.

I'm stuffed. I run a greedy finger around the rim of my plate picking up the last of the crumbs. I raise my finger to my lips which is sticky with jam and cream. Mum goes to the loo. I watch her weave between the tables, her long skirt brushing chair legs and dragging over bags left on the floor. I look around protectively to see if anyone else is watching her. The cafe is busy. People are drinking and eating and chatting, absorbed in their own little worlds. A toddler totters between these worlds, bumping into the tables, smiling at strangers, then looking terrified when they smile back. I still feel like that a lot of the time. I want to ask Mum if she minds people staring at her, but it is a stupid question. Who would be okay with it? She has caught me staring a few times when I thought she wasn't looking. It's hard not to notice it. The scar on her face is not very big, but her lips twists up a little in the corner where it's still tight. The doctors said that the scar would look better in time. It will flatten and look less red. She massages it every morning and night with a special oil. Maybe things will get back to normal eventually. Then I remember that Mum is still waiting for test results to make sure they removed all the damaged cells. If they haven't, she will have to have more treatment. I don't know what that means. The worry sits in the bottom of my stomach like a heavy slice of cake.

Mum is taking a long time in the toilet, there must be a queue. I twist around in my chair to see if she is coming. Our waitress is laughing with two old ladies as she places a pot of tea down on their table. They are sitting in the window and the sun shining through the glass illuminates their silvery hair like glowing haloes. They chuckle at whatever the waitress is saying. One of them gives a little scream and the sound carries across the cafe. She bats the waitress's arm playfully. The waitress's laughter makes me angry. I clench my fists and focus on the tablecloth which has a smudge of jam from my scone. At school the counsellor told us that if we were feeling stressed we should concentrate on things around us that we can see and hear. However, the smudge of jam is blurring. The little burning hole inside me is spreading. Under my makeup, under my sunburn, my cheeks start to burn as well. *I'm going to say something to the waitress.* People shouldn't stare and make Mum feel self-conscious. It's just a little scar, she's not deformed. The waitress probably had a good laugh at me and my sunburn as well. I know it shows through the foundation. *I'm definitely going to say something.* Where is Mum? I look over towards the toilets again. The waitress isn't there and the old ladies are pouring their tea. The sun has gone in and their grey hair looks darker like clouds gathering rain. I twist around in my seat scanning the rest of the café to see if Mum has gone somewhere else.

'Here you go.'

A voice makes me jump. The waitress is right next to me. The sleeve of her old-fashioned black and white uniform reaches around me, and she gently places two glasses of water on the table. Mum asked for them ages ago. I'm afraid to look up but I have to speak. My chest feels tight and my palms are a little sweaty. My breath is hot like steam as I spit out the words.

'She's had cancer you know!'

'Sorry?' the girl replies, sounding surprised.

Of course, it meant nothing to her. She probably doesn't even remember. Angry, I finally lift my head to face her.

'I said, she's…' my words falter.

It's a different girl. She has a thinner and sharper face. She's older than the original waitress and her hair is brown not blonde. *Oh no*.

'Sorry, what did you say?' The new waitress is trying to be polite but I don't think it comes naturally.

'Nothing,' I mumble. To avoid looking at her I grab my drink which spills. It runs underneath my fingers down the glass and on to the tablecloth. I watch the dark stain spread until I'm sure the waitress has disappeared. Mum comes back. She's put some concealer on her scar. It looks odd, more noticeable than before.

'Can we go?' I ask quickly.

'Sure, where do you want to go first?' says Mum. 'We can have a look around the shops if you like.'

'No, home. I mean back to the caravan.'

Mum looks surprised.

'I'm tired,' I add.

She nods, understanding but not understanding. We gather up our bags and jackets. Mum goes to the counter to pay. I head for the door. I don't want to see that waitress again. Outside, I link my arm through Mum's and pull her towards me. I'm cold and her body is warm next to mine. The sky is much darker now than when we arrived at the cafe. Mum looks up at the bruised clouds.

'It's going to rain,' she says, 'We'll pick up some cakes and get straight on the bus.'

*

'Any luck, love?' says Dad to Mum.

He barely glances up from his phone as Mum comes in closing the caravan door.

We're all plugged in, lying on the sofas, Dad and me on our phones and Ella on the laptop. Ella is lying on her tummy playing a game and listening to music with headphones on. She is humming along to a song only she can hear. Mum's hair has a mist of rain. She shakes it off. She had to go outside and walk a bit to make the phone call, you can't always get a good mobile reception in the caravan.

'No,' she answers flatly. 'I rang the cafe again, just in case anyone was there but I got the answer machine again. It's their early closing day but I thought someone might still be there cleaning up or something. I rang the bus company but that was voicemail too. They close at four.'

'Okay', says Dad.

Mum chews her lip anxiously, the non-scar side.

'I want to check the car again. Can I have your keys?' she asks.

'Love, we looked in the car, your hat's not there,' says Dad still distracted by whatever he is watching or reading on his phone.

'I want to check again, where are your keys?'

Mum stands over him. Dad pats his pockets with his free hand keeping one eye on his phone.

'They might be in the bedroom,' says Dad vaguely.

When he doesn't move. Mum tuts and treads heavily through the caravan to their bedroom and then back again. The floor vibrates sending shock waves across the caravan with each dull step. Dad doesn't seem to notice what is happening until Mum opens the caravan door again and the cool air creeps in from outside. I shiver.

'Lizzie, wait,' says Dad sitting up. 'Don't bother going now, you're already wet. I've checked in the car and your hat's not there.'

'I just want to have one last look,' she insists.

Dad did pick us up from the bus stop because it was raining, but I don't think Mum's sun hat is in the car. I don't remember her having it on the bus either. It's more likely she left it in the cafe. We left the cafe in a hurry because I was embarrassed about snapping at the wrong waitress, not that Mum knows that. The sun hat must be still on the chair tucked under our table out of sight. I feel guilty, I should have remembered.

'Then let me look,' says Dad hauling himself off the sofa and stuffing his phone into his back pocket.

Mum stares at Dad meaningfully. She doesn't have to say that she doesn't trust him to have looked properly. The temperature inside the caravan keeps dropping as Mum stands holding the door open.

'No, it's fine,' she says, her voice tight.

'Love,' says Dad. 'Let's leave it until the rain stops. It's not like you need a sun hat when it's raining.' He shrugs and grins as though it is funny. 'It's not important.'

'*Not important*?' repeats Mum.

Ella and I catch each other's eye nervously. Even if Dad can't hear it, we can sense the tone in Mum's voice like the threat of rain, and Ella still has her headphones on.

'I think I can decide what is *important* to me,' continues Mum.

Mum and Dad's argument goes from 0-100 mph in a matter of minutes. They don't row much but when they do it always seems to be about the stupidest things. Ella and I stare shocked and silent as though a dormant volcano has suddenly erupted from the floor of the caravan.

'Stop trying to make an argument about something that doesn't matter!' shouts Dad.

'That's right,' yells Mum. '*You* say it doesn't matter, so it *doesn't* matter! *Everyone* says it doesn't matter. That's because it's not happening to *them*!'

'What are you going on about?!' yells back Dad. 'It's just a hat! I'll get you another hat if you calm down and talk to me properly.'

'Don't you tell me to calm down!' shouts Mum.

Mum starts to really lose it. Her face and neck are scarlet as though lava is flowing under her skin. I tap Ella on the leg and signal towards the door. Ella picks up the laptop and follows me. Mum and Dad stand facing each other in the middle of the room. We slip through them, ducking our heads as the angry words fly backwards and forwards. Safely in our bedroom, we flop on the beds in the cramped space and close the door. Anything is better than listening to that.

*

Rain: a thousand impatient fingers drumming on the roof of the caravan. Dad and Ella are tapping a message back on the edge of the table. They don't know they are doing it and the habit drives Mum mad. Eyes fixed on the game, Dad and Ella are waiting for Mum to lay a card. They are so competitive. They are almost as bad as Luca and Marco, who are officially the most competitive people I've ever met. Even more so than super-sporty Grace Barker who is in my form at school. She made Sophie give up her place in the sports day relay team, even though Sophie wanted to do it. However, Grace was worried our form would lose. *Who cares?* Sophie had to do javelin instead which she hated.

Ella is jiggling around in her seat clutching her last card. She has a massive grin on her face, confident that she's about to go out. We're on our fifth, or it might be our one hundredth and fifth, game of Uno. The weather is rubbish today. Not that I want to go out. I still don't want to see Luca. I just want my phone, but I can't have it because we're having 'family time'. So annoying.

This end of the caravan, where we sit around the table and lounge on the sofas, is surrounded by windows. The curtains are open despite the ever-darkening sky. The windowpanes are like mirrors reflecting everything back into the room as though the only thing that exists in the world is our family playing cards around the table. The glass is blurry with condensation. On the window nearest to me I rub a small circle like a spy hole. I can see the door to Luca's caravan. *I wonder what he's doing.* Then I feel that hot embarrassment prickles my skin again as I remember everything.

Ella's triumphant shriek makes me turn around. She slaps down her winning card and jumps up knocking into the table. All the drinks spill. 'Idiot,' I snap. 'Chloe…' says Mum with a warning in her voice. I reach behind me for the kitchen roll to mop up the puddle of juice. Ella pushes her bottom in my face as she does a victory wiggle past me. I push her away. 'Girls...' Mum warns again. Dad chuckles in that way when he finds something funny but knows that he shouldn't. Mum looks at her watch, maybe even she's had enough. I certainly have.

'I need to pee!' shouts Ella.

As she moves the 'other Ella' sticks out her tongue at me from the last scrap of uncovered mirror, and then pulls a silly face. I can just about see the 'other Chloe' over Ella's shoulder in the mirror. She is making a face too. Ella and I smirk at each other. We have been getting on much better today but the 'other Ella and Chloe' are always there, waiting to get us into trouble. Ella starts dancing in front of the mirror, copying the 'other Ella's' every move. The 'other Chloe' and I sigh at our identical flaming cheeks hoping it is just the light in here and the stuffy atmosphere that is making them look worse. I might need to touch up my makeup. A gentle tapping at the caravan door makes me jump. It's hard to imagine that there could be anyone or anything out there in the thunderous rain. Mum looks at her watch again.

'Who can that be?' she says.

'Salty Dog!' says Ella excited. She rushes to open the door.

The damp evening has wrapped the caravan in mist bringing the salty scent of the sea creeping around our door. When Ella and I were little, Gran used to tell us that the smell came from a big, friendly dog that would come sniffing around the caravans on rainy evenings. His damp shaggy coat smelt salty because he loved to swim in the sea. His fur was full of sand from rolling around on the beach. He liked to run up from the shoreline under cover of the mist and explore the field and caravans. If Gran said it was a 'Salty Dog' type of night, Ella and I would rush to the caravan door, looking this way and that, and then complain that we couldn't see him. *Look harder*, Gran would say. We squinted through the mist into the dark night hoping to see his sandy-coloured head nosing up to the caravan steps looking for treats. Gran swore she had met him when she was a girl and we desperately wanted to see him too. I think Ella is still hopeful but obviously I know it's just a story. Gran always found ways to make it fun here. Even when the weather grew chilly, we were too excited about seeing Salty Dog to be disappointed that it was raining.

Ella pulls open the caravan door letting in the smell of a thousand wet, salty dogs. Framed in the doorway, her dark hair merging with the night sky is Auntie Helen. She is smiling and asking us if we would like to go to the cinema. It is the first time I've seen any of the others since yesterday and that feels like a million years ago. I focus on my hands resting on the table, fingers curled tightly around the playing cards. Auntie Helen chats in her usual quiet way and doesn't mention my red cheeks or talk directly to me at all. I still don't think anyone knows what happened with Luca. Mum thinks she knows but really no one knows except me… and Luca. My stomach sinks. *I can't see him.* I could stay here and tell everyone my head hurts. Mum, Helen and Dad's conversation is rumbling on about what's on at the cinema and what time to go. The film they are talking about is supposed to be good. Sophie's going to see it this week with some girls from our form. I feel a stab of envy. I wish I was with my friends now, laughing in the dark, throwing popcorn at each other.

There's something weird about the way Mum is sounding all surprised about the cinema and talking to Dad as though they need to 'think it over'. We always see a film on holiday, particularly on a rainy day, it's a tradition, *another* holiday tradition. Ella is ecstatic and shouting about how she can't decide what flavour popcorn she wants; she always has sweet. I think about Mum looking at her watch just before Auntie Helen came to the door. *Could they have planned it?* A flush of embarrassment sweeps down my body. My legs feel shaky. I put my Uno cards on the table. I turn away from the noise of everyone making plans and start drawing a face in the condensation on the windowpane next to my spy hole. The face is too smiley, so I rub it out with my hand making a smeary mess. I watch the drips run down the glass. I thought I could just hide out in the caravan for at least one more day.

*

110

We meet up with the Rossis at the little old-fashioned cinema in the village. It only has one screen and the front two rows are a collection of battered sofas instead of normal cinema seats. There's a counter in the foyer that sells bags of sweets and drinks in cans and bottles, and they have an ancient popcorn machine where you can see the popcorn jumping around inside a glass box as if it's part of the show.

I've checked my make up a thousand times to see how my sunburn looks. Mum says it is hardly noticeable now but she's probably being nice. She didn't even tell me off when she saw how much foundation I had put on to cover it up. She hates me looking 'unnatural' as she calls it. She doesn't understand. I follow loads of YouTubers who have amazing makeup channels.

I am so nervous about seeing Luca. There's a knot in my stomach as tight as those impossible tangles you get in a necklace when the chain wraps itself into a little metal ball. I keep telling myself it will be all right but then I remember how Luca ran from the beach and that metal knot inside me tightens again.

When we arrive at the cinema the tiny foyer is packed with people. Helen, Toni and Luca are at the front of the queue for snacks. Toni waves to us to shout over our order.

'SWEET POPCORN!' yells Ella jumping to be seen and heard over the crowd.

Toni gives her a thumbs up. Luca is facing the other way. All I see is the back of his dark head and his broad shoulders dressed in a light grey sweatshirt. As we wait, more and more people cram into the foyer. The noise level swells like rising water. A bell rings and we are hustled towards the cinema doors by a wave of people moving behind us. I hang on to the back of Ella's T-shirt to stop her being swept away. The Rossis are still quite a way behind us. The crowd slows as tickets are checked at the door and then we drift slowly forward again as people are let into the cinema. I crane my neck behind me trying to see where Luca is but there are too many people in the way. We stop again and Dad tries to put his arms around Mum, Ella and I squeezing us into a tight circle. It's uncomfortable.

'Here we all are,' he beams. 'Me and all my girls out together.'

I think he is trying to make up for Mum and him arguing earlier. They are doing a good job pretending but things have been weird between them since Mum lost her hat. I feel a stab of guilt as I think of the hat probably still sitting alone on the chair in the closed café.

Things get a bit awkward when we find our seats. I still haven't spoken to Luca yet and every minute that passes makes me more nervous. I think he's gone to the loo. Mum and Dad, joined by Auntie Helen and Uncle Toni, who are laden with armfuls of sweets and popcorn, shuffle sidewards along the row towards their seats apologising to the people already sitting down. Ella and I are edging towards our seats in the row in front. We always sit like this, adults behind and kids in front. I am struggling to hold my drink and balance the over-full bucket of popcorn that Ella and I are going to share. I don't realise that Luca is behind me until I hear his low voice. 'Shall *I* hold that?' The words make me jump and popcorn spews everywhere, some into the hair of the woman sitting in the aisle in front. Luckily, she doesn't notice. Luca and I exchange looks trying not to laugh. It's so normal, like nothing's happened.

I forget about feeling awkward or 'playing it cool'. The woman raises her hand and brushes her hair absently, but one bit of popcorn is trapped in her curls.

'Come on,' said Ella impatiently shoving me from behind. 'Move up.'

She always pushes into the middle of any group; between Mum and Dad, or me and Mum. Now she is squeezing in between me and Luca. This would have annoyed me a couple of days ago but now I am relieved. Luca hasn't said anything else to me and I can't think of anything to say back. The awkwardness has descended again like mist on a rainy evening. He doesn't seem annoyed with me though, or weird. Maybe he wants to forget about it as much as I do. Irritatingly the memory of him running away from me across the beach flashes into my mind as it has a million times. I feel caught in that moment, as though I'm reading the same page of one of those stupid *Kute* magazine 'photo stories' over and over again. In my mind there's a black and white photo of Luca running across the beach and me sitting on the sand with my mouth open and a speech bubble over my head shouting: 'Wait! ' I wish I could just turn the page or even better rip it out completely.

Lost in my embarrassing thoughts, I am surprised to hear Luca successfully persuading Ella to let him sit between us and hold the buckets of popcorn. Ella starts to make a fuss but when he says he would stop me eating too much popcorn, *and* she can share his sweets as well, she looks ecstatic. She points a finger at me saying 'Ha! In your face!' loud enough for Mum to look over crossly. I don't care. I just want to hide in the dark, watch the film and not talk to anyone.

The lights fade in the cinema and there are a few cheers from the audience. Time for the trailers – my favourite bit. Popcorn is melting on my tongue, and my lips are already shrivelled from too much salt. *It's the law that you have to eat most of your popcorn before film starts, isn't it?* I sip my icy drink and the sweet fizz mixes with the salty taste in my mouth. Delicious. I put the bottle back in the cup holder letting my arm relax there. The fabric covering the arm rest is prickly. I like it though. The soft, scratchy feeling against my bare arms reminds me of all our summer trips to the cinema. I don't use the arm rest on the side nearest to Luca but keep my arm tightly pressed to my side. I'm being careful not to touch him. I'm settled in for the film now. It's a relief to know that everyone is watching the screen and I can just disappear into the dark for a while. No one is asking me how I am. No one is staring at my stupid red face. I was dreading coming to the cinema because of Luca but it's okay. The worst bit is over, I think.

I keep my eyes fixed to the screen. Luca is a dark shape to my right. I am afraid to dig into the two big buckets of popcorn that he is holding in his lap. However, every now and then Luca shakes the tub in my direction. Without turning to look at him my hand reaches in and scoops out as much as I can hold, so I don't have to do this too often. It's hopeless though. More popcorn drops into my lap than my mouth. My hand is like those big metal claws in the amusement arcades where you try to grab a cuddly toy, but it falls out immediately the claw lifts up again. I don't know whether Luca can see how clumsy I am.

Everyone is laughing at one of the funny bits in the film, not just our group, the whole cinema together as though we share one big booming voice. I forget where I am and put my arm on the divider between Luca and me. It's not prickly anymore. It's warm and tickly and confusing and...

Oh no. *Oh no!* My arm is on Luca's arm. I pull away like I've been burned whispering, 'Sorry, sorry,' into the darkness next to me. Luca whispers back, 'It's okay, we can share.' Luca shifts his arm over slightly. I pause, not sure if I understand. Then feeling more confident I gently place my arm next to his. I try to take in the familiar feeling of the prickly armrest and the unfamiliar softness of Luca's skin against mine. Now I can't breathe. Now I'm back on the beach but this is a different page of the photo story. Why doesn't *Kute* magazine or anyone else have advice about what to do when your arm is glued to the arm of the boy that you thought you liked and used to be just a friend, but then you kissed him and freaked him out, and now you are freaked out and embarrassed and want to forget about it. *That doesn't fit into a catchy headline does it?*

We're walking back to the little car park around the back of the cinema. Everyone is talking, well talking over each other mostly, about their favourite part of the film. Luca starts doing an impression of the main character finding a dog in his bed instead of his girlfriend. Ella is laughing so hard I think she might wet herself. I think she's trying to be in hysterics so everyone will look at her. She's such a show-off. Luca has done his impression three times now because Ella begged him too. The others are starting to laugh at her as much as Luca. She loves the attention. They are all watching Ella now, everyone except Luca. Luca is studying something behind me. I glance behind to find a high garden wall. *What is he looking at?* When I turn back, Luca looks away quickly and seems desperate not to catch my eye. My heart sinks. I thought things were okay between us but obviously not. *Is it my sunburn, or the too much make up, or is he remembering how awful it was on the beach?* (Well, it wasn't, but then it was.) I sneak a look at him. He doesn't look angry. We pass under a streetlamp and Luca's face is lit up in the sudden spotlight. His face is flushed. It's mainly two red circles of colour on his cheeks. It looks like Luca is blushing. I've never seen him do that before. No, it must be sunburn, or the light, and if it makes him look red, I must look awful.

6

THURSDAY

The rain has stopped properly this time, no more drizzle, no Salty Dog sniffing around the caravan. Mum opens the caravan door first thing and smells the air.

'Someone's washed the field,' she says inhaling deeply. 'Nice fabric conditioner… grass cuttings, daisies and... a sprinkling of sand.'

I join Mum on the caravan steps. The sun makes the recently rained-on caravans shine like new. The sky looks clean with all the grey washed out of it. Mum sniffs the air again. Her nose wrinkles making her freckles dance. She has a very neat nose that turns up slightly at the end. Ella has Mum's nose. I have a bigger nose with a blob on the end. *Thanks, Dad.* Mum puts an arm around my waist. I rest my head on her shoulder. I am almost as tall as her now. We both stare up at the cool blue sky. The heat has gone out of everything. Even my face has simmered down from red to pink. It's as though nothing has happened and everything. Everything has changed and nothing.

Mum leaves the door open when we go back in for breakfast. I crunch the same cereal I ate yesterday and the day before. I chew slowly as though reluctant for anything to begin. A chill morning breeze sneaks around the caravan. The pictures Mum has stuck to the mirror flutter as though invisible hands are running their fingers through the drawings, maps and postcards, lifting the corners curiously. Sitting at the table, I wrap my dressing gown around me and pull my knees up into its warmth.

It feels cosy in the caravan and even Ella doesn't want to rush outside like she normally does. We both stay in our pyjamas, curled up on the sofa watching cartoons. There's no WiFi so we watch whatever is on TV. After an hour or so, Ella starts dragging out all the board games. We haven't had a proper session all week. Ella sets up one of our favourite games, 'Guess Who'. We each choose a person and then guess who it is by asking questions about what they look like, but you can only answer 'yes' or 'no'. It's an old version that we bought from a charity shop in the village. The faces in the game are faded and wrinkled. 'Just like me,' Gran laughed when we played with her. We play with one eye on the game and one on the TV, chuckling and singing along to *Horrible Histories*.

'Do – you – have a beard?' asks Ella, face screwed up in concentration.

'No,' I say rubbing my chin and we snigger at the familiar joke.

'Do you have red hair?' I ask her.

'No, ha, you're the ginger!' she points at me and we belly laugh together.

All the old jokes, funny for not being funny anymore. In the corner of my eye I catch a movement in the doorway. Luca. He is holding two tennis rackets. He is dressed in sports gear as usual, shorts and a T-shirt, and a different pair of very clean trainers. I am conscious of still being in pyjamas and my old fluffy dressing gown with the rabbit ears. It is a bit tatty but I love it too much to throw it away.

'Hiya,' he says. 'Who fancies tennis?' he holds up a racket hopefully. His quiet voice reminds me of Auntie Helen and how you don't always know she is there until she speaks. Ella and I blink at him as if woken up. I think we had forgotten about the rest of the world. I don't want to go but Ella rushes off to get ready. She loves sports. She's in a million sports clubs at school. Mum follows her to help her find her trainers and shorts.

'Sure you won't come?' asks Luca.

He is looking straight at me swinging one of the rackets in a mock backhand as though the ball could hit me between the eyes. I am surprised at the directness of his gaze and I think so is he. We both look away as though suddenly caught by a bright light.

'No, I'm just going to – like – chill,' I reply, my voice trailing off. There's a pause where neither of us says anything. I reach into my dressing gown pocket for my phone so I have something to look at.

'Er, Chloe,' says Luca. He hesitates then the rest of the words stumble out. 'The other day on the beach...'

My heart squeezes tight in my chest. *I don't want to talk about it. I don't want to know what he thinks.*

'I'm sorry...' Luca continues.

He falters as I look up startled.

'... you got sunstroke,' he finishes and sighs as though he has run a mile. He is looking down at the tennis racket in his hand.

119

'It's okay,' I say feeling a rush of relief. Maybe I wanted him to say something else but this is better.

'Yeah?' Luca replies. He sounds relieved too. 'Cool.'

'Yeah,' I add for no reason other than to say something.

There's another awkward pause where both of us look anywhere but at each other. It feels okay though and for once I'm not blushing. Luckily Mum bustles back into the room noisily. Ella is still getting dressed. Mum is asking Luca questions about the tennis coaching he gets at school. Apparently, he was chosen for a special programme, sponsored by someone famous. Luca is facing Mum but he keeps turning to look at me as he explains. He moves stiffly turning his whole upper body like an actor that hasn't learnt to be natural on stage. He doesn't look me in the eye but focuses slightly above my head. I'm trying to concentrate on what he is saying but I am starting to feel too hot and self-conscious in my fluffy dressing gown. The sun's rays are beginning to slant through the caravan windows which were closed this morning against the chill.

Luca stands between the table where I am sitting and the kitchen where Mum leans on the counter. I would have to squeeze past him to get by. The caravan feels crowded even though it is just the three of us. I notice that Luca is a tiny bit sunburnt across his nose and forehead. I didn't notice this last night at the cinema. It feels like evidence that he was there on the beach. Until he mentioned it a minute ago, the whole thing was starting to feel like I'd imagined it or read it in one of the cheesy photo stories in *Kute* magazine, our whole afternoon spread across a series of black and white photos. Some of the stories in *Kute* carry on to the next week's magazine and at the end have 'To be continued' written in a white rectangle, a bit like the speech bubbles. I still don't know what happens next in our story. Will I have to wait until next week to find out?

When Ella and Luca leave, I feel like I can breathe again. Mum is in the bedroom. I don't know where Dad is but probably with Uncle Toni. I am glad Mum didn't hassle me to go with them. I lay back on the sofa bench that surrounds the table at this end of the caravan. The beige and brown sofa cover is worn. I tuck my toes into its familiar snags and holes knowing that Mum will tell me off if she catches me. I look at my phone. There's a message from Sophie. 'How's *Kute* helping with your cute?' followed by lots of emojis. *Kute*? I sigh. I wish I had never read those stupid magazines. I wish I had never told Sophie about Luca. I wish she'd never told Hannah because now the whole school will know. I ignore her message then change my mind and type 'Friends, that's where it ends. Don't want to spoil a good thing.' She'll get that. It's the lyrics from a track we both love. The singer is so hot. She sends heart emojis back and music notes. When I'm home I'll tell her what happened with Luca. *Maybe*.

*

Mum's hat is back. The cafe owner rang this morning to say that they had found it and Dad drove to the village to pick it up. Mum and Dad haven't said anything else about it, or not that I've heard and it's hard to miss anything in our caravan. I noticed that they haven't talked much today, and he didn't make eye contact when he brought the hat from the car. Mum hasn't worn it yet. The hat is sitting on one of the

121

camp chairs outside like a visitor that everyone has forgotten to talk to.

That feeling of not being able to breathe returns every time I see Luca. I have to think too much when he's around and it's more relaxing when he's not. Things are fine between us, but he always seems to be there, in the corner of my eye, just on the edge of my vision like something caught in my eye lash. Ella and I are sitting on the grass in the shade of our caravan. The day is hotting up. The freshness of the morning has gone but the cool grass feels good against my bare legs. Luca is looking at his phone scrolling through memes which he occasionally reads out. He's leaning against his caravan opposite Ella and me. It's an odd place for him to stand, not with us but not away from us, not in my view but not out of it. I try to ignore him and concentrate on our game. Ella and I are playing 'Armella'. It's a hand-clapping game I learnt at school then taught it to Ella. Obviously, I only play it for her now I'm older. Our hands meet perfectly with every clap and we chant the lyrics together.

> *Aaar-mella, super Stella*
> *Big boys, crazy girls.*

I sometimes change the lyrics to 'Our Ella, super Smella' which Ella both loves and hates.

Our hands clap faster hoping to catch the other one out. We're killing time whilst Uncle Toni collects Luca's brother, Marco, from the station. He left ages ago but there's still no sign of their car. We could have gone off and done something I suppose but we're all feeling lazy today.

No one wanted to miss Marco arriving either, it's probably the most interesting thing that's going to happen today.

Armella, super Stella
Big boys, crazy girls.
Statue!

Ella and I cross our arms over our chests trying to stay as still as possible. The one who moves is the loser. Ella's eyes are wide and crazy. Her lips tighten as she tries to hold in the giggles. Her face is going red now and she looks like she's about to burst. I stare coolly back. I'm too good at this, she's not going to last. A shout distracts me and I jerk my head in its direction.

'Ha!' shouts Ella triumphant. 'I win!'

She grabs my arm, pulls it straight and starts thumping it above and below the elbow shouting in time with the blows.

'I – win – you – lose. You – deserve – a big – bruise!'

'Ow, get off!'

I shake off Ella and kneel up. I can still hear shouting. It's closer. I'm sure I heard my name. All our names. Luca turns towards the noise as well. 'Hello-o-o!' calls a voice from somewhere. The high hedge around the field blocks our view but I can see some of the branches to our right are shaking. Something dark starts to emerge from the thick green hedge, a shoulder in a black T-shirt pushing through the tangle of branches, an arm holding a stick like a sword. A head follows with leaves in its brown hair, *his* hair. Ella screams.

'Marco!'

Marco squeezes himself through the hedge, bashing a large stick against the prickly branches like the prince in 'Sleeping Beauty', just like we used to make him and Luca do all those years ago. The three of us rush towards him laughing with surprise and excitement.

'Hello losers,' he says.

We grab what bits of Marco we can. He is stuck half in and out of the hedge. Sharp little twigs tug at his T-shirt and jeans as if they don't want to let him go. One foot is caught behind some tree roots. Ella drops to her knees and crawls half into the hedge to help release him. We are all laughing so much we don't notice the adults arrive.

'Marco, your clothes!' says Auntie Helen in a cross-but-not-very-cross voice.

'Ma-ma!' calls Marco in his fake Italian accent. 'You miss me?'

Auntie Helen folds her arms and raises an eyebrow. Uncle Toni is next to her, Mum and Dad are behind.

'The stupid boy wanted to surprise them,' said Toni. 'He made me drop him off at the bottom of the field.'

Marco pulls himself free, kicking branches out of the way, and shaking off the clinging twigs. Grinning, he stumbles into the field scattering the rest of us backwards. Ella, Luca and I surround Marco shouting questions. *Why is he in the hedge? Why is he such an idiot? How was the football? Why did it finish early?* We talk over each other, laughing, teasing, the four of us on holiday like we always have been since before I can remember, when I can only remember things by the photos that Mum and Dad show me. We weren't expecting to see him this holiday but now he is here, it feels like he was what we were missing all along.

*

We are sitting around the little camp table with the built-in benches waiting for lunch. There's just enough room for four of us, Ella and I facing Marco and Luca, like we've sat a million times before, except the seats used to feel roomier. It's not so bad for Ella and me, but Luca and Marco are a tangle of arms and legs and Luca resorts to sticking one long leg out to the side. Uncle Toni places a plastic bowl filled with salad on the table between us. Ella and I start picking out the cherry tomatoes and bits of cucumber. Uncle Toni leans between Luca and Marco, resting one arm on each of his sons' shoulders.

'So nice to see you *little children* all together again,' says Toni.

'Yeah, alright, pops,' said Marco, 'We only look like kids because you are so old.'

Uncle Toni pushes at Marco's head and messes his hair.

'Like and subscribe,' says Marco.

He makes this weird hand gesture like he is flicking something off his hand onto the floor. The boys at my school do it when they think they've said something funny. Toni rolls his eyes and heads back towards the caravan. Marco rolls his eyes too watching Toni pretend to hobble like an old man, struggling up the caravan steps to take a plate from Auntie Helen.

125

Auntie Helen says Marco looks exactly like Uncle Toni when he was a boy, but I thought she must be joking until today. Toni is so round and hairy with a receding hairline but maybe he was once slim and good-looking like Marco. However, when Uncle Toni stood behind Marco just now, I could see how their deep-set eyes are the same, and their hair which is almost black, is a similar shade, unlike Luca's which is just dark brown. Marco and Toni also both have deep olive skin (which I would love to have). Compared to me, Luca is tanned, but next to Marco and Toni he looks almost pale. Luca is definitely more like Auntie Helen. He's tall like her, she's taller than Toni, and even sitting down Luca is several inches taller than Marco who is a year older. Luca is also broad shouldered and solid like a statue, compared to the smaller, neater Marco who can't sit still for a minute, cracking jokes, pulling faces, waving his arms around, and getting excited about absolutely everything. Maybe he really is like Uncle Toni!

Marco and Luca are both grinning patiently at Ella who is telling one of her long, complicated stories which always start with 'you'll never guess what' therefore I get more time to study them both. Marco's smile is different to Luca's, it's more relaxed, no shyness, always ready to react to something. I had forgotten how different they are, or maybe I never noticed. Why would I? They were just Marco and Luca. They *are* Marco and Luca. I blink to remind myself I am in this conversation. I keep doing this more and more. I find myself watching everyone else like I'm not really here. I'm not reading about it all in a story afterwards. I am part of this group, right here, right now.

It's a noisy, lively lunch. No one stops talking for a minute. We eat Auntie Helen's yummy, homemade tortilla, crunchy bread warm from the oven, ham from the farm shop, and the big salad. (Luckily Mum is too busy joining in the chatter to notice that Ella and I have eaten all the tomatoes.) It is funny how Marco is only one extra person but our group is so much busier and louder now he's here. Marco is also the one to get into trouble. Auntie Helen has already told him off twice for swearing. I suppose she doesn't want Ella to hear but I have heard worse at school. When Helen gets really cross, Marco jumps up and cuddles his Mum and makes little boy eyes at her until she bats him away smiling.

Marco and Luca insult each other all the time. They give each other the finger, hiding it in their laps under the table, to avoid their parents and Ella seeing, but I know what they're doing. Luca calls Marco 'short arse'. Marco calls him a 'lanky git' and 'tall streak of piss'. These are just the ones that they say out loud, as opposed to the ones muttered under their breath. I might have to clap my hands over Ella's ears if they call each other 'dick' one more time. She loves it though. She's grinning ear to ear, lapping up every bad word she can learn.

Marco never stops teasing Luca, he cusses Luca's clothes, his football team, his aftershave, says he is taking up too much room in the bedroom and that it's like sharing with the Incredible Hulk on a bad day. He says Luca had better move his stuff off Marco's bed before Marco sells it on eBay for 10p because that's all it's worth. They fight over the last chicken drumstick, the last chunk of French bread, and the last piece of cheesecake, pushing and elbowing each other until the table nearly tips over. Auntie Helen scolds them but Uncle Toni just laughs.

Marco and Luca have always been like this, competing, fighting, two little boys rolling around on the grass outside the caravans. They're not so little now, though. Marco and Luca take the fight over the cheesecake on to the grass and take turns holding each other's face into the ground as they try to make the other submit. Auntie Helen yells at them but they are lost in their fight. Meanwhile, Ella and I cut the last piece of cheesecake in half and wolf it down.

Marco's arrival also means that Dad, Toni and Luca have another chance to discuss in detail the start of the football season. Ella stands on the edge of this group nodding wisely as though she is part of it. When she says that 'Guardiola is taking chances with his team' which is probably something she heard Dad say earlier in the week, they all laugh loudly. Marco puts his arm around her shoulder and gives her a little hug. I used to feel jealous that Marco and Luca always fussed over Ella and therefore must like her the most. Mum explained that it was because she was the baby and they were just looking out for her, but they thought of me as an equal, a friend.

Marco is talking to Mum now. Ella is glued to his side as he chats easily to everyone about everything. Marco is an inch taller than Mum. She lifts her chin a little as she talks and smiles, but her pale face looks exposed in the bright sunshine. I suppose I'm not used to seeing her outside without her hat. I hope she's wearing sun cream. Marco keeps her talking for a while and I can see the tightness around her mouth beginning to relax. She doesn't have to hold her mouth like that anymore, not since the stitches came out, but it's become a habit. I can't see Luca but then I can, he's a long shape at the side of my vision, closer than I think. I get that feeling again, that awkward tightness in my chest but it's getting easier. I'm hoping that it will go soon. Today is a new day, I tell myself. We're friends. Friends is good. I sing the song in my head that Sophie and I love, 'Friends is where it ends.'

Ella marches over shouting, 'Chloe, Marco says I'm loud!'

I just raise my eyebrows and stare at her calmly which infuriates Ella and sends Marco into hysterics.

'You see,' he gestures, 'You are loud! You're gonna bust my ears with your big mouth.'

Ella is loud. She shouts even if she is sitting next to you. Mum says all little kids are loud and I was too. I don't remember that.

Marco continues to tease Ella. 'And you two,' he gestures to Ella and me. 'You are like opposites, man. Chloe's as quiet as a mouse, and you are a loud, LOUD little monster.'

Marco's words shock me a little. *Is that how he sees me?* A quiet little mouse. *Is that how everyone sees me?* I know I'm not the life and soul of the party like Marco, but... a 'mouse'? Ella shrieks and dives at him, arms raised to play fight to the death. Marco grabs her skinny wrists trying to fend her off.

'You see, you see! Monster!'

Marco manages to hold both her wrists in one of his hands and then tickles her ribs with the other until she screams.

'You think everyone's quiet,' said Luca suddenly to Marco. 'Because you never shut the f– up.'

Marco lets go of Ella and jumps at his brother grabbing him around the waist, trying to pull him to the ground. They stagger around like this for a few minutes knocking into chairs until Uncle Toni shouts at them to 'pack it in' and 'stop behaving like animals'.

Quiet? People are always telling me that I'm quiet and I'm always surprised by it. There are so many thoughts racing through my head it doesn't feel very quiet to me. I don't realise that I'm not talking because I am so busy thinking. Perhaps I sometimes forget to speak. Gran gets it though. When Grandad says: 'Chloe's the quiet one in our family.' Gran will shake her head and say: 'Oh no, there's a lot going on in there.' Maybe Gran is telepathic or something.

Teachers write on my school report card that I should speak up more in class. I thought I was, but it doesn't always come out of my mouth. Sometimes I'm afraid to speak, particularly since I went to high school. Something can sound okay in your head but when you say it out loud, and the whole class laughs or stares at you, it's awful. Then I go red and that's even worse. Blushing is like having to wear all your thoughts on the outside whereas most people get to hide their feelings inside. Everyone knows when I'm upset or angry or embarrassed because my skin shows them, and there's no traffic light system, no green or amber, just straight to red. When I've been upset about school or friends, Mum and Dad have told me that I need to 'grow a thicker skin'. *Yeah, right, because that's easy. I'll just grow one right now, shall I?* I would if I could. If a thick skin will stop the feelings getting in, maybe it could stop them leaking out as well so people wouldn't tease me. 'Ooh, look, Chloe's blushing.' I'd love to not hear *that* every other day at school.

There are two days left of the holiday and we are talking about what to do. It's crazy but Marco arriving feels like we are starting the holiday all over again. We're going to have to do it faster though to fit everything in. Marco's also catching up on what he's missed. Ella takes charge of this and has to mention my sunburn *of course*, and that I was as 'red as a tomato'. *Thanks*, I think. Marco laughs easily at what Ella is saying and shrugs sympathetically in my direction but that's it. He's more interested in hearing about the theme park they went to while I was in bed. It's a relief. I daren't look at Luca but I'm sure he feels the same. Marco hears about me playing golf and my one amazing shot of the day. *Did that really happen?* It feels like weeks ago not a couple of days. Ella tells most of the story even though she wasn't there. We let her.

'Nice one, Chloe,' Marco says. 'Looks like things have changed a bit since I was last here.'

He says it casually, like he says everything, however, there is something different about the way Marco looks at me. It was as though for the first time since he arrived, he really notices me, and he doesn't look certain. A tiny crease appears between his black eyebrows. His eyes meet mine for only a moment but it feels longer. The look goes right through me. I like it but I don't. I squirm a little and look down at the table. Marco seemed surprised himself and the crease between his eyebrows deepens before he shakes his head slightly and turns back to the rest of our group. He

131

immediately starts winding Luca up about his golf skills even though Luca is almost as good as his Dad. I don't understand what just happened. I can still feel his gaze as if he'd touched my face; my cheeks burn.

*

We're at the swimming pool. The lifeguard is slumped down in his seat. He is sneaking a look at his phone, holding it just out of his pocket at the side of his shorts. He's supposed to be watching the swimmers. If Mum was here, she would go over and tell him off, but luckily, she's not. Taking our chance, and on Marco's signal, we all kick off our shoes, run across the wet paving stones and jump into the pool.

SPLA-A-A-A-A-SSSHHH!!

One huge bomb, four bodies, eight arms, eight legs. The wave must have been gigantic. I can hear the lifeguard's whistle from under the water. We come up gasping, shaking the water out of our hair like dogs. Marco whoops. There are a few disgruntled cries from the handful of swimmers already in the pool. The lifeguard gets out of his seat to shake a finger at us like an old man. It's funny because he's about the same age as Marco. Marco gives him a cheery wave whilst the rest of us collapse into hysterics.

The jump into the pool has woken me up. As I came up from the water my head felt clear as though the haze of the last few days has finally been washed off. The colours of the pool are sharp, people's swimming costumes stand out against the sparkling water in pinks, greens, reds, blues. We form a tight circle treading water while we chat. My legs kick against the gentle pull of the moving water around and below me. We stay like this for a few minutes until the splashing starts. The boys kick back widening the circle then scooping up water to fling at each other and then at Ella and me. I blink as cold water hits me in the eyes and runs down my face into my laughing mouth. Ella and I chuck water at the boys, me with one hand on the back of Ella's swimsuit to stop her from sinking.

Marco and Luca race each other up and down the pool. Ella and I join in but we can't keep up. Luca easily beats Marco stretching his long arms to reach the edge of the pool first. We play Marco Polo of course. Although Marco ruins the game by shouting 'What?' every time someone shouts his name. It is hilarious though.

*

We're playing football on the beach. Sand kicks up in every direction. Dad and Uncle Toni are playing too. They've got some skills, but they turn too slowly with the ball like they are playing under water. Marco and Luca dribble around them throwing insults at their Dad every time they get the ball away from him. 'Too slow, old man,' shouts Marco tackling Toni and sending his Dad stumbling. Toni laughs and tries to grab the back of Marco's T-shirt and the boys yell, 'Foul!'.

The hot sand scorches the soles of my feet. I wish I'd kept my sliders on, but they fall off when I run. I dance from one foot to the other around the edge of the game. I wave my arms and call to them to pass to me, secretly hoping they won't because I'm so rubbish at football. Ella's in the middle of the game holding her own. 'Chloe!' I turn my head to see Luca gesturing. He kicks the ball so it lands perfectly at my feet. I strike at it clumsily, bare toes bruising on impact, and the ball veers back towards Dad and Toni. Ella runs into the middle, scoops up the ball with one sure foot and scores a goal. She cheers, gives Dad a double high five, then screams as Marco and Luca rugby tackle her to the ground. I run in to help her and get pulled into the pile of sandy, sweaty arms and legs.

*

We're running up the steep path from the beach. Marco and Luca are racing to the top, elbow to elbow, but Marco is quicker. Ella tries to keep up with them, arms pumping like a sprinter, feet leaping nimbly over half-buried stones. Dad and Uncle Toni puff behind us but lose interest eventually, slowing down as they start to chat. It's only as I reach the top that I remember the last time I chased Luca up this path. The memory stings as though I've stepped on something sharp. I run across the soft grass to catch up with the others, hoping I can leave all those feelings behind.

*

We're lying on the grass between the caravans, stretched out and exhausted on the cool ground. So hot from running, so sweaty from football. Mum hands out rainbow-coloured ice-lollies which we accept like precious treasure. The cold lolly on my lips is heaven. Mum passes one to Dad without saying anything. He takes it silently. She places the next lolly on Uncle Toni's hairy mound of a belly where his T-shirt has ridden up. He gives a high-pitched shriek.

'You!' Toni points up at Mum, glaring comically. 'If you were less beautiful and I was less tired then I might come and stick one of those cold ices down your neck. See how you like it.'

Mum unwraps her own lolly slowly and relaxes back into one of the shady camp chairs, a little of the old mischief twitching around her eyes.

*

The day is passing like a film in fast forward, a film that started like a repeat of everything we had done in the previous five days but has now taken us on a different path. Our new cast member, Marco, has spun us into an alternate universe and I don't think we've stopped laughing since he got here.

*

We're in the arcade now. It's a windowless room just off the bar at the modern caravan park next door to our field. The dimly lit space is confusing after the bright sunshine. It takes a few minutes for my eyes to adjust. In every direction are flashing lights and clashing electronic music playing the same short tune over and over again. Mum doesn't like us hanging around here. She says we spend all our pocket money in five minutes. We came here earlier in the week,

135

but it wasn't as much fun. In our new universe, Marco has an endless supply of pound coins which he feeds us to keep the games going. We hold out our hands greedily like addicts.

Mum asked us to go to the shop on the main road to get stuff for this evening's barbeque and we, well, Marco, decided we should stop off at the arcade on the way back. Luca and Ella are playing the basketball game, he tall, she small. She stands practically under his armpits and they take turns to grab the basketballs and throw them in the hoop. The points are racking up, and the electronic voice is telling them they've hit the high score. I'm standing with Marco while he shoots robot aliens on the big lit up screen in front of us. We were both playing but I'm out. Numbers are counting down on the screen and the words, 'Continue – Insert coin' appear over the graphics. Marco tries to pass me another coin without taking his eyes off the screen but I don't want it. I can't be bothered to play anymore. I don't think I've hit a single alien so far. I'm half watching him, but also looking at my phone. I can pick up the WiFi here from the bar next door. I'm scanning my form's WhatsApp group. Everyone is talking about which teachers they think they're going to have next term. So boring.

'Hey, Chloe,' says Marco.

His arms are stiff, stretched out in front of him holding the gun. His eyes are focussed on the screen tracking the robots that are crawling spider-like across the wrecked hull of a spaceship.

'When I arrived today, for a moment, I didn't recognise you.'

What? I look up from my phone surprised.

'I know, crazy. Woah!' he flinches as a bunch of alien robots get too close and he has to rapid fire so as not to lose a life. 'Yeah, you look, I don't know… different.'

'Oh.' I didn't know what else to say.

'Maybe it's your hair,' he shrugs, 'It's longer, right?'

'Yeah,' I nod, confused. It's hard to know when Marco is teasing you, he's too good at it and loves winding people up. He's like an annoying big brother, or how I imagine an annoying big brother to be if I had one. I've often wished I had one rather than a stupid little sister. I smooth my hair down self-consciously. It is a bit longer I suppose. I am different though, I am, and no one else seems to get that. Maybe Marco is the only one that can see. I look back at my phone, smiling to myself. Marco continues shooting alien robot spiders until a sudden blast erupts on the screen and wipes him out the game.

'Mother F…'

We are leaving the arcade. I step out into the sunshine and shiver. The late afternoon sun has an edge to it. Gran always says that the summer ends in the last week of August. The days in the tail end of August are just as sunny and hot but there's a chill in the evening. It's the thing that brings Salty Dog to our door, puts the nip in the air. A warning, Gran, used to say, it's a sign that 'something is coming, and something is ending'. This scared me when I was little. 'What's coming?' I asked looking around in fear, 'And what's ending?'

'Summer', Gran said, 'Summer's ending, but don't worry, they'll be plenty more. Summer has to make way for Autumn and Winter. That's who's coming. Time for change.'

Gran grew up in the countryside, by the sea, not far from the caravan site. That's why she and Grandad bought the caravan. He said that Gran grew up with nature and she felt things strongly. It wasn't right for her to be in the city all the time which was where they lived and worked after they got married.

*

We're waiting for the barbeque. We're all starving and moaning about it, snacking on crisps, and being shooed away from the salad and bread in case we eat too many tomatoes or 'fill ourselves up'. Something is wrong with the burners on the barbeque, the gas is not working properly. Everything is taking ages to cook. Toni and Dad are fussing over the controls, exchanging ideas about how they can fix the problem. Normally this would make Dad stressed and irritable but with beers in hand, he and Toni are not letting it bother them. Mum and Auntie Helen are already on the wine. Mum balances a large glass on the arm of one of the camp chairs. She stretches out her legs in front of her and rests them on top of the cool boxes.

The smell and sizzle of burgers and onions floats over to us followed by laughter. At least something seems to be cooking now. Toni is preparing his special sticky ribs, just like our first night barbeque, and now on our first night together with Marco. Finally, the burgers are ready and there's a rush to the table with Ella and Marco elbowing themselves in front of me. I push at them annoyed but Luca just hangs back and waits. Marco takes another opportunity to wind up his brother.

'Bro, don't you miss it?'

Marco takes a huge bite of his beefburger. A line of grease dribbles down his chin and hand and then drips into the grass at his feet. Marco pushes his face close to Luca's and chews. His mouth is so full that bits of burger and bread spill over his lips. It's disgusting but it's making me hungry. Luca pushes him away and swears quietly at his brother so his mum and dad don't hear.

'Luca!' scolds Ella hearing everything and grinning.

I nudge her to shut up. Amazingly she does but then she doesn't want to be left out.

'Veggie sausages are ready!' shouts Dad. 'I think,' he adds. He peers at the pale shapes on the grill. 'It's hard to tell.'

Luca steps forward, puts two veggie hot dogs in one roll and starts adding ketchup and mustard.

'Mate,' says Marco peering over his shoulder, 'You better empty that whole bottle over those babies if you're going to get any flavour.'

Luca ignores him.

'Anyone else,' says Dad looking at the full tray. 'Any takers?'

'Better stick those in the bin, John,' says Marco.

It's odd to hear Marco call Dad 'John' as though they are friends.

'I'll try one,' I say.

'What!? No! Not you as well, Chloe,' Marco grips the sides of his head dramatically as though the world is ending. I smirk at him. It's worth it just to see the look on his face. I don't mind veggie stuff anyway. Mum cooks it a lot at home because she says it's healthier and will help save the planet. Lots of girls at my school are veggie and vegan which is fine but they do go on about it all the time.

'Just thinking about my carbon footprint,' I say smugly, helping myself to a veggie sausage.

I am quoting my friend Abby who is an expert on all things eco. She was my partner in the big science project last term about climate change.

'Don't you know millions of acres of forest are destroyed to feed farm animals. It's ruining the planet.'

'Yeah, yeah,' says Marco. 'Bet you'd rather have some real meat though, Chloe. Come on, I've seen you put away the ribs.'

Marco's right, I'll be having a burger and ribs later, but for now I'm happy to annoy him. He watches me take a big bite.

'Enjoying that?' he says in disbelief.

'I am,' I grin.

The hotdog doesn't taste like normal hotdogs but it's not horrible. More than anything I can taste the delicious dollop of ketchup, plus mayonnaise and onions. I chew happily making yummy noises for full effect. I wipe the edges of my mouth with the back of my hand where I can feel the sauce oozing. I can never eat anything without getting it all over me. Marco's expression is brilliant, his face screwed up in disgust and confusion.

'I'm having one too!' announces Ella.

She dives for the tray and dips a veggie sausage in ketchup. Marco looks up at the sky and shakes his fists shouting.

'I leave them alone for a few days and they all go... healthy!'

Dad looks into the half-empty grill pan confused.

'Perhaps I should have bought more?' he mutters. He picks up one of the veggie sausages and tries one nodding, 'Not bad'.

Thing is, Dad would eat anything.

Luca has been very quiet, although he always seems subdued next to Marco. I glance sideways at him. As usual, he's there but not there, close but slightly out of my eyeline. I think he's deliberately not looking at Marco or me. Luca is chewing a huge mouthful of hot dog. His eyes are crinkled, and the edges of his mouth turned up. He is trying not to laugh at us all winding up Marco. As though he can hear my thoughts, Luca catches my eye. For a brief second before his eyes dart away, I can tell that he is pleased I've been bugging Marco by eating the vegetarian food. A warm, shy feeling creeps over me, the kind that you feel when you've done something good, but you also feel a bit embarrassed. It's like when I got a maths prize at the end of my first term at high school. The Head of Year read out my name along with all the other pupils winning stuff. It felt good but it was a bit embarrassing as well. I didn't want everyone to stare at me. However, the worst thing was that most people didn't know who I was, except people in my form. The Head of Year couldn't see me, so she started stretching her neck this way and that. Then everyone else was looking around the hall like it was some big drama, and *who was Chloe Carter*? People in my form started pointing at me and I just wanted to disappear. My face flushed red and I wished I'd never won a prize. It was nicer talking to Mum and Dad about it later. They were really pleased when I got home and told them. They even put the certificate in a frame next to my school photo on the wall.

Marco's not a bad person, he loves joking around and he is always winding up his brother. Ella and I annoy each other but we don't fight like Marco and Luca. Those two really go for it. Luca is the calmer one which stops everything getting too crazy. I don't know how he puts up with Marco's constant teasing. Not always though. I remember one summer when we were younger, Luca had just got a new bike for his birthday. He was so proud of it. It was very shiny, and he liked to polish the handlebars like Dad sometimes polishes our car. I think this was the first time that he had had a new bike because he usually got Marco's old bikes. However, by then he was at least as tall as Marco and their bikes must have been the same size.

Marco kept taking Luca's new bike off for a ride, and Luca would be forced to take Marco's old bike to go and find his brother. Every time we all planned to go out on our bikes Marco would run ahead and ride off on Luca's bike waving and grinning over his shoulder. They had a lot of fights over it. I remember Luca crying because Marco had accidentally scratched some of the paint off the crossbar. It was odd seeing Luca cry. He told his Mum and Dad exactly what happened in a calm, sad voice, but he had tears running down his face. I remember his fists were clenched tight and afterwards we saw where his nails had dug into his palms. Little red half-moon shapes cut into the skin. Uncle Toni yelled at Marco and punished him for taking Luca's bike, but it didn't stop him. I don't think I would remember any of this now, if it wasn't for how Luca ended it. One day, we were all going to ride over to the swimming pool. Luca had strapped his towel to the back of his bike then went back into the caravan to get something. When Luca came out Marco was sitting on the new bike again, even though Ella and I had told him to get off.

'Ready?' he said looking towards Luca, one dark eyebrow arched.

Luca stood quietly in his straight upright way. He and Marco stared at each other, like two cowboys in a gun fight in one of those old Western films that Grandad likes to sleep through in the afternoons.

'Yes,' replied Luca eventually.

He picked up Marco's old bike and pushed off, riding in a big circle behind us in the opposite direction that we planned to go. He turned again and rode in another big circle further away and disappeared behind one of the caravans. We thought he might have gone off on his own. Then suddenly Luca appeared a metre or so from Marco pedalling at top speed, his legs in a whir like a cartoon character. He rode straight into Marco and also ploughed into his own new bike. Marco didn't have time to react. He was knocked backwards and Luca, Marco and the two bikes landed in a scream of legs, metal and wheels. Both were bleeding and crying. Marco never took Luca's bike again.

*

If you could only eat one thing for the rest of your life what would it be?
Burger
Pizza
Chips

*Would you rather eat pizza every day for a
year or no pizza for a year?
Easy. I could eat pizza every day. #heaven
Urgh, no, I'd get fed up.
Could I leave the crusts?
Can we have different toppings?*

*Snog, marry, kill: Harry Potter, Hagrid,
Sirius Black?
What?!
No, you can't ask us to choose.
Easy. Snog Sirius. Marry Hagrid. Kill Harry
because he'll come back to life as usual.
Smart. #PotterNerd*

*Okay, snog, marry, kill: Donald Trump,
Boris Johnson and.... Hitler?
What?!
Well, kill Hitler obviously.
Marry Trump.
What?!
Well, he's rich.
But he's orange!
So, you're going to kiss Boris Johnson?
No!!!*

*If you could only watch one TV programme
for the rest of your life what would it be?
YouTube
That's not a programme.*

Top Gear for me.
Typical. What, even the new ones?
Horrible Histories!
Yeah!
I love the songs.
Brooklyn 99
Yeah, brilliant.
Stranger Things.
I haven't seen that!

Did you see that meme about Brooklyn 99?
The one with the…
Yeah!! Ha, ha!
What about 'I love you 3000' – bursts into
tears.
Right, everyone, top five memes, go!

Would you rather have a leg for finger or a
finger for a leg?

Would you rather have carrot for teeth or
lettuce for ears?

Everything we say is served with a side order of laughter. Adults standing close to us look like they are trying to follow the conversation. However, they quickly turn away, puzzled expressions on their faces realising that we are talking in a foreign language.

The sun has dropped behind the caravans and the sky deepens into a denim blue. We eat, we laugh, we talk over each other, we argue, and we get louder and louder. It's brilliant. People turn around to look at us, people I hadn't noticed before. I hate people staring but I feel cocooned in our little group. A party is slowly building around us. Dad and Toni have invited our neighbours from the other caravans to join us. The field feels busier than earlier in the week and more cars have appeared today. People who have been out for the day, or just arrived, wander over to say hello. Lots of people have come for the last August weekend. That's what I can hear them saying over and over again to Mum and Dad, as well as *who can believe this weather*, and *what a beautiful evening*, and *isn't it nice to get together like this*. I don't understand why adults say the same things. It's so boring.

The buzz of conversation around us blends into a wall of background noise. The party changes shape around us, like a swarm of bees switching direction as people arrive and leave, move from group to group, greeting each other and helping themselves to food and drinks. Every new guest brings snacks and drinks and the two picnic tables fill up with an odd assortment of spontaneous gifts from people who didn't expect to be invited to a party tonight. There's the normal stuff like wine, beer, fizzy drinks, bags of crisps, sausages, but also packets of biscuits dragged out from the backs of cupboards, and leftovers as people empty their fridges. I watch Mum accept a half-eaten quiche that 'needs eating up'. It is covered in foil as wrinkled as the hands of the white-haired lady who hands it to Mum. Every gift is taken with warm thanks by Mum or Dad or Toni and Helen and placed on the picnic tables as though they were gifts at a wedding.

146

Normally we're not allowed to have music playing outside in the field in case we 'disturb' anyone but tonight Dad has put a portable speaker on the caravan steps. I saw Mr Jones, the farmer, chatting to Dad by the barbeque so he obviously doesn't mind the noise, or if he does, he might wait until he's finished his beer to complain. Marco has paired his phone to Dad's speaker and is secretly changing the music. Our heads are bent together whispering suggestions of more and more outrageous tracks. We know we might have gone too far when Dad, hearing the lyrics to a rap song, looks quizzically at the portable speaker as though it has gone mad. Marco quickly changes the song to something safer.

It's getting dark. The trees and hedges around the field are jagged black outlines in a navy sky. The shape of our two caravans is picked out in fairy lights with a pretty arch of lights connecting them. When people walk under the arch they are illuminated for a moment as if they are stepping out on to a stage.

There is a new family in the caravan two down from us. Dad introduces us. They have two cute, little girls both dressed in those shiny Disney Princess outfits. The dresses are too big and gape at the shoulders showing Peppa Pig vests. The skirts have muddy hems that drag along the ground after them. Ella takes charge of the 'mini-Elsa' and 'mini-Cinderella'. The girls follow her everywhere and Ella enjoys being the older one and bossing them around. She uses her teacher/mum voice from our make-believe games.

Dad also tries to get us to talk to some teenagers visiting their grandparents. We've never seen them before. We chat a bit, but conversation soon dries up and we return to our own group. They look as relieved as we do. There's a definite split between the 'kids' and the adults. Even the kids we're not hanging out with stand near us deep in their own conversations or silently looking at their phones. Ella is followed everywhere by the mini-Princesses. All the younger kids have formed into one feral dark shape that moves fast, close to the ground, and frequently causes an adult to trip and spill their drink or food.

I normally hate parties like this where the adults and the kids have to mix, and I have to talk to people I don't know. However, sitting between Marco and Luca I feel protected from all the awkward conversations. Marco has a comeback for everything which gives us all confidence. People we've known for years, stop to chat and tell us how much we've grown. Marco just tells them that we only look bigger because they've shrunk or some other stupid comment. He manages to do it in a way that they think is funny rather than offensive. They move on laughing and leave us to ourselves.

It's getting chilly now. I would be really cold if I wasn't squeezed between Marco and Luca on one side of the picnic bench. My bare arms absorb their body heat gratefully. Despite this I shiver at every sudden breeze. I cross my arms over my chest wishing now I was wearing something more than a crop top and shorts. I'm going to have to get changed but I don't want to move. Luca and Marco reach forward at the same time to grab a handful of crisps and the warmth around me disappears. My whole body shakes with cold and both Luca and Marco who are cramming crisps into their mouths, turn to look at me.

'You alright there?' mumbles Marco. 'You shook so hard I thought there was an earthquake.'

He wipes his hand on his shorts and puts his arm around me. He rubs his hand up and down my arm quickly as though he's trying to start a fire.

'Ow,' I say as Marco rubs too hard. A trace of salt on his fingers prickles my skin.

'Just trying to warm you up,' he says.

'Rub my skin off more likely,' I grumble.

He pinches the top of my arm mischievously before letting his hand rest there, then he calls out to a man who is passing our table and they start a conversation about the football results.

Marco's arm is draped around my shoulders like a scarf. I'm warmer but I need to go and get a fleece or something. I wait a few minutes for Marco to move his arm. He is still talking animatedly about goal differences to the football man. The man has a large bald head and the fairy lights strung between the caravans behind him make the top of his head shine. Something amazing happened in a match today apparently. I'm not really listening. Luca throws in a few comments too. I had almost forgotten he was there. He is half-turned away from me as his legs don't fit under the table with the three of us sitting on the bench. The goal difference man looks at me occasionally as he speaks as though I am involved in this conversation. I don't know why; I don't know anything about football. My left arm is squashed between my body and Marco's and I am starting to feel a bit claustrophobic. Then something nudges my right arm. I look to the side in confusion. Luca has untied his white hoodie from around his waist and is pushing it roughly onto my lap. I stare at it confused.

'Here,' he says. 'You said you were cold.'

When he speaks, he doesn't make eye contact with me but looks down at the hoodie. There's an odd gruffness to his voice. I mumble 'thank you' and wriggle away from Marco who drops his arm but not the conversation about football or his eye contact with the man. I pull the hoodie over my head pushing my arms into the half-warmth left by Luca.

I settle back between Luca and Marco protected from contact with either of them by the thick fabric. That's better, I think. I feel a bit more back in my own skin. Marco looks straight ahead listening and arguing cheerfully with the shiny-headed football man. On the other side of me Luca sits looking straight ahead as well, but not moving or speaking now. I don't know whether he is listening to the football conversation or just staring at the people opposite us crowded around the food table. I can't think of anything to say. I sigh. Today's been a good day and I was hoping we could just forget about the thing on the beach but maybe Luca can't.

I think about us, Luca's body underneath mine, my toes curled in the hot sand, and the burning sun on the back of my neck. The memory itself seems to give off heat. Then I remember the kiss, and that awful moment when I opened my eyes and Luca was staring at me. That's the awkward part, I can't seem to get over that. *What was I thinking?* A familiar hot flush of embarrassment overwhelms me. I really hope he is still not feeling weird about it all. Only a few minutes ago I was thinking about how fun and easy it is for us all to hang out on holiday. I don't want anything to spoil that. We've had a great day all of us together. I can be myself here. It's nice to be with friends without having to think too much about what I am saying or doing, or *not* saying or doing. It's not like this when I'm with my new friends from high school. They are great and everything, and they are some of my best friends now, like Sophie, but I've known Luca and Marco forever.

Everything's so different now I'm at secondary school. It's not like primary school when everyone knew me, and I knew who my friends were. At secondary school I can go into school on a Monday and discover that over the weekend someone has said something to someone else and now all the friendship groups are different from where we were on Friday. It's like memorising a map and then blinking and finding all the streets and roads have moved so that you have to start learning where they are all over again. It's so easy to get things wrong. You also can't be friends with the person your friend has fallen out with. If you are then everyone starts ignoring you even though you've done nothing wrong. Half the time I don't understand why 'we're' not speaking to them. It's exhausting.

Then there's the judging, you get judged for everything, your hairstyle, your makeup – too much, too little – your accent, whereabouts you live in town, what music you like, what set you're in for maths, whether you are cool or not cool depending on who is doing the judging, whether you've dated anyone, or whether you like anyone, or whether anyone likes you, or if are you straight, gay, bi, trans, pan, etc. That's why I hate it when I go red because when I get asked things people can see what I'm thinking or

151

feeling, before I've had a chance to say anything. Then the stares and laughter make it worse as though they are feeding the colour in my skin. It rises up my cheeks and spreads across my chest until I'm practically sweating. My cheeks get so hot sometimes I think it will burn right through me. Nothing is secret or private for me. I can't hide or pretend. Everyone knows whether I'm embarrassed or afraid, as though my skin is transparent, and they can see right through me. It didn't use to be this bad. I used to be able to control it or just laugh it off. I don't remember feeling so out of control at primary school. Everything's different now.

Something hurts. I look down at my clenched fists as white as the folds of Luca's hoodie. I turn them over and rub my palms. There are red marks in the skin where my nails have been digging in, like Luca's hands when Marco stole his bike. I push the sleeves of his hoodie higher up my arms and look at the pale skin on the underside of my wrists. The blue veins show through my skin as clearly as if I had drawn them on in pen. I pull the sleeves over my hands again so I can't see anything of myself. Luca is still sitting next to me quietly. I think about trying to talk to him again but it's a relief not to speak for a bit. A yawn creeps up on me which I try to hide.

The football man moves on finally and Marco, Luca and I watch Ella teaching the Disney Princesses how to play the hand-clapping game, 'Armella'. I lean across the picnic table to join in. The little girls' hands are soft like playdough. I'm afraid to clap too hard in case I squash them into a different shape. The Princesses get everything wrong, but they love to cross their arms quickly and shout 'Statue'.

They push their shoulders backwards so far I think they might topple off the bench onto the grass in a pile of giggles and shiny fabric. Soon, everyone is playing the game singing along.

> *Aaar-mella, super Stella*
> *Big boys, crazy girls.*

The best part is trying to make the statues move and lose their turn. Even Luca, seems less stiff, sitting next to me. I hear him chant along with the words. I start to relax again.

It is funny to think that this morning, I was desperate to go home and now I'm sad that tomorrow will be our last proper day on holiday. Even Ella is not annoying me so much tonight. *Miracles can happen.* I will be glad to get back in my own bedroom though. Ella wakes me up too early and she snores. I think tonight is the first time I have felt relaxed since we came on holiday. I really hope Luca and I can just forget about what happened. *I am going to speak to him.*

Everyone dissolves into laughter around me. Cinderella beats Marco at the staring contest and as Luca high-fives her, his hand twice her size, she falls backwards off the bench. Luckily, she pops up giggling, only missing her fabric crown. Now he knows she's fine, Luca lets himself properly laugh although he is still apologising. Both Princesses come round to his side of the bench and attack him. It's funny to watch. I *am* going to speak to him *properly*. Just later.

*

There are cheers from the barbeque. There is the scent of something delicious in the air, and the anticipation of more food on our lips. I lick mine tasting salt. I've eaten a mountain of crisps and some salad but I'm hungry. Dad and Uncle Toni have really gone to town with the food, and they are barbequing anything brought to them. I'm sure I saw Toni hold up a donut on a toasting fork but maybe he was just mucking about. Dad and Uncle Toni are both in a good mood, laughing and joking, wearing their matching chefs' hats, and holding matching beers. They've had a *lot* of beers and so have many other people. Toni cooked two huge trays of his special sticky ribs and they've vanished. I keep hearing whispered jokes about Toni's 'special sauce' followed by drunken laughter. *Do they think that we don't understand?* We're not kids. Well, we are, but you know what I mean.

It's properly dark now. You can't see the trees any more against the almost black sky. Dad has rigged up a camping light above the picnic tables using the pole from a parasol. The lamp swings slightly in the breeze. It creates long shadows that seem to multiply people as they step in and out of the light. It's much colder as well and I can feel Gran's nip in the air as though Salty Dog is lying under the table nibbling at my toes. The cool grass on my bare feet is soft and scratchy like new lacy knickers. I rub my toes over each other for warmth. I can't remember where I have left my shoes. I'm still insulated by Luca and Marco's body heat, who both have their backs to me talking to people either side of their table, however my legs are freezing. I

154

should go and put my jeans on. Ella and the Princesses are cuddled up on the other side of the picnic table sharing a bag of popcorn in a brief rest from running wild. They sag against each other looking tired, but their eyes are wide and cheeks bright from all the excitement.

I like these evenings when the grownups forget about us and no one notices how many Cokes you've had to drink or whether you had any vegetables in your burger or what time you go to bed. Mum's not fussing around us, making us put on something warm as the night grows cold. She and Auntie Helen are in the centre of the crowd chatting just as they normally would, but it seems odd after how Mum has behaved this week. They are both laughing at something Uncle Toni is saying. Mum's cheeks are flushed. Guests satellite around them stopping to joke and talk before moving on. Their wine glasses are never less than half full. They are not the only ones drinking, there's a constant clink of glass hitting glass as more empties are dropped into the bin bag which has now toppled over spilling the contents on to the grass. No one clears it up.

*

Things are burning. 'Something's burning!', someone shouts followed by laughter. It's not the first time we've heard this. Dad and Toni make a big fuss out of doing the barbeque, but no one seems to be paying attention now. Normally I would expect to see one of them running to the barbeque to rescue the food or prevent the caravan site burning down. Instead Uncle Toni, beer in hand, ambles over, casually picking up overdone sausages from the grill.

155

'It's fine', he jokes. 'Chargrilled.'

More laughter. He leaves the barbeque unattended again and saunters over to lean up against his caravan. He, Dad and Luca and a couple of other men are listening to Marco tell a story about a football match he played earlier in the week. Luca's slightly on the edge of the group listening. He's the only one not holding a beer. I'm surprised Marco's allowed one as he's only 14 but Uncle Toni winked at him and said: 'Just the one.' He said it quietly so Auntie Helen wouldn't hear but Marco's not hiding it. Everyone at school tells me how their parents let them drink and buy them alcohol, but I don't think Mum and Dad would let me. Luca glances towards me and out of habit I quickly look away. I should have just smiled. He probably thinks I'm the one who is being weird. I just can't get it right. I have to say something. *Later.*

*

The caravans are shrouded in darkness, the sky lowered like a veil above the roofs. The crowd is thinner. The music softer. Ella and I are sitting on the bench with the two princesses slumped against us like two old rag dolls whose stuffing has started to come out. I stroke their tangled hair. Their parents come and lift them away from us to take them to bed. The good nights are beginning. 'Good night, good night.' Ella takes turns giving the little girls hugs and waves until they are back in their caravan. 'Good night, good night.' More people are disappearing into the dark field around us. It's late but no one has mentioned bed. Ella yawns. It's just her and me now on our bench. She goes off to the loo and I feel self-conscious sitting here on my own. I look down at my phone. I'm worried people will stare at me. I can't see Marco and Luca. *Where did they go?* I feel tired and left out. Half an hour ago I was so happy and now I feel miserable and alone. *Why do things change so quickly?*

*

'Time for bed, Ella-Bella,' says Dad.

'No-o-o-o-o-o! I don't want to go to bed!'

Ella's shoulders slump forward, and her arms hang low at her sides as though they are filled with lead.

'I know, sweetheart, but little girls need their sleep,' says Dad. He's normally much more impatient at bedtime with Ella who kicks off every night. He speaks carefully and slower than normal as though the words don't fit in his mouth.

'It's late, poppetty-pop,' he adds.

'It's not late! I'm not ti-i-i-r-r-ed.'

Ella yawns the last word and Dad chuckles. Then Dad and I yawn too because everyone knows yawning is catching.

'It's not fair,' moans Ella. 'Chloe's not in bed.'

'Well, she will be soon. Luca's gone to bed already and he's a big boy,' says Dad.

What? I assumed Luca was with Marco. I haven't seen him for a while either, but I doubt he's in bed. *Why did Luca disappear without telling me?* I should have spoken to him. I feel miserable. I yawn again.

'You see, Ella-Bella, Chloe's tired too. We're all tired but you...' He taps the end of her nose with his index finger like he's trying to pop a balloon. Ella bats him away crossly. 'Need to go to bed.'

His voice is starting to fade like a battery losing power. I don't want to stay here on my own, and I know Ella won't want to be alone in the caravan, so I agree to go to bed as well, pretending that I am doing everyone a favour. There's no point in staying up without the others. And I'm cold – my legs are covered in goosebumps – I never did change into my jeans. Ella is happier that I'm going with her because she's not going to miss out on any fun. She throws her arms around my waist in a sleepy hug almost knocking me over. She's grown so much. I hope she's not going to be taller than me. I think of our height chart at home and how her marks are always higher than mine at each age. Ella thinks it's brilliant, or course.

'We can have a midnight feast!' says Ella.

The excitement briefly brings her back to life. A second later she is leaning into my waist, her head half-buried into my armpit. I might have to drag her to the caravan if she's going to fall asleep standing up.

'Thanks, love,' says Dad. He pats my arm for far too long then starts to walk away putting his feet down carefully as though he has forgotten how to walk.

'Dad!' shouts Ella.

He turns around absently, his eyes hooded and unfocussed. He's been trying to hide it, but he is definitely drunk. Ella holds one arm up towards him keeping the other dug into my waist.

'Kiss-s-s!' she says pleading.

He leans over and gives us both a kiss on the cheek, Ella first then me. His chin is rough, and he smells of beer. He wobbles a little when he stands up straight again and his voice finally slips.

'Night, night, gorshous girlsh,' he slurs.

*

Ella is in the bathroom. I can hear the buzz of her electric toothbrush and the little tune she hums when she cleans her teeth. I wait for her in the sitting-room, where I can stretch out on the sofa. There's a pink fleece blanket of Ella's that I pull over my cold legs. This end of the caravan has windows on all three sides and below this the long sofa, with the worn beige and brown cushions, that wraps around the room. The party is still going on outside. People are standing close to the caravan on the other side of the glass chatting and drinking. I haven't turned the light on so I doubt anyone can see me. It's like being at the party but invisible. Just to be sure I shift along a little to where I am partly hidden by the curtains. I like being able to watch without having to join in or make conversation. Things are winding down outside, a smaller crowd now, but their voices are loud, fighting with the music.

I yawn, one of those big jaw-clicking ones that come from nowhere. I feel like we've packed seven days into one today thanks to Marco. I can see him outside, so he hasn't gone to bed. He's standing under the swinging light that Dad put up. He is talking to two men. I don't know who they are. They must be staying with someone as we pretty much know everyone on the caravan site. Marco talks confidently waving his arms around just like his Dad. If you didn't know him you would think he was older, he looks so comfortable with the adults. He's one of them but he's also one of us. Ella calls to me from the doorway and I follow her to the bedroom. She doesn't like being on her own.

Ella arranges her cuddly toys around her bed before wriggling down under the duvet with her favourite toy, Leo the Lion, tucked under her chin. She will have kicked off the duvet and knocked all the toys on to the floor within ten minutes of being asleep.

'Aren't you going to get in bed?' she asks.

'In a minute,' I say.

I'm sitting on my bed, tired but not sleepy.

'You're not going to leave me?' says Ella, anxiously burying her chin in Leo's fur.

'No,' I sigh. 'Go to sleep. I'm just going to look at my phone for a bit.'

'You're *addicted*,' says Ella primly.

She manages to make herself sound just like Mum. It's funny but I don't laugh. I curl my feet under me on the bed, lean back and touch the smooth phone screen, as familiar as my own skin. The screen lights up, but I used up my last bit of data earlier today. Why can't we stay somewhere decent where I can at least get WiFi! So annoying. Quietly, I pull open the little drawer in the table between our beds and feel inside for my headphones. My fingers close over the tangle of wires. Buds in my ears, I lie down on the bed again and open one of my playlists. Music replaces my thoughts. However, I have it turned down low so I can just hear the voices and faint music outside.

Ella is silent for a while then I hear her voice, a mumble across the darkened room. I think she must have fallen asleep and then woken up again. Her messy mop of hair is just visible amongst her cuddly toys, bathed in the dull glow of her night light. She asks me to close the window because the music is keeping her awake. I don't want to because it will make our tiny bedroom stuffy. It's not enough with the door opened a crack tonight. However, I can't be bothered to argue as Ella is always grumpy when she's tired and I am not in the mood for a row. I kneel on my bed and pull the flimsy curtains aside to close the window. The curtains are patterned with Disney Princesses. Gran put them up for Ella and me years ago. I'd like to change them, but Ella still likes them. I trace my finger around the shape of Ariel's red hair – she was always my favourite.

Our bedroom window is on the side and looks out on the wide grassy space between our caravan and the next one along. The grass looks dyed black by the night. There's no glow from the next caravan's windows and the sky above looks lighter than the caravan's dark, crouched shape. When I was younger, I was afraid to look out of the window at night. I didn't want to see anything that would scare me. Now I crane my neck to the left, interested to see who is still up. I can hear more than I can see.

There is a group of people who move in and out of the brightest space at the end of the caravans where Dad set up the light. The constant movement makes it hard to see who or how many people there are. I think I can hear: 'Goodnight, goodnight.' More people are leaving. To let them pass three people step backwards into the shadow between the caravans. Their shapes become more sharply illuminated by the lights behind. The shorter, stocky shape looks like Uncle Toni. His face is turned towards the light. He is standing with a thinner man, no, not a man, someone younger, and although his face is in shadow, I can tell it is Marco. The other figure is Mum. I don't need to see her face. I would know the shape of her anywhere. Just like I recognise her voice on the phone or the sound of her footsteps on the landing at night when she pauses at my bedroom door to say goodnight.

The shapes of Mum and Toni lean slightly towards Marco as though they are listening intently. Toni lets out a loud laugh which I can hear even with the window closed. He slaps Marco on the back who pushes him away then grabs his arm and pulls his Dad closer as though to tell him something even more exciting. I can't see Dad or Auntie Helen, but they must be close. I watch them for a bit, but they are talking so I sit back down on the bed feeling bored. I pick up my phone automatically but again, remember that I don't have any data. Irritated, I slap it down next to me. I keep my hand on it and run my fingers over its bumps and scratches. I must get a new phone case.

I open my eyes. I must have nodded off. Not sure, but yes, I check my phone which is still under my hand on the bed next to me. It's 1.17am. Ella is asleep. Her soft breathing has lengthened in a gentle snore. She lies face down, hair, arms and legs spread in different directions as though she fell from a height. The duvet is half-kicked off already. I might as well get undressed. I can't hear any music now from outside. It must be all over. I kneel up again and pull the curtains back slightly to check. It's hard to see, but in the dimly lit gap between the two caravans, there are now two figures: Mum and Uncle Toni. Marco must have gone to bed too. Mum and Toni are just dark shapes. If I didn't know their outline, I could easily mistake them for other people, standing close together, having a different conversation. Then I realise that, yes, I must be mistaken, because these shadows can't be Mum and Uncle Toni. The man has his arm around the woman's shoulders and his face is close to hers, almost touching. Her head hangs down as though she is talking to her feet. The man bends his head even closer and their shapes merge where their heads touch. The woman puts her hands to her eyes in a swift urgent movement. The man pulls her to him, and they hug. I think the woman is upset; she might be crying. Her shoulders are hunched, and her hand keeps touching her face. The hug doesn't last long then they separate. The man keeps his hand on her arm. The woman looks up at the man who is only a tiny bit taller than her. He is round in the middle and even rounder next to her slim shape. She lifts her hand to *his* face now, and then around the back of his neck pulling him towards her. She must want to tell him something, something that has to be whispered. No one moves.

There is a pause. I am sure it is only a moment, but my chest hurts from the effort of holding my breath in tightly. I wait to see what happens next. Then everything starts to go into slow motion. The man moves his face to meet hers and their two shapes become one. *They are kissing.* My stomach drops 10 metres. 100 metres. 1,000 metres. It feels like my insides have fallen through my body, past my feet, through the floor of the caravan and straight into the centre of the earth. The weight of it all is pulling me down into a darkness that feels like it is opening up below me. I feel dizzy and sick and although I'm kneeling on the bed, I feel like I'm about to fall. The darkness is going to swallow me up. I shout 'Stop, stop' but the words stick in my throat. I think they might choke me, but they are not real words and I'm not shouting at all. It is all locked inside me like a horrible dream. All I can do is watch what is happening outside my window, like a nightmare when you can't call out or move your arms or legs to stop the bad things from happening.

They are still kissing. Stop. *Please.* Stop. I can't bang on the window because it will wake Ella. I glance down at her protectively. I envy her so lost in sleep. I close my eyes to see if I can wake up. Perhaps I am dreaming. I look out of the window again. They are not kissing. The man has his arm around the woman's shoulder again and she is back in that hunched position as though staring at her feet. He pulls her towards him and hugs her again, patting her on the back. She rests her head on his chest.

How could she? How could he? Why? Why!

'*Bitch!*' I spit the word towards the window. Ella stirs below me, an arm shifting defensively across her chest. I clamp my hand over my mouth in horror at what I'm saying. This is Mum. I can't say that. But no, it can't be Mum. It was someone else. Not Mum and Toni. Just two dark shapes. *What is going on? Why would they do that? Why - why - why - why - why - why!* Words seem to rain down on me and I move my hands over my head as though trying to protect myself from a violent storm. I can't watch anymore. I pull the curtain across and sink down on to my bed. I turn my face into my pillow and cry. Deep angry

164

choking sobs that hurt my chest and throat. I cry so much that I want my Mum. That makes me cry even more.

I open my eyes. I must have nodded off. 2.36am. *How could I sleep?* My eyes are wet, my throat is dry but for one amazing moment I have forgotten what I saw. Then the memory comes crashing in and I feel like I'm choking again. Those two familiar shapes merging in the dark. I see it again and again, playing over and over like a terrible meme.

Was it a dream? Ella has crazy dreams that stay with her when she's awake. She will sit up in bed looking normal and fully awake then ask me something random like 'I thought you were going bowling' or 'where's my doughnut?' Saying things aloud often snaps her out of it but sometimes she can look confused for ages, her mind half in and half out of a dream like someone who is stuck getting out of bed. I drag myself up from where I am slumped in the corner of my bed on top of the covers. I peek around the edge of the curtains. My stomach churns and my heart is speeding up. I am afraid of what I will see. However, there's no one out there. No figures merging in the darkness. The party is over.

The field is silent except for the sad cry of a fox. *Did I dream it?* I wish I could believe that, but I know what I saw. How *could* they do that? I start to cry quietly. There's nothing else to do. I can't scream, I can't throw things, I can't undo it, so I just let the tears run down my face. I slide back down on to the bed, pulling the thin duvet over my legs even though I'm not cold. I reach over to Ella's bed and grab one of her cuddly toys. I don't care which. I wrap my arms around Mr Rabbit – they all have stupid names like that – and squish my face into the space between his floppy ears. I stay like that feeling his fur getting wetter and wetter. The only sound comes from Ella, tiny rhythmic snores like a dormouse from a cartoon who is tucked up cosily in bed.

What does all this mean? Was it just one kiss? Or two? Are Mum and Toni having an affair? The word makes me feel sick. They can't be. They live too far away. Surely, we would know? But people don't know, do they? People hide things. And what about Dad? *Poor Dad.* Something twists in my chest. Dad throwing things around the barbeque this evening with Uncle Toni, both joking together and clinking beer bottles. Dad and Toni have been friends forever. *Does Dad know? Are Mum and Dad splitting up? Does Mum love Dad? Are they happy?* I've never thought about it before. They argue a bit but not like other parents. Grandma and Grandpa, Mum's parents, argue much more than Mum and Dad and they've been married for over 50 years. *What would happen to me and Ella if they split up?* More tears prick my sore eyes. I look protectively over at Ella who is now curled up in a ball with her back towards me.

I think about Lauren who is in my form at school. Her mum and dad split up last year. She often gets upset at school about it all. She says the worst thing is that she can't talk about things at home in case it upsets her parents. That sounds crazy to me when they are the ones that have caused it. Lauren told us that her parents used to argue so much that she had almost stopped noticing. When her Dad moved out, it wasn't a relief to not hear them arguing, it was eerily quiet. The first night he moved out she started a row with her mum deliberately just to fill the house with noise. Then

I remembered something else Lauren told us all at breaktime one day. Since the split, her mum and dad were trying to make everything as easy as possible for her and make her feel like both their houses were her home. They decorated her new bedroom in her dad's house exactly the same as the one she already had in what was now her mum's house: same bed, same duvet cover, same wallpaper, lamps and furniture. Lauren understood what they were trying to do even though it was a bit weird. However, she told us that it was impossible to have two of absolutely everything, and she was always forgetting things and leaving something in the other house – her homework or PE kit, a favourite lipstick, or her iPad. Lauren said that she realised that the thing she wanted most would probably always be in the other house, and that she just had to get used to the feeling that something was missing, just as she had got used to her mum and dad arguing when they were together. I don't want Mum and Dad to get divorced. I don't want to always feel like something is missing. I don't want to get used to something that doesn't feel right. I wriggle down into the bed and curl up around Mr Rabbit closing my eyes into his damp fur.

I open my eyes. I must have nodded off, just for a moment, maybe longer. It's still dark in the room. 4.15am. My eyes feel crusty and sore. I close them again and see what I want to forget: two dark figures merging together. Two shadows moving like those Chinese puppets that are just silhouettes. I saw one of those plays at school. I screw my eyes tighter, but the image is in my head. *Why did they kiss? Are they in love? Were they drunk? Will we ever come to the caravan again?* My head hurts. I put my hand to my forehead as if trying to stem the flow of thoughts. There are more and more questions like a magician pulling an endless stream of scarves from his sleeve.

5.43am. Weak light filters through the curtains. My eyes feel sore and I struggle to keep them open. My mouth is dry and tastes disgusting. The chill of the night has passed, and the room is close and stuffy again. I drag myself up to a sitting position and then crawl on to my knees at the window. I glance across at Ella, who is fast asleep face down on the bed, arms and legs in all directions. As predicted, she has now kicked her duvet, toys and pillows completely on to the floor. Trying not to make any noise I open the window and thrust my head outside. I turn awkwardly to push my shoulders through the narrow space so I can feel the cool air on my bare arms. I gulp down the air, drinking it deep into my lungs until it hurts. Gran says that things always feel better in the morning. Not this morning though. My eyes fill with tears. I can't see the seagulls, but I hear them crying overhead. I look up and let out a hoarse sob into the morning sky.

7

FRIDAY

I'm floating on my back in the swimming pool. If I open my eyes then I will see another blue sky, just like yesterday's. The sun nudges my eyelids wanting me to look, showing off. Another perfect day. *Yeah, right.* My head is hot and aching from lack of sleep. The water laps around my forehead like cool fingers trying to stroke all the heat and hurt away. It's nice but it's not going to work.

I'll be in trouble when I get back. I'm not supposed to come to the swimming pool on my own. Stupid rules made when Ella and I were little. Well, I'm not little anymore and no one else seems to be following any rules. An image flashes into my mind – the dark shape of two figures, separate then coming together. I wince as though the memory burns. This morning I left the caravan before anyone else was awake. My eyes and face were red and puffy: I didn't want them to ask why. Ella and Dad can't know. The secret sits heavily in my stomach and I kick my legs in the water trying to stay afloat under the weight of it all.

It was odd to be the first person up this morning. Mum and Ella are always up before me and always up before Dad who is *not* a morning person. The caravan looked abandoned. The usually tidy kitchen was full of unwashed dishes and leftover food that hadn't been put away last night after the party. There was a pile of hot dog rolls, dry and hard at the edges, next to a bowl of yellowing coleslaw. A fly buzzed around it. A half bottle of wine slumped amongst an army of empty beer cans, some tipped on their sides. Mum's normally spotless kitchen worktops were smeared. Outside the caravan the barbeque stood with its lid up like a gaping mouth with half-eaten meat on its ridged tongue. The burnt sausages and burgers glistened as the congealed fat caught the early sun. My stomach turned.

I had to leave a note so they wouldn't freak out and think I'd been kidnapped. I wrote on a scrap of paper: 'Gone swimming. Chloe.' I regretted writing that afterwards in case the others decided to come and join me, but it was too late, I was halfway to the pool when the thought came. However, after the late night I didn't think anyone would be up early enough to catch me here. Even Ella was dead to the world, her face in the pillow, one arm dangling like a dead weight over the side of the bed.

Before I left the caravan, I checked Mum and Dad's room. I crept the few extra steps down the corridor trying my best not to make the floor vibrate. Their door was slightly ajar. At first l was afraid to look. I was worried that I would wake them, or worse, that they wouldn't be there. I peeked through the crack of the door and held my breath. Mum and Dad were in bed. Everything was normal except it looked like Dad had fallen asleep on top of the covers fully dressed. He lay on his side. His T-shirt had ridden up and his belly spilled over his shorts, resting on the bed next to him like a pet. Mum was curled up under the covers facing away from the door. I could only see her hair. The flash of her red hair sparked something angry in me. Suddenly, I wanted to shake her awake and ask her what happened? No, I wanted to scream at her, *WHAT DID YOU DO?!* The door was shaking. No, my hands were shaking, and I was gripping the edge of the door so hard my knuckles were white. I had to get out of there before I did something stupid. I pretty much ran to the swimming pool. I wanted all the hot angry thoughts to dissolve as I stepped into the water.

The swimming pool opens early for residents on a Friday. Apparently, it's to make up for the fact that at the weekend the pool will be crowded with visitors and the oldies don't like all the screaming kids. When I arrived, the lifeguard looked sleepy or hungover and not fit to guard any lives. It was a different boy to yesterday but still not much older than me. Slumped in his plastic chair, he waved me through without asking to see my pass which I hadn't brought with me anyway.

There are a few swimmers here with me. Two old ladies swim short widths together chatting. They have saggy arms and huge boobs that float ahead of them in the water like lifebuoys. Three men chat in a corner, wrinkled faces turned to the sun. The water laps at their bristly grey-haired chests. There is one serious swimmer, a woman with a swimming hat and goggles. She ducks under the rope separating the shallow end of the pool from the deep end so she can swim a whole length. I stick to one corner, far from anyone, leaning back in the water.

There isn't a lot of noise but the small amount of chatter around me is broken up and muffled by the water lapping around my head. My thoughts feel broken up and muffled too. I try to concentrate on something, and then it splits into two or three other thoughts. It's like when you stare at a star in the sky and it fades as you focus on it until you are not sure it was there in the first place.

> *Star light, star bright,*
> *The first star I see tonight.*

Was any of it real last night? I am sure it was but it must be a mistake. My mind runs through the same questions as last night like I'm rehearsing a script. *It can't have been Mum and Toni. I was tired. It was dark. Mum wouldn't do that. Toni wouldn't either. He and Dad are best friends and he loves Auntie Helen.* A memory pops into my head, from I'm not sure when, perhaps one Christmas when the Rossi gang were visiting us. Uncle Toni had just kissed Mum on the back of her hand, as though she were a lady in one of those costume dramas, and Mum was pretending to swoon. Ella, her forehead screwed up with worry, was talking to Auntie Helen in a loud whisper.

'I'm sorry, Auntie Helen,' said Ella, 'But I think Uncle Toni is in love with Mummy.'

Helen laughed, and then more seriously, she loud-whispered back to Ella, her face hidden behind her hand.

'Don't worry, Uncle Toni is in love with all women but I'm the lady he loves best. However...,' she paused dramatically before continuing, 'the person he loves most of all in the world is *himself.*'

We all laughed, including Toni who nodded and shrugged. *Was Helen serious? Did it mean anything or was it just the joke we thought it was?* Why can't it be easier to work out what people really think? Grownups say one thing, but they mean something else. My head is hot and spinning again. I try to arrange the thoughts and questions in order as though I am doing a test. I wish I could solve it all by doing a multiple-choice quiz or something. Ha! I wonder what *Kute* magazine would say:

> *Is your Mum having an affair with your*
> *Dad's best friend?*
> *Well, answer these questions and see how it*
> *ends...*

Maybe I should write that quiz. Well, I can't ask *Kute* magazine what to do, but I wish I could talk to someone. I don't think I would want anyone at home to know. I feel ashamed and it's not me that's done anything. Would anyone here even believe me? I don't know if I believe it. *Was it a dream? Did I really see them kiss?* Oh no, here I go again, round and round. It's like that awful ride that Ella and I went on at the country fair last week. I was feeling sick and desperate for the ride to end. When it suddenly slowed and stopped, I thought I could get off. Then it started up again moving much faster, spinning us all backwards. Ella and I screamed but for different reasons, she loved it and I thought I was going to die.

I am still floating on my back and I let the tears run down my cheeks into the water. It's a relief not to have to wipe them away. I'm always pretending that there's nothing wrong, pushing it all down inside me until I nearly choke. Here I can cry, and my tears are lost in the swimming pool. Just tiny drops in all this water. Miniscule. Insignificant. These would be good words for my English comprehension. Miss Carlisle, my English teacher, is always telling me to use better vocabulary – so glad I don't have her next year at school.

I know I can't stay here all day. My fingertips are wrinkled and white. The pool is busier now. The water starts to churn up with other people's fun. It's hard to float as the choppy water bumps me against the walls, and splashes over my face making me blink and cough. The pool is coming to life, people edge closer. I have to throw a ball back to a group of kids who shout, '*Cheers*'. The nearest boy, his hair plastered against his head, gives me a thumbs up then leaps into the air at the ball like a dolphin, splashing me more. Two girls, older than me, sit down on the edge of the pool dangling their tanned legs in the water. They glance at me. I don't like them staring so I haul myself out of the pool and head towards the entrance, wrapping a towel around myself as I go. I've only taken a couple of hurried steps before I almost fall over a toddler waddling in a bulky swim nappy. I mumble 'sorry' to the parents' feet and rush off, my face flushed, blinking back more tears.

It's funny how our field and the holiday park next door seem so much smaller this year. It used to take ages for us to walk back from the swimming pool, but it seems like only minutes until I'm nearly at the entrance to our campsite. There used to be just a gap in the hedge here, but Mr Jones has installed a gate between the holiday park and our field. It is locked late at night but stands open now. There is something white on the ground near the gate. As I get closer, I see it is Mr Jones' cat, its creamy fur spread like melted ice cream across the path. I stop to stroke him, digging into the hot, thick fur at his neck with my fingers. He doesn't purr or even look that pleased to be stroked, but anything to delay going back.

I glance up through the gateway into our field. There are small signs of life: smoke from a barbeque, caravan doors open, camping chairs moved into the sun. Luca jogs past close to the opening then disappears behind the hedge. My heart jolts. I wasn't expecting to see anyone yet. I don't want them to see me like this, hair dripping, eyes red from crying and swimming. I don't think Luca saw me crouched on the floor with the cat. I can't see him now but through the gateway I catch sight of Marco, further away, running in a half-circle then stopping a ball with his foot. I hear them shout to each other, but my view is blocked by the hedge. I'm trapped. It will take me ages to walk around to the front entrance of the field and I will bump into even more people going that way. I am going to have to bluff it out. I stand up quickly but my towel, which is wrapped around my waist, catches under my feet. I stumble, try to untangle myself, and step sideways into a hole hidden in the long grass. My ankle twists painfully. The tears come easily, and I stand here sobbing for a few minutes, then gasping as though I am out of breath. I must look like an idiot. I look around me but luckily, I am still alone. Everyone I know would laugh at me if they could see me, wet hair dripping down my neck, standing here in my swimming costume, my towel trailing in the dirt, crying my eyes out like a little baby. Well, I'm not a baby! I tug at my towel angrily and wrap it roughly around my waist pulling it tight. I'm sick of it. I am angry and tired, and I don't want any of this.

I want to go home. My body sags at the thought, my legs heavy from swimming struggle to keep me upright. I wish I had my phone with me. I could ring Gran and Grandad and ask them to come and pick me up. Or maybe when I get back to our caravan, I can find enough money to take the train home. *No*. There will be a meltdown and too many questions, but I'm the one who has all the questions. I know I am going to have to speak to Mum, it's the only way to know for sure. The thought of it makes me want to sob again. I'm angry with her but afraid. I want Mum to tell me it was a mistake, that I didn't see what I did. But can she? Do I dare even ask her? *What did she do?!* My chest is tight. It feels like something is pushing hard to get out. It's hard to breathe under the pressure. *Am I having a panic attack?* I slump forward, my hands leaning on my thighs to steady myself. This usually makes me feel better but today I feel sicker. I suck in a few quick breaths before standing up right again. I rub my face to get rid of the tears and panic. I need to hold it together. If I can get through one more day, then tomorrow we go home. *I want to go home.*

Through the gap in the hedge, the field looks lush and green. The sun is shining on the caravan windows opposite me making everything glow. It looks unreal, perfect. It makes me feel angry. I hear some little kids giggling and shouting at each other, playing a game. I bet Ella and I used to sound like that. I think longingly of Ella. I wonder what

176

she is doing. Mr Jones' cat has left me and is skulking off into the shade further down the path. The sun beats down on the back of my neck. I can't just stand here but I feel shut out. The gateway to the field feels like the entrance to another world that I'm not part of anymore. I don't know if I can walk through and join in with the rest of the holiday. It will feel like I am acting.

I was in a play last year at school. I didn't want to be, but they made everyone in Year 7 take part. Mrs Duckworth, the drama teacher, kept changing the parts around because so many girls got scared about being on stage. I ended up with one of the biggest acting parts in our class because I didn't complain like the others. I wish I had.

I learnt my lines, turned up for every performance and prayed I wouldn't make an idiot of myself. Standing in the wings at the side of the stage, surrounded by shadows and whispers from the other actors and stage crew, I knew that in a moment I had to step out onto the bright stage where everyone spoke in loud voices, and pretended to be someone else. The first night I stood there in the dark, afraid, trying to remember my first line. I thought that if I could remember what I had to say then I would feel ready. However, my mind was blank. I couldn't go on stage and pretend to be someone else if I didn't know what to say or how to play the part. Then it was my cue. Urgent voices were whispering behind me, 'Go. Now!' My hands shook. *What was my line?* I couldn't do this. My stomach was churning. I imagined everyone in the audience taking pictures of me puking on the stage and sharing them online. That made me feel even sicker. Then someone was nudging me in the back and before I realised what was happening, I was in front of the audience blinking under the harsh stage lights. As soon as I stepped into the other world of the play, I found myself saying the lines and acting out the part just like we had rehearsed.

I know I was rubbish, and I never want to be in a play again, but I did it, going through the motions every night. It's crazy that I am thinking about that stupid play, but I suppose that's what I have to do now. Step through the gate and play our 'happy family holiday' until I work out what to do next. Just one more day to get through. It can't get any worse than this. Just one more day. I pull the towel around me, my face an ugly grimace as I step forward on to my twisted ankle.

*

The second I open the caravan door, Ella is in my face all wide-eyed and dramatic.

'Where have you BEEN! I woke up and you were GONE. You've been SWIMMING?!'

'So?' I snap.

I'm already cringing at the volume of her voice which is getting louder and more annoying with every question. I suddenly feel exhausted after my long swim and sleepless night.

'WHY didn't you tell me where you were going? You KNOW I love swimming. WHY did you go on your OWN? Why didn't you WAKE ME? YOU MUST HAVE LEFT REALLY EARLY!!'

Her questions come at me at a hundred miles an hour as though she has saved up every thought and feeling since she woke and is firing them at me like bullets. I want to throw my hands in front of my face as a shield. I try to manoeuvre around her but my limp slows me and I stop to rub my sore ankle. Ella is snapping at my heels.

'What's WRONG with your FOOT?! Did you hurt it swimming? Was it busy in the pool? Was that lady there with the funny swimming hat? Have you had breakfast? Did you get a CROISSANT from the shop? You should have got ME-E-E ONE?! I had boring cereal. Do you want to play a game?'

Shut up! I shout at her in my head. I quickly scan the room for Mum. She's not here. I'm both disappointed and relieved that I don't have to talk to her yet. My stomach has that up-down feeling that you get on a seesaw. Dad is in the kitchen, his back to me, slumped over a sink full of dishes.

'But we didn't KNOW where you WERE?!' Ella says even louder dancing around in front of me blocking my path. She hops from one foot to the other without a pause. I swallow down the scream that I want to let rip, and spin around and she stops dead in order to not bump into me.

'Yes, you did,' I say in a low voice that sounds dangerous even to me. 'You read the note. I went swimming. I can leave without your permission. Now back off, I need a shower.'

The words are hard, and it feels like I can lean right on them. Something fearful passes over Ella's face and wipes the next battery of questions off her lips. I glare at her and she quickly looks away. I head towards the bathroom again. Dad turns from the sink and gives a half-hearted, soap-sud covered wave. There are bubbles stuck to the front of his damp T-shirt and halfway up his arms. His voice is tired but

179

cheerful as usual. He can't have heard what I said to Ella otherwise I'd be getting told off for being mean. It's always my fault.

'Morning, Chloe-bear,' he says. 'Ella, let your sister get in the door. We're all knackered and you're like a bloody jumping bean. Come here and help me dry up.'

Ella gives me a resentful glance then skips over to him to snatch up the tea-towel he offers her. She stands close to him, her blonde head leaning into his arm and stares sulkily at me. Dad doesn't notice the looks passing between us. He sags against the sink and sighs as though someone is letting all the air out of his body. His face is grey and the fine lines under his eyes have deepened into folds. He is definitely hungover. At least he's not telling me off for going out. Maybe he didn't notice. I think of last night and what else he doesn't know. *Poor Dad*. A desperate feeling rises in my chest. I blink quickly to stop a tear escaping. I keep my head down and pretend to look for something in my swimming bag. I can't look at him, he might see I'm upset. He might see *everything* in my face.

'You ok, love?' says Dad.

'I'm fine.' I say. I can't stop myself asking, 'Where's Mum?' The sound of her name feels like a cut. My arms hug my body as if to protect me.

'She's gone to the shop to get some bits. I'm surprised you didn't bump into her,' says Dad.

The thought of the near miss makes me panic even though it never happened. I don't want to see her, but I have to see her. The cut stings deeper.

'I'm going for a shower,' I say and disappear straight into the bathroom before anyone can answer.

After I have washed my hair and body at least three times in the shower using mine, Ella's and Dad's shower gel, I stay in our bedroom for as long as possible with the door closed. No one comes to find me, luckily. Eventually I need to go into Mum and Dad's room to find the hairdryer. If I don't blow dry it properly my hair will be frizzy. There is a large suitcase on the bed surrounded by neat piles of folded clothes. On the floor filling the gap down the side of the bed is a much larger heap, a messy tangle of clothes and towels that must be the dirty washing pile. The hair dryer is on the floor behind this. I have to half-scramble over the clothes mountain to reach it, disgusted as my hand touches a pair of Dad's pants. *Urgh.* Hanging on to the bed, fingers digging into the cotton duvet, I pull myself back up to standing clutching the hairdryer to my body. When I spin around to leave, I find Mum blocking the doorway. I jump and my heart feels like it has thrown itself out of my chest. The hairdryer is a dull thud hitting the floor.

'Clumsy,' says Mum bending down to pick it up. 'Sorry, did I scare you?'

I stare at her, shocked and unable to speak Over the past few hours Mum has transformed in my mind into some sort of monster that I have to confront. However, everything that has been torturing me is out of place in the ordinariness of us bumping into each other in the bedroom. I feel wrong footed and unsure. Mum looks just the same as before. *Normal.* Mum-like. A moment passes that feels like an hour as she waits for me to answer. The bedroom curtains are half-drawn against the glare of the sun. Dust dances in the one arrow of light from the window. I feel caught in the moment like the dust particles. In the dim room, where we are standing – too close – Mum's freckles are dark against her pale skin. There's no make-up, not even a smudge of concealer on her scar. I try not to let the red twisted shape draw my eyes towards it. Her face looks naked, transparent, but I can't read her expression.

'Did you have a nice swim?' she says.

I was expecting a row. *I want a row.*

'I'm old enough to go on my own,' I say.

'We're packing this morning,' she replies looking around the room.

Did she hear me? I can say more. I want to shout at her and tell her what I saw, what she did. *Why did you do that?!*

'Put the hairdryer back in the suitcase when you've finished,' she says.

Her gaze settles on me for only an instant as she scans the items on the bed, her mind mentally organising what still needs to be done. She always insists we start packing early. It's stupid as we're not leaving until tomorrow.

'Mum.' I croak the word up from a throat as dry as sand. It's a desperate noise.

'Yes?' Her voice sounds as far away as her thoughts.

Why did you kiss him, I think. The thought of saying it releases a horrible sickening fear that pools in my stomach. *What do I do? What do I say? How to begin?* My fingers clench and unclench as indecisive and anxious as me. I need to say something now. I want her to explain. I realise that I am still hoping that I didn't see what I saw, and that there's a reason for all this. *Tell me it didn't happen. Tell me I'm mistaken.*

Mum bends to pick up some clothes that have slipped on to the carpet, probably when I grabbed the duvet. Her hands move quickly returning the neat folds to the fabric before dropping them into the suitcase. The normality of it is confusing. I want her to show me that she is different so that I can understand. How can she be so normal after what she has done? *Who are you?* I think. *What were you doing last night? I hate you.* It doesn't feel like I hate her though.

'Chloe?'

She's waiting for me to continue, one eyebrow half-raised. Unable to meet her gaze, I stare down at my hands as though I am looking to them for courage. They are occupied with twisting the bottom of my T-shirt into a tight roll then releasing it. I watch them repeat this, my fingers painful as the fabric pinches unexpectedly.

'Doesn't matter,' I mutter.

I can't. *I'm pathetic. I'm a failure.* I hate her for making me feel like this. A spark of fire flashes inside me. *Good.* There it is. I can only be brave when I'm angry. That's when I stop worrying about what will happen. I want her to light the furious little fire that's been smouldering inside me since I woke up this morning. However, Mum doesn't say anything, just carries on folding clothes, and I stand here like an idiot, an idiot that can't speak. Luckily Ella interrupts us and brings something as good as a match.

'What's this?' says Ella. 'I found it when I was packing. It's funny and old – look at this girl's hair!'

She stands in the narrow doorway to Mum and Dad's bedroom flicking through a magazine, pointing at the crazy 1980's hairstyles. It's the December issue of *Kute*, the one I took from Sophie's loft after we did the 'Who's your Prince Charming?' quiz. No one knows I have it, not even Sophie. Hot red shame floods my face.

'That's mine, you bitch!' I yell.

I spit the words at Ella and snatch the magazine from her hands. A page rips leaving Ella holding a torn corner. I quickly hide the magazine behind my back, my hands trembling. No one must see.

'Hey!' shouts Ella.

'Chloe!' shouts Mum. 'Do NOT speak to your sister like that.'

'She's been in my stuff again!!' I shout back louder.

I want to scream and cry at the same time, wrestling embarrassment and rage.

'It was on the bed.' Ella bites her bottom lip, a sure sign that she is lying. 'I found it when I was packing.'

I impersonate Ella's sly whine, *'I found it while I was packing*… liar!'

'I did!' She sounds more desperate.

'It was in my bag, and *you* took it,' I poke her hard in the chest on the 'you' and she shrieks.

'Ow! Ow, Mummy, she hurt me!'

She scutters over to Mum who instinctively puts her arms around her. I watch them jealously.

'I hardly touched you, you baby,' I sneer.

'Stop it,' says Mum.

'I never get any privacy,' I rant. 'She's *always* in my stuff. Don't tell me it's my fault.'

'I didn't mean to take it.' Ella makes her voice wobble, but I know she's faking. 'I didn't know it was important. What is it?'

'None of your business!' I snap back.

'Girls,' warns Mum.

'It was on the bed,' says Ella.

'It wasn't on the bed, it was in – my – bag,' I snarl.

'Well, your bag was on the bed,' says Ella. 'And your stuff was all over, so how am I to know!'

Her mouth sets in a stubborn line but her eyes are wide and unsure. We face each other like two snapping dogs on leads.

'Thief.'

'Shut up.'

'You're a liar,' I say.

'I hate you.' she whines.

'Good, because I've always hated you, ever since you were born.'

Ella bursts into tears.

'Chloe, that's enough!' snaps Mum.

But I don't want to stop.

'Yeah, yeah, whatever, take my phone, ban me from breathing. She's still a pathetic liar. Taking my stuff. Spoiling everything as usual.'

'You're the one that spoils everything!' wails Ella. 'No one likes you!'

'I – said – STOP!' Mum's voice rings out like a shot. I imagine all the seagulls rising off the caravan roofs as though a gun has gone off.

Ella and I are shocked into silence.

'Chloe! You will apologise for being rough with your sister. There's no need for that, particularly when she is younger than you.'

'Typical!...' I interrupt but she cuts me off.

'Quiet! Ella you can apologise for taking Chloe's things without her permission – that's the second time this holiday. You can't share a room unless you respect her privacy.'

185

No one moves. No one speaks.

'Well?!' says Mum. Her tone is as sharp as a razor, her narrowed eyes flit between our sulky faces.

'For goodness sake, this is the last day of our holiday! Just say sorry and try and get through one more day without killing each other!'

We both mumble 'sorry', not meaning it, shooting daggers at each other with every glance. I am still holding the copy of *Kute* magazine behind my back. The pages are scrunched tight in one aching hand. I try to unclench it. My fingers stick to the shiny pages.

Mum's voice is whispered and serious. 'This is our family holiday. One day you will realise how lucky you are to spend time together, for us to be a whole family. Things can happen...' She pauses and there's a noise in her throat that sounds like something is caught there. She clears it and continues. 'Things can change.'

'They already have,' I say glaring at her.

'I know,' says Mum. Her eyes flick away for a second. 'But it's important that you two are friends.'

'Huh, yeah, right,' I sneer at Ella.

'You're mean,' says Ella. 'I hate you.'

'No, you don't,' says Mum, 'you just think you do because you've had an argument. No one hates anyone in this family.'

'That's what you think,' I mutter.

Mum sighs and replies in a tired voice, 'What's that supposed to mean?'

There is fire raging inside me, but my words are made of ice. I pick them carefully.

'People might hate you if they really knew you.'

186

There is a long pause and the words hang in the air between us like an unhappy birthday banner, too high for me to reach down. Mum says nothing but there's a flicker, a tiny dent in her expression. She looks at me and I stare right back holding her gaze for as long as I dare, which is only a few moments, but just enough.

Words seem as light as paper, but they can hurt if you throw them right. I remember when Ella and I were younger we were making paper aeroplanes in the caravan on a wet afternoon. Gran and Grandad had a drawer full of coloured paper and we had got bored of drawing. The two of us knelt on the floor, leaning over the coffee table at the far end of the caravan, folding the coloured paper into different shapes. The aim was to see which type of aeroplane would fly the furthest. We sent them everywhere, floating in all directions, bouncing off the chairs and ceiling and disappearing behind the kitchen cupboards. Some just spiralled up for a few seconds then dropped to the carpet with a thud. Others sailed across the room in an elegant arc crashing into the mirror at the other end of the caravan.

As we got better at folding them, learning which styles flew best, we changed our game. I stood at the other end of the room whilst Ella launched the planes at me to catch. I missed a lot and caught a few. Then one paper aeroplane, folded from Gran's blue writing paper, thrown with all Ella's might, sailed gracefully across the room but with a speed I wasn't expecting. I stretched my arms and flapped like a bird trying to get high enough to catch it, but the plane hit me in the face just under my eye. It was as painful as a knife although you could barely see the cut. Dad said that if it had hit me a couple of centimetres above it could have damaged my eye. It stung for days. I think of that cut now as Mum's face twitches and two spots of red appear on her cheeks. My words hit their mark.

Taking advantage of the momentary silence, I walk towards the door of the bedroom then half-turning back to Mum, I say, in a voice as innocent and light as I can make it, 'Oh, and Mum, if you've run out of concealer you can borrow some of mine if you like. I've got some really thick stuff that you can use on your lip.'

*

Mum is making us do stupid chores before we go to the beach. I'm sitting on the floor of the caravan, knees bent to one side, tidying the board games and DVDs back into the cupboard under the TV. Ella is with Mum in the kitchen, just a few feet away but I feel like I'm in another world from them. Dad's outside somewhere probably pretending to clean the barbeque but more likely to be sitting in the front seat of the car checking the football scores on his phone. Mum and Dad are always going on about me spending too much time on my phone, but they are much worse. Dad checks the sport about every 10 minutes and Mum is constantly texting her friends.

Mum likes to do most of the packing on the last morning so it 'doesn't spoil the rest of the day'. I've always hated this, a sign that the holiday is almost over before it truly is. It doesn't bother me today though, as I can't wait to get out of here and go home. She is emptying the cupboards in the kitchen, working out what food to take back with us and what to use up before we leave. Cereal boxes line up like a wall on the kitchen counter between us. No one has said anything much to me since our row earlier. I know I'm in trouble. *I know they all hate me*. For once I don't care.

I haven't seen Marco and Luca this morning. Apparently they left early with Uncle Toni to have one last game of golf. I don't feel like hanging out with them anyway and I don't want to see Uncle Toni. *Toni.* I haven't thought much about him, but I should hate him as much as Mum. He's the other shadow in last night's nightmare. It's just… I can't imagine him ever doing anything to hurt anyone. Not that Mum would either… deliberately. It's so confusing. *Why did this have to happen?* It's like a terrible song going round and round my head. I hit the side of my head with my fist as if trying to knock my jumbled thoughts into order. I lose my grip on the Scrabble box that I'm holding. The lid comes off as it hits the floor, the little plastic pieces clattering together like chattering teeth.

Ella looks up at the noise but realising it is me, scowls and turns away. She is removing the pictures that Mum has stuck on the huge caravan mirror. I watch her peel away our holiday bit by bit, first tugging at the corner of a map of the village until the blue-tacked corners pop free. Next is the fish and chip shop opening times, and then the scorecard from our golf day. Ella's drawing of the beach, with our heads bobbing in the sea, starts to tear so she picks more carefully at the sticky tape. Postcards, receipts, tickets, and more drawings are all removed. She keeps going until the mirror is clear and our holiday is a roughly stacked pile of memories which Mum sweeps into a drawer.

With the mirror clear we can see the 'other family' again. *Have they had a good week's holiday?* The girl with

189

the red hair looks angry. The younger girl with the blonde hair is sulking. Seeing me watching her, the blonde girl sticks her tongue out then turns to confide in the red-haired woman in the kitchen who pats her arm. The woman is barely visible, surrounded on all sides of the kitchen surfaces by food containers and plastic bags that overflow with half-loaves of bread, crumpled boxes of teabags, near-empty bottles of cordial, crisps, an odd selection of vegetables, and anything else that's been dragged out to be used up today.

I expected the caravan to feel bigger with the pictures gone and the mirror clear. Instead there is something oppressive about seeing the 'other room' again and the 'other family' staring back at us. None of them is speaking to each other. I watch them in the mirror wrapped up in their own individual tasks. The girl with the red hair sits alone at the far end of the caravan. The red-haired woman stops moving around the kitchen for a moment. She turns to hand a soft cloth and a plastic bottle of cleaning fluid to the blonde girl, presumably to squirt on the glass. The girl shakes the bottle vigorously and with an enthusiastic sweep of her arm mists up a large part of the mirror in a long swoosh of spray, then another, then another. She coughs and flaps her arms to clear the air around her. I can smell it from here. I can't see the 'other family' anymore. It's a relief to disappear for a moment. Then the spray condenses into liquid and begins to drip down the glass in great long streaks. We start to appear again, bit by bit, our faces distorted in the glass.

*

There's a stillness about our group on the beach today, no breezy laughter, no gusts of activity and games. Except for Ella, and maybe Marco, the party last night has left everyone flat like half-drunk cans of pop left to go warm in the sun. Luckily the usual stupid beach rules of 'no phones on the beach' and being forced to take part in 'family activities' such as cricket or sand-castle competitions have been abandoned. No one has even asked me if I've put sun cream on. Instead of our normal beach picnic of home-made sandwiches and little boxes of chopped up vegetables and fruit, we're eating chips and hot-dogs from the cafe, and an assortment of caravan leftovers. Ella is in heaven. She would eat ice cream for breakfast if she could. I've eaten nothing. Something heavy is sitting in my stomach and there's no room for food.

The heat is thick like you could cut slices out of it. It's not the 30 degrees or whatever we had at the beginning of the week, but it's more intense. As soon as we got to the beach, I flopped under one of the umbrellas. After the rain and the chill that's crept into the air on the last few mornings and evenings, today the heat feels desperate. Sweat lines the creases of my body, the top of my legs, the bends of my elbows and knees. I have a disgusting wet patch between my boobs, which I try to wipe with the heel of my hand when no one is looking. Even the waistband of my shorts feels damp where it touches my skin. 'It's so-o-o hot!' the adults sigh, exhaling the words as though using them to cool them down. They sound surprised, as though it's not August, and the sky isn't blue, and it's not our 'Last Chance Beach Day'. That's what Gran calls it. She says that it doesn't matter if the weather has been miserable all week,

191

it will always be hot and sunny on the last day of our holiday. I wish she were here now. She would know what to do.

As soon as we got to the beach, I made sure that I positioned myself as far away from Mum as I could manage. I turn my body away from her, everyone else, and the sea. Mum is sitting at the other end of our rough semi-circle of beach mats and chairs. Auntie Helen is squashed between Uncle Toni and Mum. Their three sun loungers are pulled close together under the shade of one large red umbrella. It would be hard for Helen to escape without one of the others moving out of the way. I want to go over there and pull her free. It looks so wrong seeing her stuck in the middle of them.

Uncle Toni has been asleep since we got to the beach, one arm thrown across his face. His shirt is unbuttoned and tufts of dark hair escape at the neck. His chest rises and falls deeply with each long breath. Mum and Helen, eyes hidden behind sunglasses, lie back in their chairs with their heads angled slightly towards each other. Murmurs of conversation drift over but I can't hear what they are saying above the general beach noise around me: children calling out to each other, the trudge of feet on sand as people pass by, seagulls crying, music from the distant fairground, the thud of bat hitting ball and then a cheer. Over this, always lapping at the edges of everything, is the sound of the sea, the waves turning over and over. There's something turning over in my head as well, thoughts rolling against the shoreline in my brain, a voice narrating everything I see. *How can Mum and Toni act like nothing has happened? Are they just going to ignore it? How can they sit with Helen and chat and laugh? What's going to happen?...* I've been watching Mum and Toni on and off all afternoon, spying I suppose, waiting to see a sign, further evidence that something has happened, that something is different. That's what they do in detective TV shows isn't it? It's not enough to have seen it, you need evidence, and you need other witnesses. However, there's only me, and I can't tell. I don't want the others to feel like I do – afraid I might see something but too scared to look away.

A can of Diet Coke lands on the beach mat in front of me nearly knocking my phone out of my hand.

'Hey!' I say.

'Amazon delivery,' says Marco. 'No need to sign for it.'

I squint up at him, shielding my eyes with one hand. It's awkward because I'm lying on my stomach. I shift my weight on to the other elbow, the beach mat is scratchy as I lean harder into it. The can rolls against the bare skin of my forearm. It's icy and gritty where the sand has stuck to the condensation.

'We've got a whole cool box full of them, so drink up,' says Marco. 'Dad's worried we might take home more than we brought with us.'

'Thanks,' I reply.

I hook my finger around the ring pull enjoying the snap as it gives. I take a deep swig and the icy fizz hits the back of my throat. Heaven. I can feel the chill inching its way down the inside of my body down to my stomach. I wrap my hand tighter around the can, desperate to absorb as much of the cold as possible. With my free hand I pick up my phone again. I am disappointed when Marco drops into the hot sand in front of me. I don't want to talk.

I'm lying under a beach umbrella protected from the afternoon heat. Earlier, when I was waiting for Dad to set it up, the sun on my head felt like I was standing under one of those outdoor garden heaters, the ones that you worry will set your hair on fire. However, the sun doesn't seem to bother Marco. He pushes his hair out of his dark eyes unblinking at the cloudless sky. It's hard not to but I try not to stare at his tanned chest and stomach which now fill my eyeline. Marco might look like Uncle Toni but he's not the same shape as him. He's skinny and his chest and arms are toned. I guess he works out; he and Luca play a lot of sport. Marco tilts his head and watches me.

'Whatcha doin'?' he says in a mocking sing-song tone.

'Go away,' I say.

This must be the fourth time he's been over to bug me. The first time was to see if I wanted to play cricket. The second time was to get me to help him carry food from the beach shop. Luckily Ella volunteered so I didn't have to move. The third time, I can't remember what he wanted, maybe football, and now he's here again. Marco's so restless. Luca, on the other hand, has taken my approach to the afternoon, although probably not for the same reasons. He is stretched out on a sun lounger, almost too long for it, reading something on his phone. I haven't spoken to him much yet today but I don't care. He can be pissed off with me if he wants. That all feels like nothing now. Kid's stuff.

'Go play with Ella if you are bored,' I say to Marco.

'She's burying your dad again, and I don't think she needs any help,' replies Marco nodding behind me.

Over my shoulder I watch Ella decorating Dad's half-buried legs with long strands of dried seaweed. I had

194

wondered what they were laughing about but I didn't want to turn around. Dad is pretending to sneeze: 'Ah-ah-ah-ah…' On each loud 'Ah-choo!' his legs kick up in the air scattering sand and seaweed. Ella giggles, 'Stop it, Daddy!' She pushes more sand over his legs until she is satisfied that they are covered again. The lacy seaweed is then laid carefully on top like the final flourish on a cake. Ella and I love watching those crazy baking shows where they make cakes look like anything. The seaweed could be the sugar decorations, and Dad's legs made of sponge covered with fake sand icing. Ella leans back on her heels admiring her work. It's the kind of thing we normally do together; burying dad, building sandcastles, digging tunnels to let in the sea. Dad starts his preparation for a sneeze, 'Ah-ah-ah-ah…' 'No!' shouts Ella. 'No, Daddy, don't you dare!' She wags her finger at him sternly. 'Choo!' Up fly Dad's legs scattering sand and seaweed again. A few shells fly in my direction. Ella screams in pretend outrage at Dad then falls to the floor in a giggling heap. I look away to make sure I don't start laughing myself. When I twist back to face Marco my neck cricks. I dig my fingers into the sore spot, a tight string that stretches between my shoulder and my ear. I must have been lying in this position too long with my shoulders hunched over. My phone vibrates. I have data. I scroll through my messages again, thumb and screen working as one.

'Swim?' says Marco.

I shake my head, eyes on my phone.

'Come on,' pleads Marco. 'Don't be boring.'

'You're boring,' I say.

He laughs, almost a cough. There's a pause and I think he's going to finally leave me alone. Instead he surprises me, his voice softens, and he asks as casually as he can, 'You okay?'

I hate it when people say that. There's only two ways you can respond. You either tell them what's really on your mind and then they freak out, or you say 'fine' and they get offended that you won't tell them what's wrong.

'Yeah, fine, I just want to chill,' I mumble. *And not talk.* I can feel my cheeks reddening so I keep my eyes on the phone screen, praying he will leave now.

Marco is oddly quiet again so that after a few minutes I glance up to see if he is still there. He is stirring the sand with his fingers, as though trying to mix the salt and pepper-coloured flecks into the gold. He scoops up a handful of grains then spreads his fingers. We watch the sand trickle through them like an hourglass. The moments pass, each second stretching out like an hour. It's how everything feels today. Long, and languid and lethargic. I smile at the alliteration. My English teacher would be proud of me – if she didn't hate me. Marco interrupts my thoughts.

'Ok, loser,' he says, 'I'm going for a swim.'

He scrambles to his feet showering me in a spray of sand. I can only see the bottom of his legs now. His footprints are obliterating the neat circles his fingers had drawn in the sand. The moment is gone. Then his feet are gone, and I hear him rounding up the others behind me.

'Bro! Swim.'

Marco again, insistent, 'No, now. Get up!'

Luca's voice. 'Ow! Get off. Okay.'

Ella's voice rings out. 'I'm coming!'

There's a collection of getting ready and moving noises behind me: chairs creaking, clothes and shoes being pulled or kicked off. A ball of conversation about nothing much that gets passed between them as they prepare to leave our camp. Then their voices grow fainter as I follow them in my mind down to the shoreline. I can just hear the splash and shrieks as they run or dive into the sea. I can almost sense the shock of the cold water on my own body, but in reality, all I am is hot and envious. If I lie very still, I can just about feel the air moving across my skin and pretend it's a breeze.

Pain throbs in my temples. I wish I'd taken some paracetamol before we came to the beach. Mum probably has some in her bag but there's no way I'm asking her. My phone vibrates again. I tuck it under my folded arms and rest my head sideways. I can see the beach stretched out before me side on, everything turned 90 degrees wrong. A thin layer of sweat quickly forms between the skin of my cheek and arm. It's hard to relax on the hard ground. When you walk across the beach the sand is soft, your toes sinking deep almost tripping you up. However, underneath me now, the sand is solid and unrelenting like I'm lying on rock. A stone or something sharp digs into the top of my ribs. I wriggle around until I am more comfortable. My eyes flutter. Eventually, the tightness that seems to be holding my body together, shifts a little. The heat is seeping under my skin. My eyes are closed.

There's a movement to my right, and a shift of light, then the heavy sound of someone flopping down next to me with a grunt. The beach mat shifts underneath me. *What? Who?* I lift my head a few centimetres. *Was I asleep?* My head is a fog. I struggle to open my eyes. The sharp light makes me feel sick. Irritated, I snap.

'Can't you just leave me alone?'

'Someone's a bit grumpy.'

Not Marco's voice, Dad's voice. I turn towards it. He's lying on his front next to me, bare-chested, patches of sand stuck to his shiny skin. He smells of sun cream, sweat and Dad.

'Thought I'd keep you company,' he says.

Why is it when you just want to be left alone everyone wants to talk to you? My mouth is as dry as the beach. I run my tongue over my lips.

'Was I asleep?' I croak.

'You weren't snoring if that's what you are worried about,' he grins.

He's lying half in and half out of the sun, one eye closed against the glare. His hair is lit up on the side furthest from me like a spiky halo.

'You okay, Chloe-bear?' he says.

That stupid nickname. Isn't it time he stopped using it? I'm not a baby. He sounds too bright and cheerful, like he's talking to a toddler, probably trying to cover up his hangover. However, he's not that good at pretending. Maybe Mum has sent him over to talk to me. The thought floods me with so many different types of anger, but I try not to let it all bubble to the surface at once. It's not Dad's fault.

'Yeah, fine' I say.

He nods at my phone.

'What you looking at?'

My phone is welded into my hand. I loosen my grip; my fingers are stiff and sweaty. I must have been holding it while I was asleep.

'Just a YouTuber that I like,' I lie.

'Great,' he nods.

'Makeup and stuff,' I say. 'You wouldn't like it.'

'OK,' he says. 'Is that on In-sta-gram.'

He says the word slowly like he's learning a foreign language.

It's so awkward. I'm desperate for him to go. He carries on nodding whilst turning over a white stone in his palm that he's fished out of the sand.

'Actually, I'm just really tired, Dad,' I say. 'We went to bed late and I have a headache. And I'm sad that the holiday is nearly over.'

'Oh, poppet,' he says.

His face is a mixture of concern and relief that there is an explanation for why I haven't said a word to any of them all day. *Job done.* He hugs me, a hot gritty arm around my shoulders. I'm faking all this, so I don't understand why my eyes prick with tears. I try to blink them away before he notices.

'You poor old thing,' continues Dad. 'Yeah, we're all feeling a bit off today. That's what I said, I mean... that's what I thought was bothering you.'

He looks anxious that he might have revealed too much. He wipes his free hand across his forehead. Sand sticks to his sweat covered face. He looks like one of those sand pictures we drew in the beach last year, the ones in the photo stuck to the caravan mirror.

'So bloody hot,' he says. 'This is the best weather we've ever had down here.'

'Last Chance Beach Day,' I say.

'That's right, Last Chance Beach Day!' says Dad. He looks sidelong at me smiling and then plants a too warm kiss on the side of my head just above the ear.

'Urgh, Dad,' I complain. 'You're all gross and sweaty.'

'We're baking,' he says, 'Baking like bloody jacket potatoes.'

A long shadow falls across the sand in front of us. It has Mum's voice at the end of it.

'Hi you two,' she says.

'All right, love,' says Dad.

Dad shuffles up further on to his elbows to look up at her. I keep my head down. I can only see the dark copy of her stretched across the sand. It reminds me of the two shadows last night by the side of the caravan. I feel sick.

'I'm going to walk to the loos,' says Mum. 'Do you want to come, Chloe?'

I tense. We usually go together. The toilets are right at the other end of the beach, and there is always a queue. There would be plenty of time to talk.

'Chloe, I said…'

'I'm fine,' I interrupt.

'Sure?' said Mum. 'You've not been since we got here.'
What, has she been monitoring me? I'm not five.

'I don't need to. I'll go when I'm ready.' I try to keep my voice even but there's an edge to it.

'Ok,' says Mum. 'Just thought I'd ask, you know, if you fancied a walk.'

Is that the best I can do? *I'll go when I'm ready.* What about everything else I want to say? I've been trying to pluck up the courage to face Mum. I could have spoken to her in the caravan when I was drying my hair, and there's been lots of opportunities since. Sometimes I think she's been making them for me, asking me to look for something in the car with her, getting me to carry things with her, sending Ella and Dad on errands. Every time I have felt paralysed. I keep coming up with excuses for why I can't speak, *not the right moment, Ella or Dad might hear,* but I know it's because I'm afraid. *Is Mum having an affair? Are Mum and Dad going to split up?* Dad's arm is still draped over my back, hot and sticky, but I don't want to push him away. I can't bear the thought of us all not being together, not being on holiday together. But I can't talk to her, I can't even look at her. I just keep seeing those two shadows by the caravan becoming one. You think you know people but then you see something that *is* them but is *not* them. I hate myself for being such a failure, but I don't want it to be my fault that they split up. I just can't ask her.

She's gone. She might have said something else to me, but I didn't hear. I breathe slowly trying to calm myself down. There are tears at the back of my eyes, but I don't dare blink in case Dad sees them. Dad waits a few moments before speaking then turns his head closer to me and says in a softer voice.

'Chloe, I know you are probably worried about your mum, but you know you can talk to me any time, about anything. I know we'll have good news when we get back, but I know there's a bit of a shadow over things this year.'

What?! I start slightly at the word 'shadow'. Does he mean? *No.* No, of course, he means Mum's skin cancer. The doctors sent a sample of skin to be analysed to check they had removed it all leaving only healthy tissue around her scar. I don't like any of these words: cancer, tissue, scar. They are so out of place on the beach, under this perfect blue sky, on our Last Chance Beach Day.

'The doctors are very confident that they got it all,' he finishes.

I feel guilty for not remembering that we are waiting for the test results. Dad shifts his arm across my shoulders in a clumsy hug. Neither of us speak. We stay like this for a while, with me weighed down by guilt and his arm which feels heavier and hotter as each minute passes. Then, after I don't know how long, Dad speaks again.

'It's been hard for all of us,' he says.

I could have missed it; he spoke so quietly. The words came from him but they seemed to catch in my chest. I want to turn and look at him, but I am afraid of what I might see. Instead I press my fingers on the warm skin near my heart and hold them there, on the bit that now feels heavy like something is stuck. We sit in silence for a few more minutes.

'Chloe!'

A shrill cry. Dad and I both look up. It sounds like my name but seems to come from above, carried on the wind, or maybe dropped by one of the seagulls circling the beach.

'Chloe!'

Someone *is* shouting my name, throwing it hard across the beach, an impatient scream. Ella, of course. Dad slides

202

his arm from around my shoulders and we turn in unison to sit up and face the sea, Dad lifts his hand to shield his eyes and chuckles pointing.

'Someone's trying to get your attention.'

Ella, who seems to have forgotten that she hates me, is waving and beckoning to me. She is bouncing up and down, the water splashing higher around her waist with each nudge of a wave. I hope the boys have noticed that she is getting too deep. Marco has a pink plastic bucket, probably stolen from some poor child on the beach. He is throwing water at Luca and Ella in glittering arcs lit by the sun. Luca jumps backwards to avoid being hit and slips under the surface. He comes back up laughing and coughing, water pouring off his head and shoulders, trying to wrestle the bucket out of Marco's hands. Ella uses her hands as a scoop and sprays more water over them both. I watch them all kick and splash playing in the water like little kids. Marco catches me watching them. It's too late to lie down and pretend to be asleep. He waves impatiently. 'Come on!' he shouts. I shake my head, slow and exaggerated, as though I am the one who is moving through water. Marco pretends to be fishing and mimes throwing a rod towards me and then reeling it in. Ella copies him and finally Luca does the same. As they coordinate the move, they look like they are performing a strange dance to pull me into the water.

'I think they are trying to tell you something,' says Dad. 'Go.'

'I'm tired,' I shrug sadly. 'And my ankle still hurts.'

I can't leave him. The umbrella has shifted position and I am now sitting in the full sun. The heat presses on my head and shoulders. My legs are folded up to my chin which I rest on my knees.

'You're fine,' says Dad, poking me in the ribs.

'Ow!' I cry.

He jabs me again in the ribs.

'Go. For. A. Swim!'

Each word is punctuated with another jab until I am squealing. I try to fight him off tipping over on to one side and kicking with my legs.

'Oh,' he says suddenly looking over me across the beach. 'Here comes your Mum.'

I'm up. I kick off my sliders and quickly wriggle my shorts over my hips, treading them into the sand. I'm running. After sitting hunched in the heat, it feels amazing to stretch out my legs as though I had forgotten what it feels like to move. There's a slight twinge in my ankle but it's nothing. Ella, Luca, and Marco start cheering. To everyone on the beach I know that this will look like I'm running towards something, but I know that I'm running away.

Sand scorches my feet. I weave between the groups on the beach, jumping over sandcastles and half-dug holes, toes catching on discarded spades, tangles of seaweed and food trays half-buried in the sand. I reach the edge of the water and plough into the cold. My feet scratch on the shingle, a strip of crushed shells and stones at the edge of the water, and I push through that first shock of the cold water hitting my toes, then calves, then thighs. The others splash towards me, the movements of their arms and legs exaggerated. Then there are two shrieks, both of which come from me. The first shriek is the shock of Marco's cold hands wrapped around my bare waist, and the second is him lifting me up to throw me into the sea.

*

The swim has taken the heat out of everything, and for the first time today I start to relax. I've almost made it, nearly the end of the worst day of my life. Just tonight to get through, and then tomorrow I can go home. I don't know what happens next, but I don't want to think about that now. Ella is slurping and gulping down another can of Fanta.

'How many of those have you had?' I ask.

'One,' she lies.

Then, she pretends to think about it and changes her answer to something she thinks is more believable.

'No, this is my second,' she says, smiling at her own cleverness.

She takes another irritating slurp, followed by another, and then burps without covering her mouth. She's disgusting, I can smell it. However, the swim seems to have washed away our argument over the magazine and I haven't got the energy to row about anything else. Luca and Marco catch up with us nudging in either side of me, so that Ella is pushed slightly ahead. We're heading for the far end of the beach to the fairground rides. There are only a few old rides that have been there forever but it's something to do.

The sun is low now, making it hard for me to look ahead. The four of us, me, Luca, Marco and Ella, are making our way slowly along the dark, flattened sand at the water's edge, bumping against each other, laughing and chatting. Ella and I drag our feet through the shallows,

205

splashing each other with gentle kicks and giggles. Luca and Marco are sometimes ahead and sometimes behind us involved in one of many competitions like jumping over the tiny waves as they hit the sand or seeing who can skim a stone the furthest on the now almost flat surface of the sea. We watch them bounce one after another across the blue-grey water leaving steppingstones of ripples, before disappearing with a final splash.

Ella is pouring the contents of her can on the ground. She is transfixed by the orange puddle bubbling up at her feet then disappearing into the sand.

'It's orange then it's gone,' she says. She burps loudly again then laughs.

'Don't waste it,' says Marco.

He takes the can and chugs it back. He then throws it in a long arc down the beach. He and Ella chase it like dogs.

'Hi,' says Luca. 'Okay?'

I didn't realise he was walking so close to me. His voice is soft and casual but its unexpected sound makes me jump. I wish people would stop asking me if I'm okay. Or maybe he just means 'hello'. Either way I nod and force a small smile. At least he's talking to me. I'd been so wrapped up in thinking about last night, I had forgotten about Luca being weird at the party. All that seems like nothing now. He chats about which ride looks to have the shortest queue but before I can think of anything to say Marco appears and they argue about what to go on first. The queue for the Waltzers is longer so we head for the Twister. Even that wait is too long for Ella. She jigs on the spot swinging her arms from side to side like a rag doll. She looks feverish. Her fringe is tangled and stuck to her damp forehead. Her face is flushed with what could be sunburn, her nose shiny and raw looking. Did no one put sun cream on her today? In contrast with her pink face, her lips have a white dusting of sugar from the doughnuts that Marco bought when we first started queuing. I couldn't eat anything. There's no room for anything inside me today. Marco tried to tease a doughnut near my lips, but I batted him away, trying not to show how irritated I was.

We're close to the front of the queue now. The music for the ride is deafening. The speakers distort the sound as if it's trying to escape from the black heavy boxes hung above our heads on the side of the ticket booth. I can just make out the words of the song. The vibrations thud in my chest painfully. There's a metal barrier separating the queue from the Twister. I curl my fingers tightly around it as though I'm on the ride already. The paint is peeling and prickly, but the metal underneath feels cool.

'Nearly there, nearly there!' says Ella jumping up and down to get our attention. 'Me on first! Who's with me?! Who wants to sit with *Chloe*?'

Her emphasis on my name indicates that I am the booby prize.

'Me,' say Luca and Marco in unison.

They look at each other surprised. There's a pause as we all take this in. Luca looks embarrassed. Marco styles it out, hands raised in a defensive gesture mouthing 'Mate?' at his brother. Luca mouths 'whatever' looking away. I feel the beginnings of a blush, that horrible, embarrassing heat that starts somewhere within me and before I know it will have spread up my face and across my whole body. Ella is already red in the face and furious.

'What?!' she wails. 'Why doesn't anyone want to sit with *me*?! I don't want to be on my own-n-n.'

She drags out the last word with all the weariness of the day.

'I'll sit with you,' I say quickly.

'I don't want to sit with you,' she whines.

'Then choose, anyone, it doesn't matter,' I say, trying hard to keep the impatience out of my voice.

The queue is shuffling forward, we're up next.

'I'll sit with you,' says Luca.

He steps forward and puts his hand on Ella's arm above the elbow, guiding her up the steps that seem too deep for her short legs. The flashing lights throw rainbow streaks on to her blonde hair.

'I don't know, I don't know,' she says, not liking being rushed onto the ride. 'I want to sit with Marco too-o-o.'

A man who could have been the same age as us or ten years older, a lumpy money belt strapped to his waist, points at a seat and I climb up into it. It's Marco that jumps into the seat next to me. The sound of Ella complaining is lost in the music which is even louder now we're on the ride. It's the same song over and over again. *One Last Time.* The bar comes down squeezing me across the waist. As soon as the ride starts, we swing backwards and outwards, and Marco is pushed towards me.

'Woo, hoo!' shouts Marco.

I clench my teeth as the ride whips us round faster. Marco's hip presses hard into mine. He reaches further up the bar to try and pull himself away from me, laughing with the effort. He can't help it. It's something to do with centrifugal force. I learnt about that in science this year. I should have tied my hair back; it cuts across my face and I breathe in a few strands and cough. As my hair is thrown back again Luca and Ella's seats cross close to us. Before they move further away, I catch sight of their unhappy faces. Luca has his arm around Ella and her face is turned towards his chest but she's not smiling or whooping like she normally is. Perhaps she's still sulking about everyone wanting to sit with me. *What was that about? Weird.* Oh no, we're speeding up again. I grip the bar tighter, my knuckles white and tense. Marco has given up trying to separate himself from me and he is welded to my side. At least if the ride is speeding up that means it's nearly over. I want to close my eyes but know that will make me feel worse. Instead I see Luca and Ella swoop towards us again. Ella's face is distorted, her mouth gaping open. Luca is trying to hold her body up above the bar.

The ride ends and Ella just makes it to the bottom of the steps before she throws up. A revolting fountain of puke erupts from her mouth falling on to the sand. Luca jumps back so he is not caught in the splatter. Marco runs down the steps and grabs Ella's heaving shoulders. He pulls her hair away from her face but not before something gloopy gets stuck in it. My stomach turns and I am afraid that I am going to start to retch. I know it's horrible of me, but I hate people being sick. As Ella pukes again, I clamp my hand over my mouth as though it might come out of me too.

Ella is sobbing hard, her shoulders shuddering violently. There's another explosion of vomit, then another, then it stops. She cries harder for a few more minutes, clutching her stomach, while Marco makes shushing noises. Then she takes a few big gulps of air and draws her hand across her mouth. Sticky trails of sick hang from her fingers which she shakes to the ground. A lady rushes forward pulling handfuls of tissues out of her bag, asking if Ella is okay. Luca has found a bottle of water for her to drink. Ella gulps the water down so fast I think she's going to make herself sick again. It dribbles down her chin and she wipes her mouth with the back of her hand again. She looks less feverish and even manages a smile as the lady hands her more tissues. I should step forward and help but I am paralysed at the top of the steps. People are starting to push past me to get on the ride, having taken a wide circle around the dark stain of vomit on the ground below.

'Ugh, that is rank,' says Marco.

'Disgusting,' says Ella half proudly.

They all stare at the pool of sick at Ella's feet. It has a faint tinge of orange like the Fanta she drank earlier. I look away. Ella pours the remaining water on to it as if she's going to make a sand pie on the beach.

'Stop it,' I cry out and start making my way down the steps.

Marco pulls Ella away and Luca kicks sand over the vomit. Away from the ride, we gather around her.

'That was some vom-fest, I thought you were going to empty everything out including your brain,' says Marco.

He taps her on the head, and she jumps to grab his hand.

'Feeling better then,' he says.

Ella lets me put my hand on her forehead. She's surprisingly cool to the touch. She takes my hand and keeps hold of it, smiling sweetly as we start walking.

'Sorry I smell,' says Ella. 'I know you don't like it.'

As we make our way back up the beach, I keep glancing at her to check she's okay. She's a different person to the one before we went on the Twister. It's as though she's been purged of everything, all the fizzy pop and junk food, the ride, the sun, the anger over who to sit with, and all the over-excitement of the late night and our last day. I look at her enviously. I wish I could feel like that. I wish it was that easy for me to feel empty and light again.

*

The adults are going out for the evening – *without us* – this is new. They are leaving Marco to 'babysit'. Marco folds his arms across his chest and smirks at his brother. Two spots of colour appear on Luca's cheeks, and his lips almost disappear as he presses them together in a narrow line. I just roll my eyes. *Who cares?* Mum and Dad leave me at home on my own, so everyone knows it's only Ella who needs babysitting.

They have booked a table at a restaurant in the village: Mum has always wanted to try it. It has white tablecloths and looks dark inside even when it is open. Each table has its own cute vintage lamp that sheds a little pool of light around the people eating as though all the tables exist in their own separate worlds. Mum said it looked romantic. *Are you looking forward to it?* I think nastily. *Who do you want to be romantic with?* Without warning I have stupid tears in my eyes again. Angrily I blink them away and exaggerate rubbing my eyes to pretend I have something caught there. I hate feeling like this. I glare at Mum. She is standing by the kitchen counter taking a long time to organise the inside of her handbag. She keeps taking things out – lipstick, keys, phone, tissues, hairbrush, purse – rummaging around inside for something, then putting the items back carefully as though she is counting them. The others are waiting. Toni stands by the caravan door, a jacket folded over his arm. Helen shifts from one foot to another. She is wearing a fitted black dress and gold sandals with little heels which look amazing but totally out of place in our old-fashioned caravan. Dad is wearing his one shirt and jacket that Mum makes him take on every holiday 'just in case'. His shirt has two creases down the front where it was folded in his bag. For possibly the 10th time, Dad says, 'You ready, love?' Mum looks deep in thought staring into her handbag. The corner of her mouth is caught between her teeth, twisting the scar above her lip even more. I remind myself not to stare.

Just go, I think.

'We don't want to lose that reservation,' coaxed Helen.

Please go, I silently beg. The thought of a few hours not having them here – not having *her* here – is heaven. One more evening. *One Last Time.* Then I can go to bed, wake up, and go home.

'Lizzie, love, come on, you've got everything,' says Dad.

He touches Mum's elbow gently and it seems to wake her. She nods slightly and picks up her bag. People start to move. Toni, his hand already on the door handle, pushes it down and with a click, cool air steals around the room touching each of us in turn. I shiver as I feel the chill on my arms but it's not just the cold, something else seems to have crept into the room, a feeling of excitement and anticipation of a night without the adults, something different from our usual holiday routine. I can feel some of the tension of the day slipping away from me. *This could be fun.*

Dad puts Mum's jacket over her shoulders. Out of habit, Mum turns to the caravan mirror to have one last hair and makeup check. The maps and pictures that covered the mirror have been stripped away and the other Mum's reflection is back where it belongs. However, when Mum sees her, she turns away quickly. Her hand moves to her scar, then quickly drops before her fingers touch it. At least she's put more concealer on it although you can still see the redness underneath.

I glance at my own makeup in the mirror. I set up a YouTube video in our bedroom earlier and tried some new techniques. I love my eyes. The shading has worked really well, and my eyebrows are perfect. My foundation looks much smoother too; you can hardly see my freckles. I lift my phone up to my face and take a couple of quick selfies, staring straight into the camera. I might post them later – maybe. I'll try taking some more in the bathroom where the lighting is better. Ella keeps blowing kisses at herself in the caravan mirror admiring her cherry lips.

Mum wasn't very happy when she saw Ella's makeup. She also tried to blame me for Ella being sick. The second we got back from the fairground rides, Mum laid into me, saying I should have been 'looking after my sister better'. I think we could all feel that this was going to blow up into a massive row, in the same way that you can feel the tingle in the air before a thunderstorm. We stood face to face on the beach. I pressed my tightened fists against my bare legs. Mum's face was half in shadow under her wide-brimmed hat, but I could see her colour darken as I told her that it wasn't *me* that let Ella stuff herself with junk food all afternoon and get sunburnt. Everyone was packing up the beach things around us, strangely quiet for once. It was like that silence you get before the first rumble of thunder. However, before Mum could reply, Ella pushed herself between us and insisted that none of it was my fault, *which it wasn't*, but no one ever cares about the truth do they? Ella said Marco gave her the doughnuts and fizzy drinks *which was true*, and she told Mum that I had told her not to have them, *which was not true*.

Mum stared at us both her expression believing and not-believing. I met her gaze and for once did not feel afraid. This was something I could argue about. As Mum finally turned away, Ella squeezed me on the arm and pushed a secret thumbs-up into my stomach. I slapped her hand away, but only gently, whispering 'You need to clean your teeth, stinky face, I can still smell the puke'. Ella chuckled and trotted off to collect the buckets and spades she'd scattered across the beach like giant confetti.

Before the adults leave to go to the restaurant there is a last-minute shower of dos and don'ts. Mainly don'ts. *Don't use the oven... don't light the barbeque... don't overheat anything in the microwave... you can order pizza but ask who it is before you open the caravan door... you can sit outside but not when it's dark... don't play loud music... don't leave the caravan site... don't leave the caravan... don't fight... don't argue... call 999 if there's a problem, then ring us.*

'Yes, yes, yes,' says Toni pushing everyone towards the door. 'Come on, come on, I can hear the taxi.'

Before she disappears, Auntie Helen fixes Luca and Marco with a dangerous look, one eyebrow raised a millimetre higher than the other. She waves a warning finger at them, and keeps it pointing at Marco a fraction longer. Marco's easy smile shrinks a little, then almost disappears as she holds his gaze just that bit longer. Then her face relaxes, and she smiles and blows a kiss to the room, hurrying out after the others, into the night.

Outside, car doors are slamming. There is the rev of an engine and the crunch of tyres turning on the gravel path. The sound grows fainter until all I hear is my quickened breathing. Ella kneels on the sofa bench and lifts one of the lacy curtains. It forms a veil above her head. There is a glimpse of red lights receding into the darkness. Finally, *finally*, they are gone. No more dos and don'ts, no more tension. I have a sudden urge to giggle hysterically but before I can make a noise, a voice I don't recognise cuts through the silence.

'Right,' says Marco, his tone is business-like, grown up. We all turn to look at him as though a headteacher has walked into the room.

'I've promised Mum and Dad I will look after you properly. I don't want to let them down so this is what's going to happen...'

His expression is deadly serious... *what is going on?*

'...I'll order pizza...'

Marco looks around the room without making eye contact like when people are practising giving presentations at school.

'...We'll play a few games of cards and hopefully, there's time for a movie – PG of course.' He nods at Ella.

215

'And I want you all to be ready for bed, although, not actually in bed, by the time our parents get back.'

Ella and I stare at Marco speechless for what is probably only a few seconds but feels stretched out in time. Luca takes a step forward, his body tense, however, before he or the rest of us can say or do anything, Marco's expression transforms into a broad grin like a magician revealing a trick.

'HA!' he shouts, making me jump. 'Gotcha! THE FLOOR IS LAVA!'

There's a second of delay as we all realise what is going on and then a chorus of shrieks as we scramble to get off the floor. I love this game! Ella is already on the sofa bench, and I take a running leap on to a section further down. Marco has hopped on to the coffee table, which creaks under his weight. Luca has the hardest job. He was leaning up against the kitchen counter, so he leaps on to the dining table using one of the stools as a steppingstone. His other foot slips on some pizza menus scattered across the table. Ella cowers on the sofa bench below him. She folds her arms over her head to protect herself. Amazingly, Luca keeps his balance. He puts his hands on the caravan ceiling to steady himself.

'A-a-a-and MOVE!' shouts Marco, counting slowly to 10 as we all circle the room. 'And STOP!'

Oh my god, I am in hysterics. I clutch my stomach. It hurts. I also think I'm going to pee myself. Luckily, I'm curled up on one of the dining chairs desperately trying to keep my feet from touching the floor. We do this about three more times before Luca comes crashing down after attempting to leap from the kitchen counter to the sofa on the other side of the room. Even with his long legs it seems like a suicidal move. Launching himself, his back foot accidentally kicks some mugs off from the kitchen counter and there's a collective gasp as we wait for the smash. Miraculously they bounce, making a dull thud as they hit the floor just before Luca hits the floor with a much louder thud. The caravan shakes and the windows rattle. I can feel the floor buckle even though I'm not touching it. We laugh harder half out of fear that the whole caravan is about to collapse.

'Out!' we scream.

'And go!' shouts Marco. Luca rubs his leg and back and groans. The rest of us scramble across the nearest surface. Two more rounds and we are all panting and out of breath again.

'Stop, stop!' I beg, my sides aching with exertion and laughter.

I am declared the winner after Ella rolls off the coffee table when attempting a ninja slide on to a wobbly footstool. She lays sprawled out face down on the floor, shrieking with laughter into the fluffy rug in front of the fire.

The caravan doesn't have proper sofas, although it looks like it does. The sofa is more like a padded bench that runs all the way around the walls of the caravan underneath the windows at one end. Every sofa cushion has slipped on to the floor and I start grabbing at them and rebuilding the sofa enough so that I can lie down. Marco and Lee do the same. Ella is still giggling into the carpet, waving her arms and legs like a beetle that can't turn over. I lie on my side, one arm dangling towards the floor, the other running a hand across my sweaty forehead. I'm exhausted, but that was brilliant. Marco slips on to the floor, his head resting back on a sofa cushion, eyes half-closed. Luca lies full length across the sofa at the end of the caravan arms stretched out behind him. His hands and feet almost touch wall to wall.

'I think I've broken something,' he groans.

'Wimp,' says his brother.

While we get our breath back, we survey the damage to the room. The remaining sofa cushions are scattered across the room, two chairs are knocked over, and one of the curtains hangs loose from when Marco grabbed it to walk along the window ledge. Newspapers, food menus from the table litter the floor. An assortment of jumpers and coats have been pulled off the pegs by the door and lie in a sprawling heap like a pile of bodies. *Mum would go mad if she saw this*, I think gleefully. Marco is following my gaze.

'We'll sort it out,' he says. 'While we wait for the pizza.'

Pizza. Hot cheese stinging my gums and tongue. *Ow, ow, ow!* Can't stop though. Can't wait for it to cool down before I sink another bite into the scalding yumminess. I've eaten nothing today and now I feel empty. I reach over to get some chicken nuggets and practically have to fight Ella to get my hand in the bucket. She is stuffing two into her mouth.

'Watch it you,' I point at Ella. 'You'd better not be sick again.'

Ella just grins at me, her teeth full of breadcrumbs and pizza sauce. Marco and Luca are sharing a 'Hot and Spicy' daring each other to pile all the jalapeno peppers up on a single slice. Marco slips another can of beer from the rucksack he has at his feet, the one he hid amongst the piles of shoes and bags near the door until the grown-ups had gone out.

He offers another one to Luca who waves it away. I don't think he's drunk much of the one he's got. Marco is zipping up the rucksack again.

'What about me?' I ask. 'Don't I get one?'

'Chloe, Chloe, Chloe,' tuts Marco, eyebrows raised in mock horror. 'You keep surprising us. Here you go.'

He throws me one then zips up the rucksack and pushes it under the table. *Why not,* I think. I'm not a baby. Everyone at school seems to get drunk every night from what I see in their posts. I push aside my juice box, place the beer on the table, and snap open the can. The sound attracts Ella who reacts like I am about to rob a bank.

'Chloe! Oh my gosh!' she exclaims. 'You're not allowed. *You'll get in trouble.*'

'We'll all get in trouble, Ella,' sighs Marco. 'So how about you zip it unless you want us all to get arrested.'

He digs his fingers into her ribs, and she doubles over giggling and shrieking at being tickled. Backing away from him, she looks excited now by the rule breaking.

'Can I have another juice box then?' she says, helping herself to one without waiting for a reply.

Feeling that all their eyes are on me, I take a sip of my beer which is mainly froth. I try not to wince at the taste of the bitter liquid underneath. There is something sweet about it but it's also just as gross as I remember from when Dad let me try some of his. I take one more sip but tighten my lips so not much goes in my mouth. I casually put the can back on the table in front of me as though I do this every

219

day. Marco takes a big swig of his, tipping his head back, and then puts his can next to mine.

We put a movie on. There are only normal TV channels in the caravan, but we have a stack of DVDs that Gran and Grandad have collected. Ella chooses *Mrs Doubtfire*. We've seen it a million times, so it plays in the background and we only tune in for our favourite bits. Most of the time we're watching memes on Marco or Luca's phone. Luca is obsessed with them and likes to read them out in this robotic voice he copies from YouTube.

> *'Announcement: The Queen is dead.*
> *The World: Stopped existing 2,000 years*
> *ago.'*

> *'Prehistoric man is unfrozen from ice.*
> *He sees the Queen. 'Hi, Liz, weren't we at*
> *school together?'*

It's so stupid but I'm belly laughing at everything. I bet my eye makeup is ruined as I keep having to wipe my eyes. Ella laughs even when she doesn't understand half the jokes and to be honest, at one point I'm laughing just because we're all laughing.

When the film finishes Ella makes us play cards. We play a few rounds of Cheat, then game after game of Uno which is Ella's favourite. I feel like I'm back at the fairground because playing games with Ella is a rollercoaster. She shrieks with delight when she gives me a 2+ or 4+ card but wails like the world is ending when she picks up two or four cards of her own. She makes us swap places around the table so that different people are sitting either side of her as one by one we're accused of being mean or cheating. A whine is creeping into her voice which would normally get her packed off to bed if Mum and Dad were here. *But they're not here.* I hug the thought to myself. This is the best night we've had on holiday.

Ella's not the only one annoying me when we are playing cards. It doesn't matter what we do or what we play, it all becomes a battleground for Marco and Luca. I know they are competitive, but they seem particularly bad tonight. I'm getting fed up of being dragged in to decide whether something was a *cheat move*, or *who has won more games*, or *who won more games last time we played*, or *who deals faster*, etc, etc.

'Chloe, come on, I'm right,' pleads Marco.

At one point he puts his arm around me and pulls me closer to him on the bench to demonstrate I am literally on his side. Luca watches us, and there's a little pause before he speaks. I used to think he was struggling to find something to say, or not wanting to argue with his brother. He's a much quieter person than Marco. However, Marco gets so agitated when Luca doesn't respond straight away that I suspect that Luca pauses deliberately to get a rise out of Marco. Luca uses silence like a weapon. Marco often interrupts before Luca has spoken, but then Luca will interrupt him with something much more crushing before Marco's finished his insult. It's like watching an aggressive tennis match played with words and insults that feel like metal bats and bombs. It's always been funny watching them wind each other up, but tonight it's exhausting. Maybe because we are stuck inside, maybe because there is no Auntie Helen to tell them to shut up.

I think about Helen, Toni, Mum and Dad at the restaurant. I wonder if they are enjoying their meal. Will it be awkward? *Are they going to talk about it?* Is that why they went out? Fear catches in my throat; I push the feeling down to my stomach. I'm not thinking about that tonight. Nothing will happen. They've just gone out for dinner. I concentrate on our game of cards.

After what feels like the 400 millionth game of Uno, I push my cards across the table and sigh. Stretching my arms above my head I look up at the yellowing ceiling. It feels too close. I wriggle out from behind the table to get a glass of water from the kitchen. Luca moves his legs to one side to let me by but doesn't say anything. He, Marco and Ella are hunched over his phone watching, then re-watching a video, collapsing into laughter every time a kid gets hit on the back of his head with a model plane. I've seen it before.

The pizza has made me thirsty and I gulp down a whole glass of water before filling it up again. The room is stuffy. The others are loud, their voices bouncing off the caravan walls. I feel like I'm hearing everything twice.

My head is starting to ache. I walk over to the caravan door. The handle seems to release before I've even pushed it down. *Click.* A gust of cool air hits me. It's like opening a fridge on a hot day. I gulp down the cool air feeling instantly better. The breeze creeps around me, lifting the hair off the back of my neck. I feel pulled, or maybe pushed, to the top of the caravan steps where I lean on the handrail.

The field is quiet, dark and sleepy. The windows of the other caravans give off a soft glow where their curtains are drawn. The only other light is the dim, old-fashioned streetlamp that stands near the entrance to the beach path. I can't see the entrance, which is hidden in the darkness, but I know it's there. An animal calls out and the sound makes me shiver. The moon is high and bright, shining above where the beach must be. There's a movement behind me. I look over my shoulder to find Ella, Marco and Luca standing together watching me as though they are waiting for me to say something.

'Let's go out,' I say.

'We're not allowed!' says Ella quickly. 'It was one of the don'ts. *Don't* leave the caravan!'

'Where?' says Marco.

They're all staring at me. No one ever asks me. The breeze ruffles my fringe. I think of the moon over the beach.

'Dunno,' I say. 'Just a walk.'

Marco looks at Luca. Luca shrugs.

We decide to leave the lights and TV on in the caravan so it will sound like someone is home, however, I can't find the key to lock the caravan door. I open and close drawers in the kitchen and search the floor near the doorway in case the key got knocked out when we were playing 'The Floor is Lava'. Everyone has their shoes on and we're ready to go. I stand by the door wondering what to do. Mum and Dad must have taken the key accidentally. I bite at the skin around my thumb nail.

'Leave it. It'll be fine,' says Marco putting his hand on my shoulder. 'Quick walk on the beach. We'll be back in an hour.'

He's right and it feels so good to be outside. We try not to make too much noise making our way to the entrance of the beach path. It is only a few minutes' walk, but I look around nervously, worried someone will see us and ask what we are doing. We're giggling and shushing each other, infected by the knowledge that we are doing something we shouldn't. Underfoot, soft grass gives way to the gravel at the top of the beach path. I'm wearing sliders and my bare toes catch on the sharp stones. The first section of the track is wide and lit by the old streetlamp. Moths spin around the light, bumping against the bulb. We've been to the beach at night with Mum and Dad once or twice to look at the stars. I know that in a few moments the path will turn sharply to the left and the light won't reach there. I hesitate, suddenly afraid of plunging into the dark tunnel ahead. I'm conscious of the others close behind, pressing me forward. *Perhaps we should go back?* However, Marco steps forward. I can feel the warmth of his body next to me. He switches on the torch on his phone. Luca does the same on the other side of me. Finally, Ella squeezes through us and stands up front. She is wearing a head torch strapped around her hair with a thick elastic loop. The three circles of light overlap each other like silver umbrellas forming a shield between us and the dark.

'Ready?' says Marco.

I feel like he's talking to me although he probably means everyone. I'm not the leader but I've started something.

Dark hedges loom up on either side of us. The path has high stone walls which are overgrown with thick shrubs and branches that scratch my bare arms. I'm wearing a cropped, sleeveless hoodie and I wish I'd worn something warmer. The air feels cooler here as though we have disappeared underground. At least I swapped my shorts for leggings. As we shuffle down the path the cold sand scooped up into my shoes feels like water splashing my toes. I keep glancing up at the dark blue sky. The moon is only just visible above the black walls closing in on either side of us. We could probably see the stars if Ella, Marco and Luca weren't swinging their torches around.

> *Star light, star bright,*
> *The first star I see tonight.*

We walk in a tight knot bouncing off each other with jokes and comebacks. We stumble together over the uneven ground, bumping against the sides of the hedge and then each other. Marco and Luca take any opportunity to push the other into the bushes. Suddenly, Luca trips, lurching forward grabbing at anything – arms, bodies, clothing – to steady himself. He nearly brings us all down on the ground. Our shrieks quickly become hysterics. My sides are aching again from laughing. After our near miss, Luca keeps his torch aimed at the ground on the lookout for stones and tree roots that we could trip over.

As we get used to the dark, we loosen the little knot we've formed inching along in the path. Space opens up between us and Marco and Luca drop back a little while Ella is slightly ahead of me. As Ella walks, the movement of her head swings the torch light from side to side and up and down. The shadows shift with the light. It looks as though something is moving through the hedges on either side of us, sometimes ahead and sometimes dropping behind. I don't say anything, the others will think I'm stupid. I know it's just a trick of the light, but it could be Salty Dog nosing along the path beside us. There is a nip in the air. I shiver. I tuck one arm across my stomach enjoying the warmth of my own skin. I keep my eyes down following the beam of my torch illuminating my pale feet. The polish on my toenails looks faded. The night has drained everything of colour. The stones, rock and grass that make up the path are just shades of grey.

Marco and Luca fall into step either side of me, elbows occasionally bumping against me. They continue their normal teasing and arguing sometimes reaching across me to emphasise their point or deliver a random slap to the other. Then their teasing turns into play-wrestling and they crash into the hedges showering all of us with leaves. Ella and I shriek and flap at the creatures sent fluttering out of the bushes. Every time Ella turns around her head torch shines straight into our eyes and we shout at her to turn it off. She just laughs and skips ahead.

'I think I can hear the sea,' she calls over her shoulder.

I don't know how long we've been walking but she might be right. A breeze slips between us. The path is widening, and the walls fall away. Our torch light fades as it tries to light up the entire beach. Whoosh! Walking out into the open we are caught by a blast of wind. I gasp as though I've been holding my breath. Maybe I have.

'Woo hoo!' I shout into the wind.

The others take up the echo. 'Whoop, whoop, whoop!'

We can hear the gentle lapping of the waves. The sea is an inky strip across the horizon. The moon sits in a halo of cloud above. The beach feels huge, grey sand stretching into the distance before being swallowed up by the darkness. We are the only ones here. It looks so different at night. Normally the sand is broken up with beach mats and umbrellas but tonight the beach is ours. I spread my arms like wings and before I know it, I'm running in a wide circle around the empty beach. The wind rushes over my face and body. *Is this what it feels like to fly?* I run faster, flapping my arms like a bird. I feel free. I want to take off and I jump as high as I can. Ella copies me. We loop around each other swooping and leaping across the sand. I imagine myself floating in the air, gliding over the beach like we see the seagulls do every day. We call out to each other in our best bird impersonations: 'Caw, caw!' Eventually I'm out of breath and I slow to a stop, my feet shuffling in the cold sand, the grains scratching my toes. My heart is beating fast in my chest like wings. Ella carries on running up the beach. She's switched on her head torch, and the beam looks like a plane making its way across the night sky. My cheeks are burning from running in the wind. I'm panting, my heart a heavy *thump-thump*. I place my hand on my chest to feel the rhythm. I realise that Marco is watching me from a few feet away. He's smiling. I straighten up feeling self-conscious.

'What?' I ask him.

'Nothing,' says Marco.

Ella and I are running again but this time towards the sea; Marco and Luca follow us across the soft sand to the water.

'Leave your shoes here,' I say to Ella. 'If the tide comes up, they'll be safe.'

Marco and Luca are still struggling out of their trainers. I take Ella's hand as we tiptoe carefully across the shingle at the edge of the water. I hate the sharp stones but it's only a moment. Our feet slap across a stretch of flat wet sand. This is probably where our sand pictures would have been before being washed away. Ella and I splash into the chilly water, shrieking and dancing. The boys catch up with us and we grab their hands. Marco tugs us further into the sea. I gasp as the ice-cold water splashes up my legs soaking my leggings. We howl and cheer and shout crazy things into the night air. The wind seems to snatch the screams and laughter out of our mouths and carry it across the beach in a continuous echo as if there are 400 of us, not just four.

Despite the breeze, the sea at the water's edge is calm enough for skimming stones. Marco and Luca search for the perfect flat stone and compete to see who can get the most bounces across the water. Ella and I try too. She's much better than me and joins in the competition. I stand with them but I am watching the relentless rolling of the waves. How does that huge swell out at sea end with these tiny ripples lapping at my toes? It doesn't seem possible that something so big can end in so little. It's like when you've been expecting something terrible to happen, but it turns out to be nothing. I think about Mum and Toni. This feels huge but will it just be a ripple? I hope so. I shake my head as if trying to dislodge the worry. I promised myself I wouldn't think about it all tonight. I look down at my feet, the water gently washing over them. They are so cold they don't feel like they belong to me. Something brushes my arm. It's

228

Marco. He taps his phone and the screen lights up showing the time.

'I hate to kill the vibe, but I think we should go,' he says. 'They'll freak if we're not in the caravan when they get back.'

He means the parents. I'm shocked at how long we've been out and disappointed that we have to leave. I want to stay here all night. However, I nod at Marco, secretly a little surprised that he's being the sensible one. He takes a few steps away from me calling to Luca and Ella. The wind has picked up and whips around my legs. I'm starting to shake with cold now. Luca trots up with Ella riding piggyback behind him.

'I can't walk,' announces Ella, princess-like. 'The sea has turned my feet into icicles, so now Luca's my pony.'

'You mean he's an ass,' says Marco.

Luca holds his middle finger up to Marco. Luca's hand is in front of his stomach so Ella can't see the gesture from where she is sitting behind him.

'Shut up,' says Ella. 'He's a very good pony.'

She pretends to feed Luca a sugar lump which he eats from her hand then makes a whinnying sound. Ella grins and strokes his 'mane'. Luca looks deadpan at me and rolls his eyes. I can't help but laugh.

'Come on,' says Marco.

It should only take a few minutes to reach the entrance to the beach path, but I am out of breath. My legs are tired and stiff from standing in the water, and walking across the soft sand seems to suck the energy from me as I sink further with every step. Before we start walking back up the path, I turn and take one long look at the open beach and sea, trying to fix it in my mind like a photo. I want to remember that feeling of running across the beach at night, my arms spread like a bird, then running into the water and howling at the moon.

Marco walks ahead, the light from his torch penetrating the darkness. I keep mine trained on the floor to stop us tripping. We're walking uphill now. After maybe five minutes, Ella cries out.

'My torch! My head torch! I've left it on the beach. We need to go back.'

'Just leave it,' says Marco. 'We can pick it up in the morning.'

'The sea will take it,' wails Ella.

This is what Dad tells us when we can't be bothered to tidy up all our beach stuff. I think about Mum's strict packing regime. Ella's torch should have been put in her bag today. She'll notice if Ella has taken it out. There will be questions.

'We won't have time in the morning,' I say.

'Do you remember where it was?' asks Luca.

'I left it with my shoes, near the sharp stones,' says Ella.

'She means the shingle,' I explain. 'Where we were paddling. Pretty much opposite the entrance to the path. I can go.'

I don't want to go alone though, all the way back in the dark.

'Ella and I can find it,' says Luca. 'I might need a sugar lump though.'

Ella happily feeds him one. Then he tosses his head as though he is throwing back his mane, and jogs back down the path to the beach with Ella bouncing and giggling on his back. We can still hear them after they have been engulfed by the dark. Marco turns off his torch so that it's just mine lighting up our feet. It is eerily quiet with the others gone as though they took all the sound with them. My legs are aching and I rest my bum against the rock wall being careful not to lean back into the bushes. There's less growing here on the walls but I don't want to disturb any moths or bugs.

'I'm glad I came,' says Marco.

'What?' His voice is so quiet I wasn't sure he'd even spoken.

'The holiday,' he says. 'I thought it would be a bit lame turning up at the end of the week, but it's been a right laugh. Seeing you – and everyone.'

'Yes,' I say.

It has been good, despite everything else. Marco arriving made us all fit together again like the last piece of the jigsaw. Ella and I won't see him and Luca again until Christmas probably. Or will we? All day I've been desperate to go home but now the thought of the future scares me. *What will happen with Mum and Dad?* A thousand images flash through my mind as though I'm fast forwarding through a movie; Mum explaining, Mum and Dad arguing, and then the image of something worse. A wave of anxiety rises up so quickly it threatens to tip me over like a sudden swell in the sea. My legs feel unsteady. I place my hand on the cool stone behind me and try to take in a deep, slow breath to calm me down. The rock is so cold it feels wet as if that Salty Dog is pressing his nose into my palm. I'm so lost in my own head that I don't notice Marco moving to stand in front of me. I glance up into his face surprised at how close it is to mine. He stares at me intently, his teeth just catching his bottom lip. He looks – that's odd – he looks nervous but Marco's never nervous, so I wait for him to make a joke. Instead he brings his face within millimetres of mine and then kisses me lightly on the lips. The warmth feels good against my cold face, but I'm so shocked I freeze as if I'm part of the cold stone behind me. The only thing that moves is my eyelids, slowly fluttering open then closing like a butterfly drunk on a flower. Marco's mouth covers mine more firmly. His breath smells faintly of beer. My head is pushed into the moss and plants growing on the rock which tickle and scratch the sides of my face. Marco strokes the back of my neck and his fingers creep upwards into my hair. His other hand slides behind the small of my back as though he's stopping me falling backwards. The rock where I am leaning juts out at the bottom, so my hips are pushed forward, and my back is slightly arched. Marco's lower body is pressed hard against mine. We stay fixed like this for a few minutes, my eyelids and his mouth the only moving parts. Finally, he releases my lips and whispers into my hair near my ear in a husky voice that I don't recognise.

'Oh, Chloe.'

His voice sounds like he's pretending to be someone else, someone older, someone not Marco, however, it doesn't *feel* like he's pretending. His breath on my ear makes me shiver but I'm not cold anymore. He kisses me again on the lips. Marco is a good kisser. Well, I think so. I suppose he would be. Our mouths are moving together now. I presume it's the shock but something like electricity is running around inside me, starting in my stomach and working its way deeper down through my body. It feels like I want to go to the toilet but I don't. I hope not. I clench between my thighs just in case. I don't understand. I thought we were just friends. I try to think about whether we should be doing this but it's hard to concentrate. Then for a while I don't think about anything.

You know when you're on a rollercoaster that you think is going to be okay, but then suddenly you are upside down and going faster than you've ever been before? That's how I start to feel. Marco still has one hand on the back of my neck and the other is tracing shapes on my lower back underneath my cropped hoodie. The heat from his hand is intense against my cold skin. I feel like I'm watching it's progress up my body rather than feeling it. The fingers slide under the strap of my bra and pull me closer against him. Marco's mouth moves faster. I wince as his lips press painfully against my teeth. A trace of stubble, which I've never noticed before, scratches my chin. I try to move my head back, but his tongue fills my mouth and I'm pinned against the rock behind me. My eyelids flutter faster, a butterfly caught on a pin.

Marco's body presses into mine and his hips feel like they are bruising me. The rough stone is scratching the back of my legs. My phone – my torch – has dropped to the floor so there is only darkness around us. I feel claustrophobic. I can't breathe. I want to scream. Panic swells in my throat. If I could see the lighter sky above us it would calm me, but Marco's face is too close to mine blotting out everything. *Can you forget you have arms?* Mine have been limp by my sides this whole time laid against the cold, dead rock as though they had no part to play in any of this. Thankfully I remember how to use them and bringing my hands back to life, I slide them between us, my palms flat against his chest. His body is radiating heat, his T-shirt damp. I push, gently at first, as though I'm testing my strength. Marco responds by squirming against me. He stops kissing me for a second and I take a huge gulp of air as he moves his mouth over my neck, tiny kisses pricking my skin. The tingling sensation puts me back on the rollercoaster again. It's exciting and frightening but I want to get off.

Stop, I say in my head. *I don't like it now.*

He can't hear me; he can't hear the thoughts in my head. I have to tell him. The hand under my bra strap is inching its way across my back to the side of my body.

'Marco,' I croak. 'Stop.' Then finding something like my real voice, I whisper, 'Wait. Please. *Stop.*'

My hands press at him more firmly, pushing hard enough to create a small space between us.

'Marco!' I say sharply, as if trying to wake him and myself up.

'Mmm,' says that strange voice, his hot breath in my ear.

I brush my hand down the side of his body until I find the soft space under his ribs then dig my fingers in hard. Marco cries out, jerks backwards releasing all the pressure on my body. Cool air fills the gap between us. He stares at me, blinking and bewildered, as though he's come up out of a tunnel. He rubs his body where I poked him. My fingers ache from the pressure.

'Ow! Chloe! What the hell? What's the matter with you?'

'Nothing,' I say even though that's not the right answer.

'Oka-a-ay,' he says.

His face is crisscrossed with confusion and he starts to lean towards me again. I shuffle sideways like a crab using my hands to move me along the rough stone so that my back is to the path and not the wall.

'I think we should go,' I say.

It's hard to talk. There's a big lump in my throat that is trapping my breath. The mingled sounds of our heavy breathing are amplified in the dark.

'Chloe-e-e,' Marco's voice is strange again. 'Come o-o-on, stop mucking around. We've got to wait for the others so we might as well…'

Marco gestures in the dark to the place against the wall where we were kissing. It seems a long time ago now.

'No,' I say.

That's what they tell us at school. No means no. No means stop. No doesn't need any explanation.

'Yeah, but…' says Marco. 'You were having fun, weren't you?'

Maybe there are different types of no. I try to speak more firmly but it's hard when you're trying not to cry.

'Yes,' I say honestly but then seeing his face light up I quickly add, 'But no, as well, I mean, I just want to be friends.'

'Oh, yeah, right, sure.' Marco's voice is flustered but it sounds like him again and not the stranger that was talking before. We stare at each other but without really seeing, both of us struggling with our own thoughts. There's a horrible, horrible silence until he mumbles, 'Are you okay?'

I nod although I don't know whether he can see; his face is all shadows to me. When he speaks again, doubt has crept into his voice like something has crawled out of the shrubs and bushes that line the walls of the path.

'Was I not doing it right?' he asks quietly.

'Yes,' I say. 'Of course.'

I'm confused at why I am having to reassure him. Marco is always boasting about how many girlfriends he's had, or at least how many more than Luca.

'But… I don't want to do this – anymore,' I finish.

I'm edging a little further away from the rock wall where we were leaning. Marco takes a step back as well. We don't look at each other. I feel around on the sandy ground for my phone. He shines his torch on the floor to help me. I'm grateful to feel my fingers close around my phone as though I've found an old friend. Tears are welling at the back of my eyes. I blink them away while I fiddle with my phone screen. I switch on the torch, aiming it near my feet just for something to look at that is not Marco. I can hear him breathing hard. Then he speaks, his voice cracked with worry, a river of words rushing towards me.

'Oh god, Chloe, I'm sorry. Are you okay? I thought you liked it. I'm so stupid. I thought… no, I shouldn't have. I mean, we were getting on so well and… I thought… Shit. We were just kissing but maybe… No, sorry. Honestly, I thought it was okay but – *Shit*.'

Marco has his hands on either side of his head as though someone's put a gun to his back. He looks panicked.

'I'm fine,' I say. I try to smile. 'It's fine.'

'It's not fine. I thought… I mean… I forgot you were so young,' he says.

236

A prickle of irritation changes my mood. People are always telling me that I'm too old for this and too young for that. *Don't I get to decide?*

'Did I... did I hurt you or anything?' Marco asks quietly.

His voice is the most unsure I've ever heard it. I think he might cry before I do. Actually, I don't feel like crying now, I just feel exhausted. It was all a stupid mistake and I want to forget about it.

'I'm fine,' I say trying not to sound impatient. 'I just... it was a surprise and then I thought I did, but then I didn't want to. I – I like you but... we're friends. Right?'

I try to make the 'right' as upbeat as I can. It's the way Marco would say it. I desperately want things to be normal.

'Friends,' Marco says the word as if it's new to him. He rubs the space between his eyes trying to scratch something out. Then he lets out a great sigh and puts one hand flat on his chest as though he is checking the tension leaving his body. He finally makes eye contact and grins. 'Hell, yeah!' he says in a voice I recognise. 'Mates forever.'

He high-fives me then gestures for a hug. When I hesitate he laughs.

'Don't worry, I'm not going to snog your face off. This ain't *Love Island*, you know, just Dorset.'

He's being a bit fake but at least this is more normal Marco. That's what we both need.

'Are you *sure* you are okay?' he asks again looking me right in the eye. 'No drama?'

'No drama,' I repeat.

Marco hugs me in his warm lively way and we stay like this for a minute or so. I rest my head on his shoulder amazed at how calm and peaceful I feel now, however, as soon as I think this, my eyes fill with tears. Then something is fluttering and choking and rising out of my chest. I am crying my eyes out.

'Oh god, Chloe, no,' says Marco in a panic. 'I am so *so* sorry.'

'No, No,' I try to say.

'I'm *such* an idiot,' says Marco.

'No, it's not you,' I manage.

Shut up, I think. *It isn't about you*. I want to tell him what's wrong, but I can't. I can't tell anyone. I'm gulping, trying to get a breath between sobs. I want to wail like a little girl. I can feel the snot starting to drip from my nose, but I don't wipe it away. I just let the tears and snot run down my face and it feels good not to care.

'Chloe, you have to tell me,' Marco's eyes are wide with worry.

'I – I had a row with Mum,' I sob.

I can sense his relief. His hands are on my upper arms and the tension gives in his shoulders.

'Hey. Hey!' he says soothingly rubbing my arms gently. 'That's normal. You should hear the rows my mama and I have. Do you want to talk about it?'

It would be so great to share this with someone, but I can't. Gran always says that a 'trouble shared is a trouble halved' but she's wrong. This trouble will be doubled, quadrupled. I must keep this secret otherwise it will hurt Marco too. And Luca. And Ella. And Dad. I let Marco hold me and allow myself a few more minutes of uncontrollable sobbing. Then I stop. I let the storm pass.

'Are you having a good holiday?' says Marco breaking the silence.

I laugh. I can't help myself. It's only a quick snort, my face muffled in the front of his now very wet T-shirt. Marco stands back letting me take in a few deep breaths. He keeps one hand on my shoulder as if to steady me. I sniff loudly and wipe my nose across the back of my hand. Urgh, it's slimy and I rub it on the back of my leggings. I wish I had a tissue. A noise makes me turn my head. It sounds like rocks falling against each other or the ground shifting slightly. Luca is standing a few metres away from us. His white clothes glow brightly in the half-light, but his face is in shadow. I wonder how long he has been standing there.

'What's wrong?' asks Luca.

Instinctively, Marco and I look at each other, then at anything except each other. Embarrassed, I take a couple of steps backwards, turning my face away. I quickly wipe my hands across my face.

'Nothing,' I say trying to sound light.

'Chloe, are you okay?' says Luca.

'She's fine,' says Marco.

'I wasn't asking you,' says Luca.

There's no doubting the aggression in Luca's voice. A look passes between him and his brother. I don't like it. I don't understand it. It's written in a special code that only Marco and Luca can decipher, a code developed by brothers over many years.

'Where's Ella?' I ask

'Having a pee,' says Luca. 'Couldn't wait. She's just round the corner. Told me to walk ahead.'

Luca is watching me, a strange expression on his face. His eyes flick between me and Marco. *What did he see?* I think. *The kiss, the sobbing, the hug?* I work my way back frame by frame through all the things I don't want Luca or anyone to have seen. Ella arrives a moment later, out of breath, kicking up stones as she skids to a halt.

'I had to pee, but no one saw. I didn't have a tissue so I had to shake it.'

She demonstrates, shaking her bottom, expecting us to laugh. She looks round at her silent audience, temporarily blinding us all in turn with that stupid head torch.

'What's going on?' Ella asks. 'Have you been crying, Chloe? Are you *okay*?'

'I'm fine!' I snap. I wish people would stop asking me that. Then seeing Ella's face fall, I add more gently. 'I stubbed my toe, and it really hurt. But I'm okay now.'

'Poor you,' says Ella. 'I stubbed my toe once and it was AGONY.'

'Come on,' I say walking quickly ahead. 'We need to hurry if we're going to be back before Mum and Dad.'

There's a very different vibe now from when we walked down to the beach. It's a quiet trudge uphill, no chatter or laughter to make the journey quicker. I start out in front, but Marco and Luca soon overtake me. My leggings are soaked and cling to my aching legs. It's an effort to lift them. I can't believe what's happened in the last hour. *What did Luca see? Why did Marco kiss me? Has he always liked me?* It already feels like something that must have happened to someone else, like a story in a magazine. I've been over the scene with Mum and Toni so many times in my head, it feels like I'm reading one of those stupid photo stories in

Kute magazine. The black and white pictures even remind me of how it looked at night, all colour drained away. Now I can add the story about Marco kissing me to my own special, tragic edition of *Kute*.

> *Kute Magazine. August 2019*
> *Caught getting off with your best friend by*
> *your other best friend?*
> *Will this holiday drama never end?*

I can see this one set out in photos ending with Marco and I being discovered by Luca, 'the boy she kissed a few days ago' the caption will read. Then 'To be continued…' *I hope not.* Why does everything have to be so complicated?

We've reached a narrower stretch of the beach path where it's easy to stumble on the uneven ground. I take Ella's hand although she's skipping along like a goat. The beam from her head torch cuts the darkness back and forth like a light sabre fight. The boys are in front of us. I'm not sure how it starts but either Marco or Luca trips and bumps into the other. It's dark and I'm concentrating on watching my step, so I don't know who gets bumped first. The one that gets bumped pushes the other one roughly, who retaliates even harder. They are not play shoves like they normally give each other. Each push sends the other brother crashing into the hedge on either side. Tiny dark shadows are sent fluttering out of the bushes making Ella and I squeal. We flap our hands above our heads until the moths or whatever they are spiral upwards into the night. The fight, for I think that's what this is now, is starting to spiral as well. I squeeze Ella's hand and pull her out of the way as the boys stagger together across the path towards us.

'Cut it out,' jeers Marco at Luca.

I don't think Marco has realised he's in a real fight. He's trying to laugh off the fact that Luca has both arms around his waist and is trying to hook one leg around Marco's ankle. Luca is taller and probably stronger, and Marco topples over with Luca landing heavily next to him. Marco is quick though; he rolls over and scrambles to his feet. He dances backwards grinning at Luca. There's not a trace of humour in Luca's stony face. He sprints from the floor, like an athlete, and runs straight at Marco. Marco steps aside and Luca bumps into the side, where the bushes are thin. His elbow thuds against the wall and he cries out in pain. Marco's expression says, 'you had that coming'.

'Stop it!' yells Ella in her 'Mum' voice. 'You're being stupid.'

Marco laughs and turns his back on Luca to start walking again. Luca watches him for a moment. Then calmly Luca takes a step forward and lifts one of his long legs heel first towards Marco. Luca kicks Marco hard striking him in his lower back. Marco cries out and is propelled forward by the blow. He staggers but I think he's going to keep his balance. However, his feet seem to get tangled around themselves, or perhaps he's caught his foot on a tree root like Luca did on the way down to the beach. Then Marco is falling awkwardly into the dark. I hold my breath. He seems to disappear for a moment swallowed up by the shadows. He hits the ground at the edge of the path nearest the rock walls. There is a sickening crack. It's the kind of noise that you feel rather than hear. Marco lies

242

motionless. *Oh god, he must have hit his head on a rock.* None of us move. Marco is submerged in the darkness on the floor of the path ahead. Luca staggers a little as though he's been hit as well. Then he leaps forwards and drops to the floor next to Marco's body.

'Marco, Marco!' he says urgently.

'I think he hit his head,' I whisper. Fear seems to have stolen my voice.

'Shit, shit,' says Luca.

Ella is crying. Someone is groaning. I think it's Luca but no, oh my days, thank goodness, it's Marco. I can't believe it, he's moving. He's pushing himself up into a sitting position. I rush to help Luca lift Marco up on to his feet. Once he's standing, Marco pushes us away.

'I'm fine,' he growls.

Even in the shadows we can see the pain written all over Marco's face. Tentatively, as though he's afraid to, he touches his head where he must have hit it. Luca tries to support his other arm but Marco bats him away.

'F– off' he shouts at Luca.

I move behind Ella and put my hands over her ears. It feels like a stupid thing to do but she's already seen the fight and the fall, she doesn't need to hear the rest. She's whimpering. Her shoulders shudder and in between each little sob she sounds like she is struggling for breath. Marco's breathing is ragged. I don't feel like I can take a breath at all. Luca is still, his hand still reaching out for his brother.

'Bruh,' Luca says, a crack in his voice. 'Let me look at your head.'

There's a trickle of something that looks like black ink running down the side of Marco's face. Ella is still wearing the head torch and when she looks directly at Marco he is illuminated as though caught in a stage spotlight. He flinches at the beam. However, the torch is transforming what was shades of black and grey into full colour. We all reel in shock at the sight of Marco's face smeared with blood. Ella screams raising the hairs on my arms. A bead of blood bulges from a gash above his right eyebrow. Ella screams again and again. The blood seems to run faster as though she is controlling it with her cries. Marco reaches up to touch the cut again but winces in pain. He stares in disbelief at the blood dripping from his fingers. Swearing he wipes his hand across his T-shirt leaving an ugly stain. I know I need to help but my feet feel stuck. I can't take a step. Ella shrieks and flaps her arms. We're like two sea birds trapped in oil. Luca grabs his brother by the arm.

'GET – OFF,' says Marco.

He attempts to shove him away again, but Luca stands firm. He shines his torch at the cut above Marco's eye. Marco protests, squinting and twisting away from the light. Luca turns to me, his face stricken.

'He needs a bandage,' says Luca. 'We need to stop the bleeding.'

I open and close my mouth, trying to process what he is saying. I wrack my brain, but I have nothing on me that we could use. Ella's cry has now settled into a high-noted wavering whine like a dysfunctional car alarm.

'Shut her up,' snaps Luca.

I spin her around to face me and wrap my arms around her tightly so that there is no space left between us. Like a flame starved of oxygen she stops shrieking. Her shoulders shake and the front of my hoodie quickly becomes damp with her tears. Luca is stripping off his shirt, pulling it over his head. Without Ella's head torch I am watching the scene in a dark monochrome. Luca's chest looks pale and vulnerable in the darkness. He bundles up his white T-shirt and presses it against Marco's head. Marco is protesting all the time: 'It's nothing, get off.' Luca holds it there ignoring him.

We are staggering up the track. I feel like we've been walking forever but it's probably only five minutes. Marco is holding the T-shirt against his head now. He's keeping up a commentary about how *he's fine, it's just a little cut, can everyone stop freaking out, let's just get back to the caravan and you can find me a plaster and a beer, little twat brother wrong-footed me, you got lucky*. His tone is all the usual swagger and sarcasm we expect from Marco, but his voice is weak, wavering at times which must be the pain.

Luca walks close beside his brother and when Marco slows down or trips on the path, Luca puts a hand out protectively. Every time it seems Marco might fall Ella and I cling tightly to each other as though something terrible is going to happen rather than has just happened. I'm half-dragging Ella who is sniffing loudly. Her head is slumped against me but there is just enough light on the ground from my torch to stop us from tripping on the stones and clumps of grass. I realise my feet are bare. I don't remember taking my shoes off. *How could I lose my shoes?* I want to tell the others and make a joke of it, but nothing feels funny right now. We turn the corner and see the old-fashioned streetlamp at the top of the path. It usually seems dim and gloomy, but tonight it feels as bright as a lighthouse guiding us home. We stumble the last few steps together, bunched close around Marco. My bare feet catch painfully on the gravel on the last stretch. When I feel the grass under foot, I know we are safe. However, of all the things that have happened tonight, the worst is seeing Mum, Dad, Toni and Helen standing outside the caravans, waiting for us to get back.

'Chloe! Ella!' calls Dad.

'Boys!' calls Toni.

They start walking towards us, but their pace quickens when they see Marco holding the T-shirt to his head and Luca supporting him. Auntie Helen's pale horrified face looms at us like an angry moon rising out of the darkness.

'Marco!' she cries out. Then seeing his face, 'Oh my god, oh my god. Toni! Look at him!'

What happened? What happened? People are repeating and talking over each other until the words muddle together into just noise and confusion. Our group splinters into two. Helen, Toni and Mum gather around Marco and Luca. Dad stays with Ella and me.

'Daddy,' says Ella, her voice tiny.

She lifts her arms and Dad scoops her up. I feel a painful stab of jealousy. I'm tired too. Mum, Helen and Toni examine Marco's cut. They are talking in low voices. Mum runs into the caravan and returns with our first aid kit. Marco is put in a camp chair. Luca sits on the grass close to his brother. Helen and Mum put a thick white pad or gauze over Marco's cut and stick it in place with white tape. Marco's face distorts in pain as they touch it. I hear him cry out. It's still bleeding, I can already see a stain leaking through the dressing. Toni has put his jacket over Luca's bare shoulders. Luca holds his blood-stained shirt in his lap. Dad, Ella and I watch silently.

'I'm sorry, Dad,' I say just to break the awful silence. I want to hear his voice.

'We'll talk about it tomorrow,' he says. 'Are you okay, Chloe-Bear?'

For once I don't mind someone asking me if I'm okay or using my baby name. Marco's wound dealt with, Mum appears at our side firing questions like bullets. 'Where have you been? What happened? Did he fall? Where did it happen?' It's too fast. My brain feels woozy. Nothing is easy to explain. I answer the only thing that I'm sure of.

'We went for a walk.'

'Don't feel bad, Chloe,' says Ella sleepily. 'It was good until it wasn't.'

'What?' says Mum glaring at me. 'Was it your idea?'

We are distracted by an argument erupting between Helen and Toni. Helen is sitting in a chair next to Marco; she has her arms wrapped protectively around him. She looks up at Uncle Toni.

'I'll tell you whose fault this is. You think it's theirs but it's yours!' shouts Helen jabbing a finger up at him like a dagger.

I have never ever heard Auntie Helen shout, but her words fill the caravan site like a roar. A light turns on in one of the caravans closest to us. I couldn't ever imagine her quiet voice being capable of this noise. It's like hearing a babbling brook scream.

'You think it's funny when they fight, do you? Like they are 'real' boys.'

I can't hear Toni's answer as he is speaking more quietly but his hands are moving rapidly.

'No!' yells Helen at Toni. 'You brush it off, but I am SICK of it. It's like you and your brothers. *Boys will be boys*, eh? Fighting! Frightening girls! Frightening each other!' She gestures towards Ella and I. '*Drinking. Disobeying their parents*. No wonder your mother was grey at twenty. I want better for these two.'

I can feel the force of Helen's words in my chest like the shockwave from a bomb.

'Look at his face,' she says gesturing to Marco. 'And this one,' she points to Luca, 'is scared to death because he thinks he's half-killed his brother.'

Toni puts his hand on Luca's shoulder.

'That terrible cut,' she murmurs anxiously to Marco. 'You're going to need stitches.'

She cradles Marco's head against her as though he is a little boy even though he is the same height as her.

'It's nothing,' says Marco. 'Don't fuss.'

It doesn't look like nothing. Mum and Helen have cleaned up his face with some wipes, but he is still streaked with blood. His eye looks swollen although it's hard to tell under the white padding they've strapped over it.

'You stupid boys,' continues Helen turning her fury on them. 'What on earth were you doing on the beach at night? Now look at you!' Then tenderly she asks, 'Are you dizzy, darling?' She strokes Marco's cheek. 'You might have a concussion.' Then angry: 'Fighting! Always trying to beat each other. You have to look after each other like brothers not enemies.'

'Sorry, Mama,' say Marco and Luca in unison.

They look shame-faced, eyes cast down.

'You never know when bad things will happen,' scolds Helen. 'You have to be there for one another.'

After she says this, I notice Helen exchanging a look with Mum who gives her a little nod.

'And don't think I can't smell the alcohol,' Helen scolds.

'That was only me, Mama,' says Marco. 'I was the only one drinking.'

That's not true, Luca and I had some.

'Are you sure you're not dizzy?' Helen whispers to Marco. Try not to move your head. 'Papa's getting the car. We're going to the hospital.

'I don't need to go to hospital,' groans Marco. 'It's just a tiny cut.'

'Shut up!' says Helen. 'You'll do as you're told for once.' Her voice softens again. 'And Luca, darling, Papa's getting you a sweater from the caravan. You must be freezing.' And then, furiously, she adds. 'Of course, if you hadn't knocked him over you wouldn't be covered in your brother's blood!'

It hurts my head trying to keep up with the changes in Auntie's Helen's mood. It's like watching TV when someone is flicking through the channels. Dad is still holding Ella. I rest my head against him. He unhooks an arm from Ella and puts it around my shoulder. I snuggle into the warmth.

'It was an accident,' says Marco. 'And it was my idea to go to the beach.'

'Well you can bloody well apologise to John and Liz,' says Helen. 'They trusted you to look after their girls.'

I don't need looking after, I think. I remember Marco's kiss and the red rushes into my cheeks. Luckily no one is looking at me. *And why is Marco taking all the blame for everything?* He knows it was my idea to go for a walk.

Toni is back. Luca pulls on the hoodie his Dad hands him. They all help Marco to his feet and walk slowly towards the car. Helen is still talking but I can't make out the words or whether she's sympathetic or furious. Dad mutters about getting us both off to bed, something I normally resist, but tonight I think it's the best thing anyone has ever said to me. I also need to change out of these wet leggings. Mum's voice cuts through my thoughts.

'What did Ella mean? Was it your idea to go to the beach?' she asks sharply.

She catches me off guard. The easiest thing would be to lie but I start to waffle.

'Er… it might have been. I don't remember. Anyway, everyone wanted to go.'

I don't like the way she is looking at me. I want to catch up with Ella and Dad. They are walking up the steps to our caravan.

'You were supposed to be looking after your sister. She's only nine. Why would you take her down to the beach at night?'

'I didn't make her go,' I snap.

'Oh,' says Mum. 'And she was supposed to just hang out on her own in the caravan while you lot go on a little jaunt.'

I don't want to talk about this. *How dare she blame me!* Her, of all people. I take a step towards the caravan, but her hand is on my arm. I shake off her touch angrily.

'I'm going to bed,' I say.

However, Mum hasn't finished her interrogation.

'I'm waiting for you to tell me why you thought it was a good idea to take your nine-year-old sister on to the beach at night. Anything could have happened. And it did! And why were the boys fighting?'

Shut up, I think. *I'm so tired.*

'I don't know,' I say. 'They were just mucking about, and then, it all just kicked off.'

That bit is true.

'So, it *all just kicked off*,' she repeats, in a tone that clearly means she doesn't believe me.

'You think it was *my* fault?'

'I don't think it's anyone's fault, I'm just trying to understand what happened.'

I explode.

'You blame me for everything! It's *always* my fault. Never Ella's, never Dad's, and never YOURS!' I yell.

'Don't be silly, Chloe,' she says. 'Marco's had a serious accident and we need to know what happened.'

I can't believe what she's saying. She's blaming me after everything *she's* done. *I hate her.*

'Chloe, what is the matter with you?' continues Mum. 'You've been in a terrible mood all day and now all this! I trusted you.'

'I trusted you!' I shout. 'We trusted YOU!'

I throw the words at her and then run in the direction of the beach path. I wasn't planning on going back there but there is no other way out of the field here, so I run down the gravel path and plunge into the darkness. I don't need to turn on my torch as I can't see anyway. Tears are running down my face blinding me.

'Chloe? Chloe?!'

Mum's voice is following me, her voice shrill and panicky. I stumble on down the track, this time holding out my phone as a torch. It's not so bright when there is only one circle of light to follow. My hand is shaking so much the light is a blur. The shadows along the walls move with me. Not Salty Dog. Not a friendly cold nose sniffing at my hand. Something that makes me not want to look left or right. Branches reach out and catch my hair and clothes. The twigs and stones pull at my bare feet. *Where are my shoes?*

'Chloe! Chloe!'

Mum's voice is high and strained. It lifts like a seagull calling overhead. I imagine the bird watching me from above, following me over the path. I don't want it to see me, but I don't want to be alone. I stop running. I hear footsteps. A figure rushes out of the dark towards me. It's Mum.

'Chloe!' Her voice is drenched in relief.

For a moment our hands grasp each other in the dark. However, when she reaches out to touch my face, I slap her hand away. I don't expect it to make contact like it does. The sound is awful and my hand stings. We stare at each other, equally stunned at the blow.

'Leave me alone,' I say defensively.

'Chloe,' says Mum. 'What's wrong? What is all this?'

The dark hedges either side of us lean closer as though they are listening.

'You're a cheat. I hate you!' I shout.

The words seem to bounce off the stone walls, repeating themselves back to me, mocking me.

'You're a cheat,' I say again. 'And a liar.'

I clasp my hands together around my phone. My chest feels tight. I try to remember those breathing exercises from school. I don't think those exercises are designed for real situations, when you are trapped in the dark, worried that your whole world is falling apart. I don't want this. *Why did any of this have to happen?*

'Chloe...'

Mum's voice is calm and gentle. It's the kind of voice people use in films to coax crazy people away from the edge of a roof when they are about to jump. Well, I'm not crazy, I know what I saw. She takes a step towards me.

'Go away,' I shout.

'Chloe… love,' says Mum. 'What is it?'

'I saw you kissing Uncle Toni after the party,' I blurt. 'Between the caravans, in the shadows. I saw you kissing. It was YOU. I know it was you.'

My words fall into the darkness between us. It's like we are standing on the edge of a deep well of silence and I'm waiting to hear the words hit the bottom. Mum says nothing. I can't see her face properly in the dark so I lift up my torch light, but I still can't read her expression.

'Did you hear me?' I demand.

'Yes,' she whispers.

'So?... Say something!' I yell.

'It was nothing,' she says eventually.

'Nothing! How is that *nothing*?' I cry.

Mum watches me with a worried expression. My breath is ragged now. I bend over and put my hands on my thighs.

I notice the bracelet that Auntie Helen gave me on my wrist, a ring of little silver seagulls catching the light from my torch. I wish I was back on the beach with Ella, flying like birds, feeling free. Now I feel trapped and sick. I think of Ella, earlier, doubled over on the beach puking out all the junk food she'd eaten. Now I've said it, and it's out of me, now I've told Mum what I know, why don't I feel better? I stare at the grey sand at my feet, its smooth, soft texture. It's nothing like the churned-up mess that Ella left behind near the fairground rides. At least with that we could kick it over and walk away. I start to cry. I hardly realise I'm doing it until my tears make a little pattern of dark indentations in the sand like raindrops. Then quietly across the dark and the silence, her words and arms reach out to me.

'Chloe…'

'No.' I push her hand away.

'Chloe, please…'

Her voice is all wrong. She should be angry, or defensive, or ashamed. Instead the words are thick with sympathy, sympathy for me. Her tone is exactly the same as if I'd told her about an awful day at school, or I'd fallen and hurt myself badly. The sound of it instantly makes me cry more. Her arms reach through shadow towards me, but I stagger backwards swinging my arms out to push her away.

'No!' I shout. 'Don't come near me. How could you? *Why?* Why would you do that? How could you do that to Dad? He loves you.'

Mum's voice is layered with tears.

'Chloe, I'm sorry, you shouldn't have seen that.'

'You shouldn't have *done* that!'

'Yes, that's what I meant,' says Mum quickly. 'I definitely shouldn't have done it. But you shouldn't have seen it.'

A sob breaks from her like something that can never be fixed.

'Then why did you do it?' I whisper.

'Oh god, Chloe, I'm so sorry. How do I explain?'

'Are you having an affair?'

I throw the question at her not wanting to hear the answer. Mum looks genuinely shocked.

'No! God, no... Chloe, it was a stupid mistake. I had drunk too much wine and...'

I interrupt her angrily.

'No! That's no excuse! People always say that.'

'Yes, but... No,' she pauses a moment 'You're right. However, sometimes alcohol can stop you thinking clearly. It's no excuse but sometimes people do silly things when they've had one glass too many. Usually when they are not feeling very brave.'

I think of the beer that Marco drank. Would he have kissed me if he hadn't drunk it? I push the thought away. It doesn't matter now.

'It's all just excuses,' I say. 'I'm not a baby. I know about alcohol and drugs.' They go on about it at school all the time.

She is closer to me now. I'd stopped backing away while I listened to her. She stares around her as if she is searching for the right words in the dark. Eventually she sighs and draws her hands down her face like she's removing a mask. She speaks softly but firmly.

'Chloe, I'm so sorry. I have been far too wrapped up in my own problems lately. It's just... it's just been hard with...' Her hand flutters to her scar but she lets it drop without touching her lip. 'But I promise, there is nothing wrong with your Dad and I.'

I'm listening carefully. Her voice is soothing. I don't want to yell anymore; I want to hear something to make it better.

'I've had a horrible time recently,' she continues, her voice a little shaky now. 'And... and I've been feeling sorry for myself, which is okay, because I'm allowed, but sometimes, when you feel sorry for yourself, and you don't feel attractive anymore, and you get upset, and a good friend tells you, you are still beautiful, then sometimes you might do something stupid and kiss them, but instantly know it's a mistake and it's embarrassing...'

Her voice trails off and she turns her head as if ashamed. *She should be ashamed.* Yet watching her face it's hard to feel angry. She runs her hand down the back of her hair then tucks it behind one ear, smoothing out the ends. The hair thing is a habit, she does it when she's thinking about something.   After a moment of staring into the darkness she looks at me again.

'That's what happened, Chloe. Nothing else. Please believe me. I was feeling sorry for myself, and I made a mistake. Toni is an old, dear, friend who doesn't deserve whatever you are feeling about him right now. It was stupid, we were drunk, and it will *never* happen again. I love your Dad, and Toni loves Helen. Very much. I'm going to tell Dad as soon as we get home. I just didn't want to tell him here because, well, I know it probably doesn't make sense to you but that kiss really was nothing. Although I can see that it has been everything to you. I just wanted to forget all about it. But I *was* – I am – going to tell your Dad.'

Mum takes a deep breath. She's closer to me now, her hand reaches out for one of mine. I want to slap it away again but when I feel how cold her fingers are, I wrap my warmer ones around hers. She whispers now but her voice is steady and calm. She looks me straight in the eye.

'I'm so, *so* sorry that you saw that. This was a very adult secret for you to try and keep. However, I don't want you to keep that secret for me anymore. It's mine, and I'm taking it back from you.'

The relief I feel is incredible. I don't have to carry the secret, that heavy sick feeling that's been sitting in the bottom of my stomach. It's like on the last day of term when the teachers make you take all of your schoolbooks home but you can hardly carry the bag. Then someone stops and gives you a lift in their car. It's such a relief not to have to carry that heavy bag those last steps home. She's hugging me. I let her.

'I'm sorry,' she says. 'I was stupid.'

I nod into her shoulder. I like the smell of her clothes. It's a mixture of perfume and her skin, maybe suntan lotion.

'It won't happen again,' she says. 'Never.'

I shake my head.

'You must have been so worried,' she says stroking my hair.

I'm crying. I don't know how I have any tears left after today, but it is so nice to cry and not have to hide it.

'There is one other thing, Chloe,' says Mum.

I tilt my head up to look at her, worried at what I will hear.

'Sometimes in life,' says Mum. 'You may kiss someone and then realise that you are kissing the wrong person. I'm not talking about what happened with Toni. I just mean all the people you are going to meet in the next few years and you mustn't worry about it.'

I think about Luca and Marco. *Does she know?* She can't. I put my head back on her shoulder. *Why are you telling me this?* I think.

'I don't know why I'm telling you this,' she says as if reading my thoughts. 'I just think at your age, you need to know that it is okay to make mistakes. People make mistakes. It's what you do afterwards that matters.'

'You're definitely going to tell Dad,' I whisper.

'Yes, I don't believe in secrets. As soon as we get home, I'll tell him. I promise.'

I can tell from her voice that she means it.

'Is there anything else you want?' she asks.

I want it not to have happened, I think. I want to go back in time to before Mum and Toni kissed. Before Marco kissed me. Before I kissed Luca. Before I found the copies of *Kute* magazine. Before I met Sophie. Before I went to secondary school. I keep going, my mind flipping back and back through memories. It's like turning over the pages the wrong way in a story until you get to the bit where you feel safe and secure. *Once upon a time...* The thing is though, there are a lot of good things that have happened since the *Once upon a time*. If I go back, I'll have to get rid of those memories as well.

It's late, 11.30ish maybe – I've left my phone inside the caravan – but not too late for Dad to decide to get the firepit going. Ella and I couldn't sleep so we all waited up to see Marco safely back from hospital. He has a cut and bruising, and a lot of explaining to do according to Uncle Toni.

'I can't believe we were seen in an hour,' says Helen. 'A&E on a Friday night where we live – ugh – that's normally a four-hour wait.'

She rubs her eyes, fingers resting on the worry lines between her eyebrows. She slumps in one of our sagging camp chairs around the fire. Her voice is back to normal though, steady and quiet, but heavy with tiredness.

'Thank goodness he's okay,' says Mum.

They are talking in low voices but as I'm sitting closest to them it's not too hard to hear what they are saying. Helen sighs deeply.

'Yes, just a cut, like boxers get. They glued it. It won't leave much of a scar, and it's very close to his eyebrow anyway. Apparently facial wounds bleed a lot because there are more capillaries or something in the skin.'

Helen pauses for a minute before continuing.

'I might have overreacted a bit,' she says with a flicker of a smile at Mum.

'No, no,' says Mum. 'It gave us all a shock. There was *a lot* of blood.'

'We have to keep a lookout for signs of concussion,' says Helen. She pulls a handful of scrunched up leaflets out of her pocket and gestures with them as though she could never be expected to understand what they say.

'He'll be fine,' says Mum soothingly.

'Don't you miss the days when a plaster and a kiss sorted everything?' asks Helen.

'I do,' says Mum, her voice is more like a whisper. 'I really do.'

She reaches over to Helen and squeezes her arm, letting her hand rest there for a minute. I fix my eyes on the flames and smoke weaving in and out of each other, so that it doesn't seem like I'm listening. I wish I wasn't now.

Our chairs are arranged in a straggly circle which draws tighter as Toni hands around the huge bag of marshmallows and some wooden skewers so we can toast them in the fire. Hands are wrapped around mugs of tea and hot chocolate. Ella, who is sitting on the other side of me to Mum, is blowing noisily across the top of her cup of hot chocolate trying to cool it down enough to drink. Mine sits on the ground next to my chair. I haven't touched it yet. Dad brings out blankets and wraps them around us one by one. They are 'Gran's blankets', that's what we call them, crocheted by her in clashing multi-coloured squares. Helen takes one as well and pulls it across her bare knees. She is still wearing the black dress she wore to the restaurant, now with an oversized fleece pulled over it. Her gold sandals pick up the dancing fire light.

When we were little Ella could never understand how Gran's blankets kept us warm when the lacy crochet pattern had so many holes in it.

'There's as much hole as blanket!' said Ella threading her fingers through the colourful net of wool.

'Ah,' said Gran. 'That's because I drop a little bit of love in each hole when I'm making them. That's what stops the cold coming through.'

'Wow,' said Ella, putting her eye to one of the loops in wonder. 'I think I can see it.'

I think she still believes it. She's such an idiot. However, as Dad tucks the blanket around my shoulders, I feel instantly cosy. I press one cheek into the soft wool and breathe in the sharpness of fabric conditioner mixed with that sweet musty caravan smell that never quite washes out. A yawn uses up what feels like my last scrap of energy. I struggle to keep my eyes open. When Toni reaches me, I jolt and wonder if I have drifted off for a few seconds. As if in a daze, I take the spindly wooden stick from him, keeping my eyes on the massive bag of marshmallows he waves in front of me. I know what Mum said about it not being his fault, but I don't want to look at him yet.

'Thanks,' I whisper taking a marshmallow.

I turn up the edges of my mouth in as much of a smile as I can manage right now. I want to hate him but it's hard when he seems just like Uncle Toni, not the shadowy figure I saw between the caravans the night before. I am so tired; I don't want to think about that anymore. I sink further into my chair, pulling the blanket up around my ears. I nibble at the squishy marshmallow; the sweetness is almost sour on my tongue.

On the other side of the circle, their faces disappearing in and out of the shifting smoke, Marco and Luca are transfixed by a marshmallow that Marco has managed to set completely on fire. Marco waves the stick in the air and the flaming ball leaves a trail like a comet. Their mouths are both open wide with laughter. Their chairs are pulled closely together, the arms overlapping. The only sign of what has happened between them tonight is the glint of white tape above Marco's eye.

Around the fire, our faces blend into the darkness, the flickering firelight giving me glimpses of who's who before they vanish again. It's hard to see where one person ends and the next begins. We look like one long dark creature curled around the fire settling in for the night. I've always thought of us like this, one thing, the Rossi-Carters. However, tonight everything feels fragile, like a curl of smoke that breaks and changes shape when the wind catches it. We've sat like this so many times before and I never thought it would be any different. Now I'm not so sure. Something brushes my arm and I'm startled, as if the smoke from the fire has reached out and touched me, or Salty Dog is pushing past my chair. It's Mum.

'Sorry,' she says. 'I didn't mean to make you jump.'

Her fingers gently squeeze my arm

'You okay?' she whispers.

No, I think but I nod, staring directly into the fire. Maybe I can be. For the first time in ages it seems possible. I stretch out my legs to try to warm my feet. Despite Gran's blanket, the hot chocolate, and the fire, the bare skin of my forearm, where Mum's hand rests, is the warmest part of me.

8

SATURDAY AGAIN

Ella's head looks cut off at the neck as she peers around our bedroom door.

'Chloe, come!' her voice is excited. 'Dad wants us.'

The head vanishes. I stuff the shorts that I'm holding into my rucksack and follow the sound of chattering voices. Dad is standing in the main room of the caravan, his arm tight around Mum's waist. She is smiling but her face is blotchy and the rims of her eyes bright red. My heart beats faster. *What's going on?* Dad starts speaking. His voice has an edge to it and I am worried that he is going to cry. Grandma Di, Mum's mum, went to our house this morning. Mum told her to open any post if it came from the hospital and she rang us straight away. After they removed the BCC from Mum's face the hospital had to test a tissue sample to check the doctors had removed all the cancerous cells. They were sure that they had but now the results are back it's definite. Mum won't have to have any more treatment. *Just time to heal*, says Dad. I can't quite take it in. I wasn't worried about this but now I've heard the news it's as though something has fallen away. Mum and Dad's faces also look lighter as if they've let go of something. Glancing at it today Mum's scar is tiny really in proportion to her face, to her, to everything, even though the feeling it gives me fills the room. It will get better though. It only looks twisted and bumpy because the stitches have just come out. The doctors said that with time and gentle massage it will flatten out and turn from angry red to a silver scar line, barely noticeable against her pale skin.

We're hugging, all of us, intertwined like one big teary game of Twister. Ella is in the middle of our tight circle, her face squashed into Dad's chest. She's too small for her arms to link with the rest of us. I'm almost as tall as Mum now so mine easily reach over Ella and around Mum's shoulders. I rest my head against Dad's. His arm is so tight around my waist I feel like he's lifting me up. There are sounds of crying and laughter all mixed up. It's that kind of day. Mum lifts her head and calls out to our speaker. She's got it set up with her phone.

'Play *Vogue* by Madonna.'

In a minute we'll all be dancing.

*

'Cheers!' says Toni.

He stands on the step of one of the caravans where we gather outside. He holds up a glass and toasts us all. We all shout 'Cheers!' back and clink our glasses together one after another. I don't know where Dad and Toni found champagne at ten o'clock in the morning. We're celebrating Mum's good news. It's nice but I preferred it earlier when it was just us in the caravan.

264

I sip my drink, it's a Bucks Fizz but mainly orange juice so it's not too gross. Even Ella got a tiny splash of champagne in hers. Now she's spinning around bumping into people pretending she's drunk. I don't know why people drink alcohol; everyone at school brags about it but it tastes disgusting. I feel like something is stuck in my throat. I take a gulp of my drink; the orange juice is sharp in my mouth. Someone hands me a plate. We're eating our last breakfast outside. It's not fried eggs on the barbeque like Dad wanted to try. Instead, we're having croissants, filled with ham and thin slices of cheese with holes in it, bought from Mr Jones's weekend shop. Dad couldn't resist toasting them on the barbeque. I take a massive bite of croissant. The cheese is melted and yummy.

'Hungry?' says Marco.

I jump as if a fly had buzzed in my ear. I hadn't noticed him move close to me. I'm leaning against the end of our caravan, just watching everyone and listening to the chatter. I gesture to my overfull mouth and chew so hard my jaw aches. I can feel sticky flakes of croissant around my lips and I try to wipe them off with the back of my hand, coughing as I try to swallow.

'Easy,' says Marco. 'I'm not trying to kill you.'

Marco looks worse this morning. The bruised side of his face is closest to me. The colours fan out from the cut above his eyebrow: blues, reds, purples. His eyelid is swollen giving him a sleepy look. Under the three strips of white surgical tape, his eyebrow is a mess of dried blood, and something shiny and congealed that catches the sunlight. It must be the glue. I want to have a closer look but it makes me feel a bit sick.

'Beautiful, aren't I?' he says. 'You should see the other fella. He's still a minger.'

He nods in the direction of Luca.

'Does it hurt?' I ask, my mouth finally empty.

'Nah,' says Marco then bringing his head towards me he whispers confidentially. 'Actually, it hurts like a bitch, but don't tell Luca cos I'm trying to man this one out. And don't tell the Mama either. I've got a club match in two days and she isn't gonna let me play if she thinks I've got a concussion.'

I laugh. The brief sound seems to fall into the space between us. We both look at the ground in silence.

'Sorry again about last night,' says Marco suddenly. 'I was an idiot and I...'

I interrupt him. 'It's okay,' I say, and it really is.

He looks so worried. That's the thing about Marco, he can be really irritating but underneath he's very sweet. I think I've always known that. He shouldn't have pushed me, but I know he's sorry. When I wanted to stop, he did.

'Cool,' he says. 'I just wanted to make sure. Also,' he falters and glances around us as though the right words might be hiding amongst the caravans. 'I'm sorry if I was getting in the way of, you know… anything between you and….'

He nods towards Luca. *What?* My cheeks flare red so quickly I put my hands up to my face as if to stop it spreading.

'No, no, nothing like that,' I say. The words rush out. I don't know who I'm trying to reassure, him or me. Embarrassed, I can't quite meet his gaze. I don't want to talk about any of this.

'Sure?' asks Marco.

'We're just friends,' I say trying to sound casual.

'Phew.' He pretends to wipe his brow, but he looks genuinely relieved. 'I've got to live with him.'

There's another pause. Are we both thinking about last night's fight? I still can't believe it happened.

'Friends is go-o-o-od,' Marco drawls in one of those weird accents he puts on when he's impersonating the gaming vloggers he follows. He gives me a little play punch on the upper arm. Then we spud each other, fists bumping gently.

'However, if you want to tell Luca what a good kisser I am that's okay with me,' says Marco.

'Shut up,' I say and whack him on the stomach with the back of my hand.

'Ow!' he protests. 'I'm injured.'

He's right though about being a good kisser. I'm going to take that memory home.

'And did you sort things out with your Mum?' he asks.

The question catches me off guard. *What does he know?* I fold my arms across my stomach.

'Last night,' says Marco. 'You were upset about the row with your Mum. I hope this didn't make it worse.' He gestures to his bruised face.

'It's fine,' I say pulling my arms tighter around my middle.

I hope it is. Mum came into the bedroom to chat to me earlier when Ella and Dad went to buy the croissants. I was still in bed, propped up on the thin pillows, looking at my phone. Mum perched on the side of Ella's bed amongst the mess of cuddly toys and books. It was awkward in the cramped space, her knees almost touching my bed. I knew I should put my phone away when she started talking but she didn't ask me. I liked the comfort of it in my hand. However, I turned the screen over and stared at the back of my hand resting on it in my lap. I preferred that to looking at Mum. She hadn't hit her head like Marco but there was something bruised about her face this morning. She had purple shadows under her eyes, and her skin was washed grey like the dawn rather than its usual freckly-white. Mum kept her voice light and steady as she talked to me but there was something sad and deflated about her like those helium balloons that trail along the floor the day after a party. This frightened me more than if she had been crying or shouting. I hoped she was just tired. Even her smile hadn't the energy to spread further than her mouth. Mum promised me that she would have a long talk to Dad as soon as we get home. She said Dad will be hurt but he would understand as they love each other very much.

'Everything will be okay,' she said and this time her smile reached her eyes.

'How can you be sure?' I asked quickly glancing up at her for a moment.

I wished I hadn't because something dark flickered across her face, a shadow passing over her skin that couldn't be hidden by the flush rising in her cheeks.

'Everyone,' she said. 'Everyone does something stupid that they regret. You understand that, don't you, Chloe?'

When she said this, I got a horrible panicky feeling that she was talking about me; me and Luca, me and Marco. What a mess. The dread feeling churned in my stomach and then the red came. It rose up quickly from somewhere deep inside me like a burning tsunami until my chest, neck and face was submerged in a deep crimson tide. I can't control it when it happens like that. I was so hot I wanted to open the window but didn't dare move. I couldn't look at Mum and concentrated on fiddling with the frayed edge of the duvet cover, trying to keep my breathing even. Then I heard her apologising for what she had said last night about her 'not feeling attractive' and 'feeling sorry for herself' and 'doing stupid things'.

'All those times I've said to you that it is what's on the inside that matters, not what's on the outside, and then you see me acting like an idiot because of a little scar. That's what Uncle Toni was telling me that night when I was upset, that it didn't matter. However, I was drunk and silly and… well, I'm not making excuses, but adults don't always get it right. I'm being a bit of a rubbish role model,' she sighs.

There's a pause and I don't know if I'm supposed to say anything. However, it feels a bit like Mum is talking to herself rather than me.

'The main thing is you mustn't worry. This will all be okay.'

Again, it sounds like she's reassuring herself as well as me. *And what if it's not okay?* What if I end up with two identical bedrooms like my friend Lauren whose parents have split up? Although that's better than my friend, Helen, in my maths class whose Dad died when she was a baby. She only knows him through photographs and the stories that other people tell her. She hasn't got any of her own stories, so she tells theirs as if they are her own. I think about my Dad and all the stories about him that I know because I was in them. I would hate to have never known him. I'll always have him whatever happens. It will be okay, I tell myself. I think it will. I hope so. That's the worst thing about all this, not feeling certain about anything. It reminds me of something Mum said on our walk back to the caravan last night. She talked about feeling less certain about some things even though you were older and you knew more. It didn't make sense at the time. I thought she just meant people of her age. She said that because it was hard to be certain you had to remember what was important, what made you happy, and what kind of person you wanted to be. She made it sound like it was a choice whereas most of the time I feel things are just happening to me and I don't have any control.

*

Marco drifted away but I stayed standing where I was, enjoying my place on the edge of things. It's weird watching everyone acting normal after what has happened. The fun and chatter are like a thick layer of skin that if you pulled it away you would see all the secrets and worries that people are hiding. It's like those horrible drawings on the wall of our school science lab which show a face and body with no skin and all the connecting muscles and tendons underneath. You know they're the reason your face can move but you don't always want to see them.

A few people from the other caravans have come over to say goodbye. Some of them are also in the middle of packing. Their cars have bikes strapped to the roof, and some of the rear windows are piled high with bedding and boxes. When people stop to talk to me, I smile and hopefully say the right thing. *Yes, I couldn't believe the amazing weather we'd had. Yes, I would be back at school next week.*

Ella meanders in and out of every conversation, lapping up as much attention as she can. She isn't shy about launching into the story of our dramatic evening on the beach path to whoever will listen. Luckily, she didn't mention Luca and Marco fighting and only says that he fell. She loves narrating the moment when she looked up at Marco wearing her head torch and illuminated his blood-stained face. It gets more exaggerated with each telling, more blood, more screams. An extra bonus for her is describing his face as 'bloody' knowing it is also a swear word, but she can't be told off for saying it. I want to forget that moment. It wasn't so much the blood that bothered me, it was Marco's shocked expression. All the swagger knocked out of him as he stared at the scarlet drips on his fingers. He was frightened and so were we.

Although I pretend not to, I watch Luca make his way over to me. I haven't spoken to him yet this morning. He weaves his way through the chatting groups, his head always very slightly bowed. I've noticed that tall people do this.

'Hi,' he says quietly.

He leans back against the caravan exactly where Marco stood next to me a little while ago. Luca's a head taller than me though so when I glance sideways at him I'm seeing mainly shoulder. There's no stain on his clothing this morning. He has that 'box fresh' look again dressed in a clean white T-shirt and shorts. A contrasting memory flashes into my mind; Luca, last night, panic streaked across his face like blood. His chest is bare and pale in the moonlight. He holds a crumpled T-shirt against his brother's head, something dark seeping quickly through the light fabric.

I still don't know whether Luca saw Marco and I kiss or whether he arrived when I was crying about Mum. If he saw us kiss, just a few days after he and I were on the beach, then what does he think of me? There are names at school for girls like that. Just the girls, not the boys, which isn't fair. I'm aware of a tension in my body that wasn't there when I was talking to Marco. I can smell the fabric conditioner from Luca's clothes mixed with something else, something that reminds me of the day we kissed on the beach. I don't want to think about that. We chat about normal stuff. Luca is doing most of the talking and I answer him. My mind races in a terrible loop – *what did he see, what if he thinks this, what if he thinks that.* The thoughts in my head are so loud I miss the last thing he says and, embarrassed, I ask him to repeat it.

'I know I probably didn't show it but I *do* like you, Chloe,' he repeats shyly. The way he says it sounds like an apology and he adds. 'Just in case you didn't know.'

I'm speechless. I didn't know – *or did I?* It doesn't matter. I know now. If he'd told me this a few days ago then... actually, I can't imagine what I would have said or done but now I feel an ache in my chest for something lost or missed. That afternoon on the beach feels like a million years ago, buried with the other fossils in the sand. Everything has happened, everything has changed. I know I should be responding to Luca, but my head feels foggy as though the mist has crept up from the sea and made everything blurry. Nervously, I tilt my head to look up at him. I'm shocked to see that contrasting with his white T-shirt, the skin of Luca's face and neck are bright red. This is not sunburn, he is blushing. A nerve pulsates in his tanned cheek and I remember seeing that nerve last night, just before he pushed Marco.

'The holiday's over,' I eventually say.

'Maybe we could hang out sometime,' he says.

I'm still trying to process what he has just told me. There's an awkward pause. Luca squints into the sun, I look at my feet. The polish on my toenails is chipped.

'It's a long way,' I say.

'Yeah,' says Luca flatly.

I could be imagining it but I think he also sounds relieved. Luca's family live at least a hundred miles away. Remembering something I heard earlier, I say, 'Mum and Dad were talking about us all getting together at Christmas.'

> *Kute Magazine. December 1983*
> *Who's your King Crush? Don't look too far*
> *from the mistletoe. . .*

I shush the familiar voice in my head. *You can shut up*, I think.

'What's that?'

Luca is watching me with a puzzled expression. I think my lips were moving.

'Nothing,' I say. I hold up my phone. 'Where's yours?'

Luca reaches into his shorts pocket. I wait for him to unlock it then take his phone from him. I find Snapchat and

Instagram and search for me, my thumbs moving quickly over the screen.

'Your phone is not just for football scores and memes,' I say. 'Here. You're following me now.'

I hand him his phone and then accept his follow requests on mine – Mum and Dad will only let me have private accounts – *of course*.

Luca stares at his phone screen, the corners of his mouth turning up in slow smile. I look over his shoulder and cringe a little as he looks at the last picture I posted. I'd better delete it before Mum and Dad see it. It's the four of us on the beach last night – before the kiss, before the fight. Our faces are bleached white by the flash and behind us the sea and sky are black. Another monochrome moment for my *Kute* photo story. There were no pictures drawn in the sand this year, but I have something more permanent to remind me of that night if I want to. Desperate to lighten the mood, I wave my phone in a figure of eight shape in front of Luca's face and say in my best Marco impersonation: 'Like and subscribe.' Luca laughs.

*

Dad says that goodbyes with the Rossi family can be longer than the car journey home what with the endless hugs and 'see you soons'. However, today the cars are quickly packed and everyone seems keen to get on the road, perhaps because we were delayed celebrating Mum's good news, perhaps because it's just time to go home. Our car finally pulls slowly out of the field with a last honk of the horn at Mr Jones. His creamy-coloured cat, scared by the noise, jumps down from the stone wall in front of the farmhouse and disappears under a hedge.

Instead of being up front with Dad, Mum is sitting between Ella and I on the back seat. When we were little, she often sat with us like this on long journeys. It was usually when we were fed up with travelling or ratty with each other. It's much more cramped than I remember. Mum and mine's legs are crossed over each other. Her arm lies next to mine, the downy feel of her skin as familiar as my own. Mum's scar is on my side and I think that's better for Ella – and for Mum. Ella has just about made room for Mum rearranging her nest of cuddly toys, special fluffy blankets, books and drawing pads. Ella's giant fluffy lion, Leo, sits in Mum's lap who hugs his waist like she would hold a toddler. Mum's other arm wraps around Ella who snuggles into her shoulder. I think Ella is already asleep but just as we are turning out of the village on to the main road she suddenly sits up with a wail.

'We didn't do a picture!'

'We've taken lots of photos,' says Mum.

'No, a sand picture, like the one on the mirror, our faces in the sand. With Salty Dog. We forgot!'

'What's that,' shouts Dad from the front of the car. 'What have we forgotten?'

'Nothing,' says Mum then quieter to Ella. 'It would have been far too hot for Salty Dog today,' she soothes. 'And we'll have different memories to remember.'

'But I wanted to do the same picture,' whines Ella. 'The same every year!'

'Not every holiday has to be the same,' I say trying not to sound irritated but it's hard when Ella is using her baby voice.

'And I didn't get to say goodbye to Salty Dog!' cries Ella.

I can't help rolling my eyes and seeing my expression, Ella says in a quiet voice, 'It's okay, I know he's not real.'

She slumps back down against Mum's shoulder and silently stares straight ahead, her mouth set in a tiny line. I feel bad even though she's being stupid. If the weather was rainy on our last day, which it often was, Ella and I would crane our necks to look out of the back window of the car, waving goodbye, hoping to see a glimpse of Salty Dog chasing the car through the damp grass. We never saw him.

Ella is soon asleep, hypnotised by the movement of a car. Her head lolls, her face half-buried in Leo's fur.

'You've almost got a tan,' says Mum.

I throw her a sarcastic look because the family joke is that 'gingers don't tan'.

'I'm serious,' says Mum.

I wouldn't call it a tan but there is a smudge of something darker underneath the sprinkling of freckles from my wrist all the way up my arm to my shoulder. Not as many as Mum though, whose original skin colour is lost amongst the thick dusting of pale brown freckles on her forearm.

'I've seen a few more summers,' she says noticing me staring.

I turn my arm over to compare the underside and she does the same. We are the identical shade of milky white with a hint of blue vein at the wrists. The veins show faintly

276

through the skin on my arm but protrude on Mum's like tree roots pushing out of the ground. Seeing how similar we look I expect her to get all sentimental and start telling the story of when I was born. The midwife said my colouring was identical to Mum's. She said that it looked like Mum had made me from a piece of her own skin and a tuft of her own hair. This always makes Mum well up but I think it sounds a bit creepy.

'You're peeling though,' says Mum nodding at my shoulder.

Already? I crane my neck to look. The skin on the top of my shoulders is dry and flaking. So much for the holiday tan, it will have disappeared by the time I'm back at school. I rub at the flakes and they scatter like dandruff. However, underneath the dead skin I don't look as pale as I did. There's something different.

'I don't want to go to Rangers anymore,' I say suddenly. The thought is so random that I surprise myself. More words follow. 'I know you went all the way through Guides but I... I don't like it anymore. Some girls in my form go to Scouts and they do loads of camping and it sounds fun. Or I could start my Duke of Edinburgh Award at school next year.'

'That's fine,' said Mum. 'It's your decision.'

'Okay,' I say.

Wow, I think. I thought she'd try and talk me out of it. I can't wait to tell Olivia and Cerys. They're going camping with the Scouts in September. Sophie might join too. My hand creeps to my phone to message them. My stomach is buzzing with excitement and my phone is buzzing in my lap as my friends reply. Emojis pop up one after another on the screen like a secret code. My thoughts are still firing randomly in all directions as though someone has let off a firework in my brain.

'Mum, do you think Gran would mind if we changed the curtains in the caravan in mine and Ella's bedroom?'

'What's wrong with the ones you've got?'

'They are really thin and let the light in,' I reply and then after a very brief pause I add. 'And they have the Little Mermaid on them.'

Mum looks amused.

'Yes, maybe you have grown out of those,' she says. 'I'm sure Gran wouldn't mind making something else. Ella might have an opinion.'

We both look at Ella, eyes closed, face smushed into Mum's shoulder.

'Chloe,' says Mum, lowering her voice. 'There's something I wanted to tell you, but I didn't want to say anything in front of Ella in case she got upset,' continues Mum.

The happy buzzing in my stomach stops, and my insides tighten. *Oh no*, I think. *What now?*

'Uncle Toni told me that they are planning to travel to Italy next year to see his family so we might not see the Rossi gang at the caravan.'

'Oh,' I say.

I am relieved it's nothing to do with Mum or Dad, but I'm shocked at the thought of not seeing the others next year. *Is this because of Mum and Toni?* I think. *Or Marco and Luca? Or... me?*

'Some of Toni's relatives are getting very old and he wants to make sure Marco and Luca get to meet them.

Toni's parents are going as well. They've been planning to do this for years and they've finally saved up enough money. They will be away for most of the summer holidays.'

'They haven't fixed the dates yet,' continues Mum. 'We might still be able to meet up for at least the bank holiday weekend if they are back in time.'

'Okay,' I say, still a bit stunned.

When people surprise me with news, I often can't feel anything straight away, but I can't say nothing or Mum will think I'm upset.

'Chloe, maybe you would like Sophie to come with us to the caravan next summer, and Ella could bring a friend too.'

I look at her confused, trying to imagine anyone else I know at the caravan with us. All I see in my mind is Marco, Luca, Ella and I on the beach, at the pool, around the campfire, arguing over the last burger on the barbeque. I see us at all different ages, the holidays overlapping with each other into one crazy blur. It's hard to imagine Sophie or anyone else in the middle of that.

'Or maybe we'll do something completely different,' says Mum. 'Like... I don't know, camping in France or something. Your Dad has always wanted to do that.'

'Really?' This is an even bigger surprise. I thought Dad loved the caravan.

'Yes,' says Mum. 'There are these campsites where they have the tents already set up for you – and even a barbeque! We'll have to look at the cost but you're studying French at school this year. I might be able to cope with the heat to help you learn a few phrases.'

Little twists of excitement flutter inside me like butterflies. A holiday abroad! I can't believe it. My hand creeps around my phone again but I'll wait until later to tell everyone.

Mum and I chat for a bit, mainly about school and did we need to go shopping for anything before the first day of term. It's hard to believe that in a few more days I'll be in Year 9. I'll be starting my GCSE options. It feels like everything is changing. Eventually the conversation is lulled by the rhythm of the car and the repetitive drone of the motorway. Mum's eyelids start to droop and soon she is asleep, head dropped against her chest. I slide down in my seat and watch the world race by the car window.

The journey to the caravan seems endless, or maybe it is because Ella and I are always impatient to get there. However, going back home today it feels like we've been in the car only a moment before the country lanes broaden into A roads, like streams joining fast-moving rivers. Now we're on the motorway with busy junctions and towns signposted in every direction. The familiar landscape rolls quickly by the window like a film watched in reverse. We'll soon be home. Dad is listening to some people on the radio shouting over each other about football. All their voices sound the same. From the driver's seat he catches my eye in the rear-view mirror.

'They gone?' he says.

He means Mum and Ella slumbering next to me, rocking with the motion of the car like an old-fashioned cradle. Their faces move in and out of the sun and shade. He shakes his head smiling to himself at another long-running family joke; the two sleepy heads who can't stay awake in the car.

'Nothing changes,' he winks at me in the mirror. 'Want me to turn this off? I can put some music on.'

I shake my head and hold up my headphones. He nods, understanding. I slip a bud into each of my ears and press play. The music hits my brain like a crashing wave. I love the way, just for a moment, it washes everything away. However, it's the playlist I listened to on the car journey down here a week ago. I keep skipping tracks until I find something new.

The car slows down, traffic queuing in front and behind us. I lower the window to let in some air. It smells of car fumes and hot tarmac but it's at least a bit cooler. My arm rests on the window frame. This year Ella forgot but normally at the end of the holiday, as we leave the caravan site, she dangles her hand out of the window saying she can feel Salty Dog licking her fingers as he runs alongside the car. I knew that all Ella was feeling was the rush of cool air and a drizzle of rain but in my mind I could see Salty Dog lolloping along, tongue hanging out with excitement. I've never told Ella that I used to be afraid of Salty Dog, and she's too young to remember. I didn't like the idea of a strange animal appearing out of the mist, especially at night. The rain would patter on the caravan roof and I would bury my head under the covers worrying that he was out there.

'No need to be afraid,' Gran would whisper to me so as not to wake the tiny Ella asleep in the next bed. 'That big shaggy old mut is just nosing around. He likes a change from the beach. Change is good for all of us; it's a mixed bag, but it's never all rain or all sun, and you need a bit of everything if you want them flowers to bloom.'

Can you have too much change? I wanted this holiday to be different but now, I just want everything to go back to how it was. Well, maybe not everything. In my mind I flick through moments as if I were looking through a photo album: *cricket on the beach; fairground rides; Mum's hat; the cold thrill of jumping in the sea; the floor is lava; slapping Ella; golf and the silver bracelet; the party; Mum and Toni in the shadows; Ella and I pretending to fly across the beach; Luca and Marco fighting; Mum's voice calling me through the darkness; marshmallows round the fire; Marco's bruised face; Mum's good news; the scout trip I can go on; maybe a holiday to France; the heat; sunburn; kisses...* I can't unpick any one moment without all the others unravelling like the loops in Gran's crocheted blankets.

The car speeds up but I leave the window down. The draft whips up my hair and stirs the pages of Ella's abandoned books. Along the roadside, trees, hedges, buildings, bridges roll by faster and faster. Mum and Dad tell us to keep our arms inside the car when we are on the motorway but my hand creeps out of the window. Something licks at my fingers but I'm not afraid. I know it's just the cool breeze. I spread my fingers and they float in the rush of air like seagulls gliding over the beach.

ACKNOWLEDGEMENTS

Thank you to Mum and Dad for the story-telling genes and my family for the endless encouragement. Thanks to Claire, Eve, Emma, Miriam, Clare and Jane for reading the manuscript at its various stages. Finally, thank you to the lovely workshop group at Birkbeck, University of London, where this story began.

ABOUT THE AUTHOR

Caroline Venetia Annis grew up in the north of England in a seaside resort, dreaming of the city. She now lives in London with her family and dreams of the sea. SKIN is her first novel.

Printed in Great Britain
by Amazon

69324953R00173